I0830370

The Girl Who was to Be Queen

Special thanks to a special person,
I spent a short time with and all those in my life!

Preface

Although this story is not the way my life is

and is made up, parts of it still connect and mirror

it in so many ways. The story was a long way from

right some time ago and I never thought I'd finish.

Every time I turned around I found it to be never

perfect and I don't know if that's a part of being a

writer. Even though it was some trouble trying to

put all the pieces in the right places, I enjoyed

creating it and I hope you will enjoy reading it as

much as I enjoyed writing it.

Introduction

IN A WORLD THAT DOESN'T

EXISTS TO HUMANS; A BEGINNING

TO A STORY THAT TOOK PLACE

ABOUT A THOUSAND YEARS AGO...

Gabrial, an angel created by an ancient

angel, (a mistake since creation), is cast down after

disappointing him in a duel with her sister,

Esmeralda. It is then that her journey begins when

she encounters a lonely lion and the two of them become best friends. Events take place that separates the two of them and Gabrial grows lost in a world that doesn't appear to be much better than the one she fell from, especially when she becomes a servant to Prince Damien, who is obsessed with angels and is convinced that she is one.

The prince attempts to force her into a marriage with him, which fails once his long-lost brother, Prince Emmanuelle, returns, and his wedding gets postponed till after a ball that will be held in the lost prince's homecoming. Not too long after the prince's return, he begins to fall for the angel, unaware of his brother's engagement and so does Gabrial. But as the two of them try to draw closer, the further away they seem to become from one another, and expressing things becomes harder

as the ball approaches, misconceptions are made

and secrets become hard to hide for the young

prince.

Table of Contents

Chapter 24: The Ball of Celebration II

10

Chapter 1

From the Sky

There wasn't a place in the world that was safe then. Angels had never sought to war with humans, only to be their friend until they turned against them. That is when the war broke out. Families were separated. Some never being brought together again. Things were so awful and desolate they thought it was the end of the world.

Of course, you could have said that since the war wasn't between humans, but between them and that of the unseen world. Eventually, they were driven to the ends of the Earth, where they were forced to return home and were forbidden to ever return. In spite of that, there was one that still walked among them in the form of a child, even to this day. Some were able to notice her, while others seemed to have forgotten the glory of an angel.

The Black Knight looked to the skies. He had encountered an angel long ago, but he was convinced that all angels were evil at this point. He would never trust one again. The next time he found one he'd be sure to kill it. He grinned a little when a star sparkled in his deep lavender-blue eyes that were full of hate and bitterness.

"Why do you search the skies, old man?" chuckled a merchant behind a counter. "Searching for angels?"

The knight turned to look at him, wondering whatever happened to the days youngsters like him respected their elders.

"Believe it or not there may be one that still lives among us. Perhaps even thousands, although we may never know it," he said, staring up at the sky. "Things that are rare are not always seen with these eyes, but that doesn't mean they don't exist."

The merchant was unable to understand what he meant and gave a little chuckle. Angels didn't exist except in fairytales like all other creatures. "If you say so, sir." He began to carve his wooden figure of the angel and lion again.

The Black Knight eyed the wooden carving. If he didn't believe in angels then why did he still carve them? "What is her name?"

He looked up from the carving and gave him a skeptical look. "Sharon. Why?"

There was no response. The knight turned around swiftly and stared up at the sky again. Maybe he was insane, but for as long as he could remember there had been a star that had looked so close to the moon it could have touched it, and now it was gone. His spirit-free eyes widened. For every star that went missing meant that an angel had been reborn into a new being at least according to the stories he had heard from the Old Fates. As far as he was concerned that hadn't happened since the beginning of time.

"You should study the stars, my friend. You could learn a lot about the past and better yet, the future," he mounted onto his dark horse, then tossed the merchant two coins, "thanks for the help." He whacked the reins and the horse trotted along to the edge of the town.

The merchant shrugged. The knight had been a peculiar man. That could have come with his age. He blew some of the little wood particles off his wooden statue and wiped it with a small cloth so it would shine. The Black Knight rode through the streets of the village until he reached the end of it. He turned his head to stare back at the village before he left into the forest, where he would start his long quest again. Somewhere out in this world, he knew he would find her. He knew she still existed and until he found and killed her he would never stop traveling. That was the only thing that kept him going. Kept him from going on a massive killing rampage as he had done before.

The forest was peaceful and so colorful with all the late spring colors of everything being in season. His head was lowered as his horse crossed a small river that had water that ran over the smooth rocks and Autumn leaves that had been trapped. A butterfly began to flutter its golden wings that looked like a piece of the sun, near his face. The Black Knight took one look at it, thinking it was something else, but was disappointed when he saw what it was.

The horse gave a deep snort when the river came to an end and they reached the land. He petted the side of the horse's neck as if to tell him they would soon be reaching their destination after all their years of traveling. Although he didn't know when he just knew that it would be someday.

****

In a world unknown to humans and less superior beast was an old angel that was a wood crafter, who could create anything from nothing and he created two sisters from the wind that blew through his palace from both the east and the west. That is after he tamed it. His name was Uri, known among all others as the greatest craftsman ever. The sisters were created the opposite of one another in hopes of raising chaos between the two. Esmeralda was the sister of evil and darkness just like the hair upon her head that would someday hang like a dark cape of night.

Her eyes were emeralds as if she were possessed and her voice was high pitched. She was given the color black to show who and what she was, along with her wings that were like those of ravens.

Unlike the first one, he thought she was perfect in his eyes, despite her ways. Gabrial, his first creation, which was supposed to be the one of good things, had had a fatal mistake when being created and it caused her to be caught between both good and evil. Meaning that she had emotions and feelings, something that an angel should never have.

For hours he had worked on creating her in his little work area. Trimming and cutting as he used a spinner-like thing to help him along. The little wheel turned as he stepped on the pedal. Being careful to make sure she had every detail down to the smallest eyelash until...

"WHAT HAVE I DONE!" he yelled when the wind had slipped away from his fingers, knocking over a glass full of water.

The crafter took a step back in horror of what he had done, nearly fumbling backward over a piece of wood. When he looked at the baby, her hair was far from being blonde. Instead, it was a glowing, bluish-gray. Her skin was like copper and she cried and cried. From that moment he knew he had messed up something and that made him feel vulnerable. He picked her up with hardly any gentleness, looking at her pale blue eyes of innocence that was full of so many tears, it was as if she knew he didn't like her. She stared at him as he growled.

"I should get rid of you," he looked at a bag eagerly and she began to cry again. "Will you be quiet? Hush! Hush! No one needs to know about you. You're bad," he whispered as he got ready to set her in a bag, instantly she began to cry without stopping.

Woodcrafter Uri rolled his eyes and just when he was about to put her in the bag he thought of something else. He thought to let her live in hopes of making her see how he felt about her and what she made him feel like because of her confusion. She would be hated by everyone since her personality was in chaos. Her eyes looked at him as he pulled her away from the bag, he began to laugh as he thought of his plan. Then he had a seat on a round piece of wood.

He gave her the color grey, although her wings were white as snow that sparkled as if stars had covered them. None of it impressed him though, every time he looked upon her it was like looking upon his errors or infirmities. Although he was convinced that he had none, making the situation very difficult and it could have driven him mad despite if he wasn't indeed already mad, in a different way.

He treated Esmeralda like a superior being, though her sins were great and some things she did were unholy. Gabrial never did at least anything worth being hated for, all she ever did was seek her father's love, something that she would never gain at least not from him. She was kind, patient, and loving, but although she upheld great virtue she was very lonely and isolated.

The only one who seemed to always stay with her despite her difference was Esmeralda. The two of them would play hours together and they had a bond that no one would ever separate. Esmeralda ran around the pillars, she could hear Gabrial giggling as she looked for her.

"I found... Esmeralda?" she said as she walked around the pillar to look for her, then she jumped when she felt someone poke her in the back.

She looked up to see Esmeralda flapping her wings as she giggled. "You're so frightened all the time," she giggled.

Gabrial looked down at the clouds when she thought she heard their father calling them. She didn't want this moment to end, not yet.

"Esmeralda!" he yelled as he suddenly appeared. "What are you doing child?"

She came down and landed on the floor. "Playing, father."

He grunted then scowled at Gabrial as he patted Esmeralda on the shoulder. "Come, child, we have much to do."

The two of them walked away leaving her all alone in the room. Later, she went to a lake where she watched a family of swans playing together making her wish she had a family like that. She lay back in the sand, resting her hands on her stomach looking up at the sky. At times she wished she were dead since her life already felt like death that only lightened up for a little while when she was with Esmeralda. One of the little ducklings waddled over to her, then climbed up onto her. It quacked as if telling her to get up and play.

Gabrial sat up looking at it. "Don't you ever wish there was a better place for you?" she asked the duckling as she petted its soft fur.

It began to quack again this time flapping its little wings. She closed her eyes trying to stop the tears from falling from them. Then she opened them when she felt the little duckling scurry away from off her lap racing to his family. She watched as he swam away with them along the lake. He had a family. One that loved him. That must have been a great place to be, a place where somebody cared, worried about you when you didn't come back, thought of you as their child, and not as their embarrassment.

****

Chilliness, something that she had never felt swept past her and she rubbed her arms trying to warm them. She was home, but she hadn't remembered ever seeing this place except for when she was very young. Her eyes saw her father's long white hair blowing behind him as he sat near the shoreline. He was so still, you would have thought he was a stone.

She touched her father's hand. "Papa?" she said with her little voice.

All she had ever wanted was for him to love her like her sister. He kept his back turned and said absolutely nothing to her. Tears began to fill her eyes, she was a curse to him. No matter what she did he would always see her as a walking mistake. His white beard flowed past him as the wind blew from off the shore.

Gabrial turned her back walking away, sniveling, when she looked back in hopes that maybe he was finally looking at her, it only broke her more to see him in the exact position she had left him in. Why didn't he just get rid of her like he did all things that were not perfect? Why was she ever even created if this was what her life was supposed to be nothing but despair?

Gabrial ran into the forest wiping the tears from her eyes. Darkness fell upon the forest. A darkness that was so dense she could feel that felt as if it were pushing down trying to smother her. Then she saw her father standing at the end of the path where there was light from the lantern he held.

"Papa!" she yelled as she tried to reach out, but was dragged away by some unseen force.

He looked at her as she suffered, then turned his head away and began to walk. The light vanished and she was left alone crying for him to come back as she sat on the ground with only her wings to cover around her for comfort while the darkness caved in around her. Wails surrounded her as if teasing her.

She hugged herself wishing someone would come, anybody, just somebody to be with her. To hold her hand and tell her it would all be over. Then just when she thought her breath was going to be taken from her she saw a glowing human with wings appear before her. The being reached out a cross to her.

"Take up thy cross and follow me," he said unto her.

She reached out her hand to take the cross, her hand shaking with weakness. Almost immediately she was revived with life and the darkness vanished. He took her hand and raised her from the ground. Her eyes were shut for she was unable to look upon him.

"We will meet again someday, Sharon. Don't give up yet." His voice was calm and gentle. "I'm still waiting for you, remember that."

Gabrial became uncurled on the floor, scared of the voice that had spoken to her. Her wings had flapped open and she had almost knocked down a shelf. She looked around, then noticed above her head was the face of a gargoyle smiling down on her. "You should just take my life, Erebus. I don't believe I deserve one, any more or if ever," she whispered as if the gargoyle had had something to do with her dream.

"Gabrial are you alright?" asked Esmeralda, walking into the courtyard, where she had fallen asleep.

"Yes," she answered.

Why did she have this dream every night? Angels weren't supposed to dream, something was wrong. And more importantly, who was that being that glowed and took her hand in the darkest hour? Would she ever meet

him? She let her eyes close once again falling back asleep.

Perhaps there was somebody out there who cared, then

why did she still feel the urge to die?

****

The time came faster than the currents of the sea

when the two sisters came of the age of thirteen that they

would battle each other. If Gabrial hadn't turned out to be

such a disgrace the battle would have never been created,

but since he wanted to see if there was still a chance that

maybe she wasn't a failed creation he decided to create the

battle. Woodcrafter Uri was one of the most ruthless men

of his kind that saw violence as key to his dilemma. The

sister who lost the battle would suffer by death in a way no

other being would imagine.

They stood about eleven feet apart, each of them

knelt and turned the opposite ways so they could not see

each other. Their wings slumped down covering them.

The place was open to the sky, there were no windows or doors. It nearly looked like the Pantheon except it was far better decorated and on the outside were clouds. This made it easy for either of them to easily fall out and into the clouds, although they probably wouldn't die.

Woodcrafter Uri strolled past each of them giving both of them a sword. When he came to Gabrial he gave her a look of disgust as if hoping she'd be the one to die. He made his way over to Esmeralda and whispered a few words into her ear that Gabrial couldn't make out.

"You know you are the superior one and no matter what happens I will choose you. I don't care if she won. Disappointed? Mmmm, a little, but she would never be fit for me," a crooked smile crept onto his face, nearly showing his teeth.

A peal of evil laughter followed after he was done speaking with her. A laugh that always came from Esmeralda when she was triumphant or about to perform something completely wicked. It made Gabrial wonder if she still remembered the good times they had shared. The memories they had created as little girls were that part of her still alive or had the evil she was supposed to be, take over?

The king clapped his hands down on Esmeralda's shoulders happily, then walked back to his throne chair, where he would watch. His face turned from his crooked smirk to a stern, angry face, when he saw Gabrial stare up at him with hopeful eyes. He quickly looked away, then instructed them.

"Swords are to be used until one of you falls dead!"

The two girls rose from their knees and turned around. Their eyes meeting each other. Esmeralda's full of hatred and evilness, ready to kill for anything as the emerald green reflected the light. While Gabrial was innocent with love and gentleness, she could only still picture Esmeralda as the person that was always there for her as a child. She couldn't abandon that thought, she couldn't kill her lest part of her should perish with her. No matter how awful she had become there was still a side of her that was her sister, that loving and protective person.

Her sister stared at her with her teeth tightly clenched together like an angry dragon ready to slay her. This was her moment, after all these years she finally got to kill the one she was unaware of hating as her eyes scanned straight through Gabrial for weakness. Their father had been speaking the whole time they were thinking until the final words slipped from his mouth like a death sentence. "Let the battle begin!"

Esmeralda opened her dark wings of nightmares. The sound of them was like the sound of an eagle taking to the air with its might. They beat against the fierce wind. Gabrial stared up at her as she flew toward her with the sword. She looked a million times more massive with her wing outstretched. And for once in her life, she wanted to get away or protect herself from Esmeralda, but at the same time, she was overtaken with fear and was as harmful as a mouse at this point. When Esmeralda came in close enough where she could easily hit her with the sword Gabrial took off running the opposite way of her dropping the sword. She wouldn't harm Esmeralda no matter how hard she tried to harm her. Her sister flapped behind her, driven by her hate.

Almost immediately their father arose from the chair. What was she doing? "GABRIAL!" he yelled, irritatedly.

Gabrial attempted to flap her wings to fly away and escape, but when she did so she found out that it was too late. Esmeralda flew straight into her, knocking the two of them onto the floor. The shrieks from her seemed to go on and on as she tried to push her sword past Gabrial's wrist that was covered in brass only protecting her arms a little. She closed her eyes as the brass began to tear and she felt Esmeralda's claws at the end of her wings start stabbing at her. They missed her a few times, but they were messing up her focus with the sword that began to slip past her wrist.

"Esmeralda please don't do this, can't you remember we were close when we were girls," she asked as a tear fell from her eyes, the pain from both the sword and her claws was beginning to sink in.

"Shut up Gabrial, you are my enemy so stop acting like you were my best friend," she pushed the sword harder against her wrist as a few droplets of blood began to fall.

The brass began to tear even more and she was beginning to feel the sharpness of the sword against her bare skin.

"That's not true and you know it." Gabrial cried, nearly choking.

A devilish smile appeared on their father's face, he was thrilled to see that Esmeralda was not failing him. He didn't care what happened to Gabrial, if she were to die that would be less of an embarrassment and affliction for him. Esmeralda pushed harder against her wrist so that Gabrial was squeezing her eyes as if trying to stop the pain.

"Fight or die," laughed Esmeralda as the sword grew closer to killing her sister, she could hear their father laughing in the background, he was so proud of her for almost freeing him from his distress.

"I can't. You are my blood and my sister and I love you more than anything," cried Gabrial and suddenly it was as if everything came to a stop, even the pain of the sword.

Esmeralda stopped pushing. A few tears rolled down her face with disappointment that her sister may not have understood what love was anymore. All their lives they had been forbidden to say such words, but Gabrial remembered the feeling, the bond between her and Esmeralda as girls. "I'd let nothing happen to you just like you'd let nothing happen to me. We promised that as girls.

Esmeralda's eyes grew wide with shock, she remembered saying that as a little girl, when she and Gabrial had been at the lake together one evening. The word love, why had Gabrial used such a strong word? Had they been that close bonded then? She released Gabrial so that she was able to rest from suffering. Her mind was so confused, unable to comprehend this, she grabbed her head and began to shriek out of fury.

Woodcrafter Uri was boiling with anger and probably would have slain Gabrial himself if he had a sword in his hands at the time. He stood up from his chair, then picked her sword from off the floor walking over to the sisters. He pushed Esmeralda out of his way, Gabrial sat up quickly as fear grew present within her as he stared down upon her holding the sword.

"Papa, please. Please. Forgive me, I…"

"You're weak and an infirmity within my eyes," he grabbed her from off the floor, recklessly as if she were nothing, but he struggled to pull her along as she dragged the opposite way trying to get away from him. "Not only that, you've been disobedient since birth and I'm sick of it." he pulled again, but she hardly moved. "Stop it Gabrial, this is your fault."

He pulled her loose eventually. Esmeralda watched as her sister was dragged away, begging for forgiveness which was something he didn't have for her. Her heart nearly broke by the thought of just letting Gabrial die by being killed by their father, but could only watch helplessly. For their father was way too powerful compared to them.

Woodcrafter Uri threw Gabrial near the edge of the balcony. "Jump you bastard," he ordered.

Gabrial gave one look below the balcony and the fall looked as though it would never end, then she looked at her father. "Papa, please. I'm sorry." repented Gabrial as she knelt on the glass floor in submission.

"You still refuse to obey me," he looked down at Gabrial as her hair flowed in the rough breeze, she was crying for his forgiveness.

For a moment everything was silent and at peace, she thought that perhaps her father's wrath was over, that maybe he had forgiven her. Then she was suddenly grabbed violently by her wings and her father lifted her up and above the great fall as if telling her to look down at her fall. He drew his sword up and above his head, raising

it toward the place where her wings were connected to her

back. Her father, who was supposed to be there to protect

her, was now the person she needed protection from. A few

more droplets of blood fell to the floor, from the places

Esmeralda had cut her.

The sword pierced across her back, slicing her

wings clean off. She screamed with pain sounding like a

banshee weeping over someone who had died. Gabrial

slowly fell from his grip and down into the bliss of nothing

but clouds and light. The only thing she heard were bells

ringing in her ears, along with voices that were like

ancient ones singing about her death. She could see her

father still standing above the edge of the balcony holding

her wings that were covered in her blood. Where she was

going she didn't know so she let her eyes close and let

herself be plunged down. Down into bliss.

Rain droplets tapped against her face, sharply like broken pieces of glass that had fallen from heaven as it tears. Gabrial's halo made of feathers came apart and her hair came loose from the whipping of the wind. And though her eyes were closed, tears slipped through them and joined the rain. Her body came thundering down from the sky and light that could be seen for miles, awakening everything and summoning superstitious people. The ground shook and the prince's coins were knocked off his table.

"What was that?" prince Damien questioned, walking toward his window, where he saw nothing but dark clouds.

"Probably just a quick quake, sir." answered one of his guards staring up at the ceiling.

The prince looked diligently outside, then noticed the large hole in the dark clouds. There was light where there were supposed to be clouds. It was as if some had dropped a massive ball down into the clouds. He was convinced that there was something else happening. "Of course," he replied.

He wasn't the only one that felt the quake. The Black Knight looked up at the sky where he saw a huge opening in the center of the dark clouds also and it had stopped pouring almost instantly.

"The angel has fallen," he muttered out loud.

Chapter 2

Tears in Paradise

Lost in a world without hope. Everything she

had ever known was gone with the others. She was the only

one left, the only one who had managed to survive at least

for now. The wings that had once been her glory had

turned to shame. They were raggedy, broken, and missing

feathers almost everywhere.

Which way was the way to light? Out of this dark

forest without end? Her hands were sore with blisters

along with her feet from walking in the forest with thorns and sharp sticks that pierced through them. She wondered how could humans call this place home. There was nothing here but death and sorrow.

They slaughtered their brothers like it was a part of life. They hated the sound of music and happiness if they couldn't have it. The girl stumbled, nearly falling. She breathed in heavily, surely there was a way out of this place. No place went on forever or did it? Her white dress was so dirty you could hardly tell that it was supposed to be white.

She could hear singing somewhere far ahead of her. She longed to be there with them, whoever they may have been. But her life had other plans before she was able to start walking again her body fell and her eyes closed. She wasn't dead, but she wasn't alive either.

Some 1,000 years later

$\mathcal{R}$ain poured down on them without mercy, crows flew around searching the landscape of dead men. Sobs mixed with cries could be heard for miles. A girl held her dying brother in her arms, rocking his body. Arrows nearly pierced through every part of him. She was injured with an arrow caught in her side and leg, but she was not dying.

"I'm going to get you out of here," she sobbed, trying to pick him up.

She fell back down with him and she heard him sigh in pain.

"You've done enough for me already, Valassillia," he cried, smiling a little with tears in his eyes.

A crow attempted to come near and peck him. Valassillia screamed and shooed it away, covering her brother to protect him from the beak of the little monster. She wished she still had her powers, then she would have been able to save him from this. She would have been able to ease his pain instead of watching him suffer and wait on death to hit.

"No, there has to be something I can do for you now," she began coughing again, breaking into more sobs as she took off his heavy armor. "You never gave up on me and I won't on you."

"You're not giving up on me. You'd be doing me enough if I knew you would leave me here and go. Run as fast as you could, before they come for us," he wheezed, touching the side of her face. "I don't want to die knowing that you died because of me."

"It won't be like that. Neither of us is going to die, we're going to be together and make a new home in a place where no one will care what we are," Valassillia's voice was nearly drowned in her sobs. "I won't go anywhere until I have you with me."

He could hear the voices of soldiers coming their way, the crows swarming around them. Neither of their enemies was going to show them any mercy. She tousled his soft brown hair.

"Go," he ordered her.

"I won't leave you, Bruno," she yelled. "You're not the only one who will die if I leave you… Bruno? Bruno wake up! Brunooo!!!" she wailed, pulling him up against herself and crying through her screams, scaring away the crows.

She looked over at his sword that was lying on the ground. Her heart felt like part of it had been ripped out.

Losing him was like losing her whole world, even herself. She picked up the sword, putting it on her own. As she walked she limped, then she pulled out the arrow that had pierced through her leg.

The world she and her brother had lived in was gone, there was a new world and that world was darker than the one she was putting behind herself. She wouldn't let anyone punish anyone or anything she loved anymore.

They had taken him away and if they thought they were going to get away with that, they were more wrong than starting this war in the first place.

She took out one of the swords from the slot that she had attached to her back, then cut the foreskin of her hand. Looking at the blood that flowed away from her hand like red tears. Her name was no longer Valassillia. No.

Valassillia had died with her brother. She would be known as Snowflare from now on. She tossed the body of her brother onto her back, she wasn't about to let the crows have their fun with him. He deserved a proper burial and she limped across the battlefield. Since they were little they had been taught to believe in angels, that they would help in their time of need as long as they were faithful. But where were they now? Why hadn't they saved her brother? He had been more than worthy of their saving. Ash fell upon them like black snowflakes as she dragged him along with her.

****

For days Gabrial lay in the wasteland that began to produce plants once more and life began to sprout. It was as if she was giving the wasteland life to produce again like reminding it of its purpose. A bluish-gray lion began to slowly approach her, his nose sniffing across the ground as if searching for something, then he stopped when his nose bumped into something soft. Flower and flower petals, bloody red, autumn gold, and sunshine yellow fell onto Gabrial's eyes, a few tears rolled down her cheek. He sniffed her face to see what she was, then he pushed her gently with the end of his massive paw. To his discernment, he thought she was a flower.

"Hello, flower. Why are you crying?" he asked, his voice was as deep as the sea.

"I don't remember," she cried.

The lion nodded as he watched her sit up in the flowers as the flowers fell from her face, she stared at him.

He seemed familiar every time she looked at him she would see the lion then someone there, it was almost like her sight was blurred or messed up. She felt safe near him although she had just met him, despite the fact he was a talking lion.

"You're soft like a flower and you have many flowers on you, then you turned this wasteland into paradise." He licked one of his paws. "Where are you from?"

"I thought I had…" she looked at her back where only bruises and blood showed where her wings had once been.
She covered her eyes and began to cry, what was wrong with her, she wondered? Why couldn't she remember anything? The lion felt sympathetic towards her and nudged her with his nose.

"I'm sorry if I said something wrong, I shouldn't have asked that a lot of us have painful pasts and places we come from and rather not remember," he told her. "Believe me, I know."

"No it's not that," she answered, he seemed to understand her a lot more though he had just met her.

Gabrial noticed a broken chain around every one of his ankles and his neck. He was bigger than any creature in the world, but sadly his wings were torn like a curtain full of holes, then she realized she hadn't asked his name and more importantly hadn't introduced herself, she had been so distracted by what had happened. "My name is Gabrial, by the way," she said, wiping the tears off her face.

The lion looked at her and seemed to try and grin. "Nice to meet you Gabrial, my name is Prince Emmanuelle," he said, lifting his paw to shake her hand.

She touched his paw, it felt fuzzy, soft, and warm, and just by touching his paw she could feel that he was very caring and loving. His golden eyes were eyeing her happily as if he had found his long-lost friend.

"Come with me if you'd like," he let his paw rest in the grass again, then walked off into the forest.

Gabrial followed not too far behind him with her eyes closed until she bumped into the back of one of his legs. She opened her eyes rubbing her head noticing the lion was staring back at her as if confused. When he turned back around she crept alongside him, quiet enough so he wouldn't hear her or so she thought. Then she saw a colorful pile of fruits that he had begun to stack.

She looked at the fruits but didn't touch them, even though she was feeling somewhat hungry, which was kind of odd for her. Emmanuelle backed up a little from his stack, then sat down, crossing his lower paws as if a monk. He picked up a massive watermelon from the pile like it was an apple, then sliced it in half with one of his claws.

His large mouth opened, revealing his dangerous fangs, then tossed one half of the watermelon into his mouth, swallowing it in one gulp. Then he noticed

Gabrial's expression and nearly choked as he said. "I'm a

herbivore so don't worry." he began to laugh, then tossed

her a large fruit that looked like it was made of feathers.

He giggled a little when he remembered how much

smaller and weaker she was compared to him when she

went falling into the grass. Emmanuelle picked up the

other half of the melon he had sliced, then with his other

paw, he picked her up, setting her upright, and then dusted

her off gently.

"Sorry about that. I'm very forgetful," he

announced, handing her half of the melon.

"Thank you," she replied as she took half of the

melon.

After a while of him devouring melons, he walked

around as if going somewhere and she went with him. So

far things had been happy with him as if this was where

she was supposed to be all along. They came to a lake,

where the trees looked greener than any place on Earth.

There were many waterfalls along with rainbows. It was so peaceful with only the sound of birds and the voice of nature. Suddenly, she saw Emmanuelle charge at the lake, he leaped into the air, his ruined wings causing him to glide for a little while, and then he fell into the lake with a big splash. Water ran all up onto the shore and Gabrial was hit by one of his waves.

His head bobbed at the top of the water. "Come join me Gabrial, you'll love it."

She was ringing the water out of her clothes, then she looked at the lake and him. He was laying flat on his back as he floated around. It appeared that he was having fun and that was something she didn't want to miss out on. She stepped slowly into the water, but she didn't go too far in.

"Come on," he swam over to her part of him in the water and part of him out when he came in close to the shore. "Why don't you get onto my back and I'll take you for a ride."

Gabrial smiled and climbed onto his back, it felt a little strange every time she felt him breathing. He seemed to be happy that she was with him as he swam through the water, it was fun like he had told her. Water splashed over them whenever he gave a quick kick. She giggled as his thick mane fell over his face.

"Are you alright?" she giggled listening to him grunt whenever water went over his head.

"Yes, never been better." He threw Gabrial into the air as he flipped over onto his back.

"Emmanuelle," she cried, laughing when she fell onto his soft stomach.

He began to laugh, feeling her up against him was tickling him. She laid down on him and the two of them relaxed in the calmness of the forest. As he floated like a raft around the lake letting the small currents take him.

****

53

The halls were as empty as a bare cabinet, with no guards or soldiers in sight. Prince Damien trotted down the hallways whistling until he came to a grand door, where he turned and went inside after looking around to make sure no one saw him. He laughed thinking about how sneaky and clever he was until his small triumph was crushed when he saw that someone had already beaten him to the job.

"Mother?" he gasped as he watched her jump, dropping her husband's things that she had taken out of his dresser.

"What are you doing here?" she demanded.

"I was going to ask you the same thing." He walked closer to where she was looking at what she was holding, then he noticed a golden compass in her hand. "And what is that?"

She growled in her irritation of being caught taking

a seat on the king's bed. "I'm his wife, I have the right to

be here and this thing right here is none of your concern."

she tossed it back into the drawer.

Prince Damien chuckled softly as a smile pushed

past his stern face. "We all know that no wife would look

through their husband's things unless they had a reason.

Now unless you want me to tell father about all this you

will tell me what you were hoping to find."

The queen shot him a dark look. "That better not be

a threat, my son, because if it is you have broken more

than the law," she snapped.

"It's not a threat at all, just the truth about what I

will do," he smirked. "Laws don't apply to me just like

they don't apply to you. I know how you've been plotting

to steal the thrown from father all this time and I think I

know how you might plan to do so."

Her mouth dropped, how did he know? "What have I raised you to be? A disobedient and noncompliant wretch."

"We learn from the best examples and our biggest influences," he explained, calmly. "They say sins from our fathers, but I find that a lot more children take after their mother's treachery." He ran one of his fingers across the top of the dresser, picking up dust as he went along. "I guess you "It's not a threat at all, just the truth about what I will do," he smirked. "Laws don't apply to me just like they don't apply to you. I know how you've been plotting to steal the throne from my father all this time and I think I know how you might plan to do so."

She looked at the window to avoid getting more annoyed by him.

"It is my destiny mother to have the throne," he chuckled, menacingly. "Now I don't think either of us would want you to end up like the other person who tried to get in my way. Dead! Would we?"

"No. Of course not," she answered, becoming nervous as he whispered into her ear.

When he was done speaking and scaring her, he walked casually toward the door but before he closed it he said. "Remember, between me and you. So let's keep this a hush, hush." he smiled, then shut the door.

The room was disturbingly peaceful once he left out. There had to be some way she could stop him. She couldn't let him be king and she couldn't ally with him, he was far too dangerous at this point, along with being sneaky. But she could pretend to ally with him, then at the right moment or right time make a sneak attack of her own. She could poison him, he would never expect it. She smiled at herself in the mirror as if praising herself, believing the old rabbit had outwitted the fox.

Damien chuckled to himself as he strolled along the hallways, saluted by any guard that came past him. He turned a corner, where a little niche was. A vase of beautifully colored flowers concealing a small handle that he pulled, opening a doorway into a secret room. He walked inside the eerie passageway that was lit by torches.

The sound of men talking flooded the passageway, some laughing, others yelling.

"Good afternoon sir," greeted the knights that sat about a round table.

"Greetings my fellow knights," he cheered as he entered the secret room. "We shall all be in power soon and my stiff-neck father shall fall along with his old traditions."

"Cheers to the age of ending traditions as we welcome new ideas," yelled one of the younger and zealous knights, standing up as he raised his glass.

The others repeated after him while Damien leaned back into his chair proudly.

"Too bad my beloved older brother isn't here today to see what I've become," he swung a little sack of sand around his fingers. "Well in a way at least I still crowned you a king."

A bunch of laughter became present within the room and the sack of sand was tossed into a wall.

****

Time had passed and after a long day of playing in the lake, Emmanuelle was compelled to go back to land. He shook himself off when he reached dry land, all of his water falling onto Gabrial. She began to laugh at the sight of his mane that was all over his eyes making him look more like a blind hedgehog than a lion, she started to ring her clothes out. The trees rustled when he yawned tiredly.

"Ow," she said with a bit of surprise. "Seems like someone needs a nap."

Emmanuelle nodded his head in agreement as he spun around a little, seeming lost until his massive body collapsed onto the ground. His eyes shut and his breathing slowed. Gabrial felt somewhat bound to sleep also. She rested her head on one of his paws and his gentle soul made her feel safe with him. The two of them slept for a long while until Emmanuelle was awakened by the smell of burning wood. His head perked up as he sniffed the air, there was a fire somewhere in the forest and it wasn't far from them now. He bumped his nose on top of Gabrial's head, her eyes slowly opened as she rubbed them.

"What's wrong?" she asked, still trying to knock off the exhaustion.

"Hop on my back," he told her, he sensed that there was more than the danger of fire coming, he had known that no fire just started on its own, not on a nice weathered day like this.

She climbed up onto his back, between his wings.

The lion took off into the forest, the wind blew swiftly at

her, nearly knocking her off and she held on tighter to his

mane. When she turned to see what he was running from,

she noticed trees being devoured by flames of fire.

Emmanuelle's eyes darted from place to place, but

everywhere he looked he saw flames. Someone had started

this fire and he had a hunch that he knew exactly who it

was and why they had done it.

Chapter 3

Moonlight on a Dream

Bells rang as if in the distance, when Sharon

opened her eyes she saw that she was surrounded by

angels, but these were not like the ones she used to be with.

These were different, every one of them wore armor of steel

and carried weapons made of iron. One of them reached

their hand out to her. She looked up at the angel with an

iron helmet that covered her eyes and almost all her face leaving only her lips and her long red hair visible.

"We are like you, don't be afraid," she assured her.

Sharon took the angel's hand and she helped her up from the glass floor. She smiled at her, the others seemed to be staring as if wondering if they should trust her.

"I'm an Armistice and these are my sisters," the woman said. "You must speak with our creator, you've been through a great deal of torment, but he will be able to make you whole once again. He's done it for us and he'll do it for you also."

Sharon nodded her head, right now she was too exhausted to care what happened to her. She wanted to fall into a deep slumber and never wake up again. Her eyelids grew heavy and she fell asleep again. Armistice picked up her body with the help of some of the other women. They flapped their wings leaving the place they had brought her to.

*D*ays passed like an hourglass, but the days were

so long without her and Esmeralda spent hours staring off

into the beautiful sunsets every day. She stepped onto her

favorite pillar and stood behind it and just looked off, she

may not have always shown how much she had enjoyed

her sister being there with her, but now it was like a

nightmare without her just thinking, wondering if she was

still alive. At times she even thought she heard her

laughing or giggling like she used to do when they were

small children, but it was never her, it always turned out to

just be inside her own imagination.

Then it would always make her sign disappointedly

and slouch back down on the pillar, looking off into the

sunset imagining what life would be like if she had never

lost her. Having power wasn't so great if you didn't have

anyone to share it with or if you weren't able to share a

laugh every once in a while. Her skirt blew in a small breeze that went by her, the black skirt reflected off the sun's light making it look like it had little orange living butterflies attached to it.

Nothing would be right until she had her sister back with her and she knew that and whatever her father thought about her didn't matter. Her long dress dragged behind her as she went inside the palace. Woodcrafter Uri was slouching in his chair as he watched some doves fly around, he was so unamused by anything these days. His eyes lit up when he saw Esmeralda enter the room, perhaps she would amuse him with a performance.

"Father, I must ask you for a favor," she said, kneeling before him.

He positioned himself upright. "Anything."

"I want to find Gabrial," she told him as his eyebrows rose at the name. "I don't believe she is dead and

I was wondering if I could find her and finish her for good," her tone was piercing like a sword.

"So what if she's not dead, I care to think that the humans will get the job done." A soft chuckle slipped from him. "But if you want to try that's fine, more excitement to see who kills her first."

Esmeralda smiled that her intentions were not to kill Gabrial as her father believed, but at least it would make it easy for her to leave without any problems. He chuckled softly as he walked around his chair.

"One other thing, father. I need to get rid of my wings lest the humans find out my identity."

"Of course. Of course. I will most certainly find a way to hide those for you," his tone was calm.

This time when she found her sister, she would be sure to let no one stand in the way of their relationship and that meant nobody, even if Gabrial cared about them. She would be the only one that Gabrial would care about and the only thing she cared about just like when they were little girls.

****

The fire of the forest could be seen for miles along with the smoke that showered ash upon the kingdom. For a while now he had waited for this opportunity, an opportunity to storm into the palace with no restraint. He knew she was there, he knew they had found her. The doors were pushed in and he stormed inside taking both of his swords from out of the halter behind him. They charged at him like the guards before the gateway he had entered and as he slaughtered them without restraint he did the same to them.

"Tell me what is your greatest fear in this world?" he held a soldier by the throat, his legs dangling as he wheezed for air.

"The darkness sir," he answered.

He felt the Black Knight's sword pierce through him and he choked. "Fear the darkness, yes, but fear the one who is darkness more." he dropped the soldier's body down to the floor and continued his parade through the palace.

Every soldier, every guard falling beneath his sword, it was like he was a one-man army. He laughed when he came upon the grand doors. The doors instantly flew back when he pushed them. Damien's eyes met his as he wondered how in the world had he come this far. To his surprise, the knight was dressed more like a samurai than a knight. He didn't wear their armor or anything.

"The Black Knight," he muttered, dropping his chess piece. "Why are you here?"

His mother hugged her husband in fright hoping this wasn't the end for the two of them.

"Guard!" GUARDS!" she yelled, panicking.

"Save your breath, they're all dead!" he spat. "I came here in search of the angel Sharon! I know you have her! Hand her over and no one gets hurt!"

Damien squinted his eyes and laughed. "What are you talking about?"

"The quake the other day, you know that was no coincidence! You knew that she had come!" he spit on the floor as he walked closer to them, his swords, side by side.

"He's crazy." whispered the queen.

"Maybe, then maybe not!" he looked up at the ceiling.

"Crazy? I'll admit I'm a lot of things, but being crazy is not one of them," he laughed. "Sharon exists whether or not you believe me or rather hide her for your own purposes such as immortality, powers, treasures, the things the mind of normal humans think of when they seek to find something that is supposedly a myth."

Damien had to listen to him now after hearing the word immortality. Who wouldn't want to live forever? He could really use this guy for his own good such as finding the place where she may have fallen if he could find a way to capture him.

"YOUR HIGHNESSES!" cried Sir Hamilton, entering the room.

The Black Knight turned around distracted, Damien used this as his opportunity to disarm him. He lunged forward at the knight with his sword, but was kicked in the back of his head by him. The two swords crisscrossed past his neck, biting into the marble floor below Damien's face.

"For a man of your status I'd say that was a pretty stupid move," he scolded as Damien choked his mother and father crying out his name.

"Don't harm the prince," cried Sir Hamilton. "Or you will be charged with more than trespassing."

"And what do you know about trespassing little boy?" he snarled as his voice deepened.

The prince staggered trying to grab his sword, then suddenly the ground began to shake a little, then a whole group of knights came swarming into the room like bees. The Black Knight laughed.

"So this is your backup when you see no other way out? Lousy. Very lousy. Because I have you as my safety deposit."

"Look I'll make a deal with you," wheezed Damien.

"Ha! Like anyone ever made a deal with darkness and survived, but I'm listening," he said.

"If I gain control of the kingdom and find your angel while you go to prison until then will you let me live?" he asked as if he would ever hand over something so valuable to scum like him, but he hoped his plan would work.

The Black Knight thought for a little while, Damien felt the swords release his neck and he was able to stand up again. The knights charged at the Black knight after dropping his swords, he was knocked to the floor and shackled around both his arms and ankles.

"Put him in prison and let him rot. Dirt like him doesn't deserve to roam our streets." he acted as they took him away.

His parents watched as the enemy was carried away. How had he come this far just to surrender like that?

It didn't seem right, at least not to his mother, who knew how Damien's mind worked. A smirk appeared on his face when he turned to meet their faces.

"Don't worry he is locked away for good this time." he knew what he meant by that and by the look on his mother's face she may have known too.

✳✳✳✳✳✳✳✳✳✳✳

The girl slipped from off the lion's back and into the grass, the little blades tickling between her toes. Emmanuelle nuzzled her with his nose, his dark, soft eyes staring at her. She looked up at him, then started stroking his mane.

"Thank you," she said.

"You're very welcome, Gabrial." the lion replied.

His ears started to twitch and his focus was shifted from her to something else. He looked around the silent forest or at least as far as she could tell, but for him, he heard something that she couldn't. He seemed to grow more frightened with each passing moment. Gabrial looked into his deep innocent eyes, there was only fear present within them. Even in the darkness of the pine forest his eyes still stood out. The lion looked at her for a long moment without saying anything, then in through the silence of the forest, she heard something too. People. She noticed a trail of torches winding their way through the forest towards her and the lion. The lion nudged her with one of his broken wings.

"We must go or they will take us both as captives," he explained.

"Captive? What do you mean?" she asked.

"Never mind, I'll explain it to you later. Now get on," he answered as he crouched down.

Gabrial climbed on as she did before, but for some reason, the lion felt tenser than before. The lion took off into the forest, his massive paws crunching the old leaves.

The sound of the people behind them was louder than before.

"THERE HE IS! OVER THERE!" he heard a few of them yell.

The forest suddenly came to an end and he ran into a small town where an assembly of people stood with their fiery torches and weapons. The assembly roared with anger and chaos as they looked upon the great beast.

Emmanuelle was so frightened he began to back down into

the forest, he shook his head trying to fight away the

anxiety that was now present within his heart, but as he

backed into the forest, the other group of people emerged

and threw their torches at him.

Emmanuelle jumped forward into more torches

that came flying through the air at him. He tried flapping

his broken wings and a current of wind blew a few of the

people down with their torches and weapons. The lion only

found himself in more frustration and torture, when his

wings were unable to work. Gabrial hugged his neck

tightly as if he were her teddy bear.

"See everyone, he's a monster! Kill him!" one of

the people yelled.

The others agreed and arose onto their feet and charged at

the lion with their torches and knives, along with other

weapons. The lion covered his face with one of his paws

trying to protect his eyes. A few times he groaned with pain when he felt their sharp weapons pierce through his fur. He suddenly stopped covering his face when he got tired of the poking, stabbing, and burning, he roared at them with all the pain they had given him. The people skidded back on their feet, but that hadn't stopped them.

"NO STOP HURTING HIM!" cried Gabrial, jumping from off his back, then running in front of him as if her small self would be able to protect him from the assembly of angry people.

The people stopped and studied her for a long moment, they were somewhat surprised that a girl would try and save a gigantic beast like him. She began to cry as if she felt the pain of the lion, then she said. "This monster as you call him is my best friend and the only friend I have. Why are you people so intent on killing him, can't you see, he is trying his best not to harm anyone, that just because he's different, it doesn't mean that he should be killed or persecuted for it. It's not like he chose to be what

he is, it's just him." she explained as her hands arose from

her side. "He's the one thing that has ever understood me

and cared, he's kind and gentle at heart."

The people stood there looking unmoved by the

words she was saying, although for a moment she thought

she had convinced them until she noticed the hatred that

glowed in their eyes like flames.

"If anyone should die, I will." she volunteered,

stepping forward.

The lion's head lifted when he heard those words,

he wouldn't let anyone harm her, even if it cost his life. He

bumped her with his nose and her blue eyes met his

golden-colored eyes. She smiled at him, then hugged his

nose since he was too massive for her to even wrap her

arms around his paw. "It's okay, I will be fine," she said, a

few tears coming from her eyes and slipping onto his fur.

"Don't leave me, Gabrial," wept the lion, a few giant tears slipping from his eyes.

"I…"

She was cut off when she was suddenly ripped away from Emmanuelle. He growled a little as he watched them drag Gabrial away from him. He moved his paw against the ground wondering what to do. Gabrial was thrown into the ground in the center of a circle of the angry mob. He couldn't see anything, but he could hear her screaming with pain.

He covered his ears trying to blot out as much of her pain as possible, but no matter how hard he tried to ignore it he couldn't. Everything she was feeling, it seemed as if he could feel it too and it felt like his heart was bleeding on the inside as long as he let her suffer. Emmanuelle ran to her rescue and pushed his way through the mob, only to see her curled up silently with her eyes closed.

More tears suddenly filled his eyes and he felt as if a knife was piercing through his heart. His tail fell down toward the ground, then he suddenly crouched down above her. He didn't understand it, how could he have let this happen to her. Emmanuelle suddenly let out a roar that sounded as if he could have opened the heavens above and the people were blown back. One of his tears fell from his eyes and onto her face, covering it completely, then soaking into her face. There was a little glow as it went inside her skin.

The lion lifted her off the ground with his nose, then slowly walked away. The angry mob only watched now, they stood by their word and left the lion alone, since she had given up her life for him. He walked out of the town, his tail dragging behind him as his head was lowered toward the ground, the darkness of the forest seeming as if welcoming him into a world of depression and sadness. He eventually came to a cliff where he dropped her off. Her hair blew in front of her face as the wind whipped past her. She was closed and she looked as if she were asleep.

Tears from the lion fell after her, nearly incaging her within the tears. Gabrial's body suddenly hit the surface of the water and everything came to a sudden stop as if someone had paused everything for one quick moment, then she slowly sank into the water. Her lips turned purple and she became pale as snow as she froze causing the lake to freeze over. As if time itself were in slow motion, snow began to fall from the sky, never before had it snowed in these parts until now.

✳✳✳✳✳✳✳✳✳✳✳

Damien stared out his window at the falling snow, he didn't know how long it would take him to find her, but however long it took he knew that it would be worth the wait since there was a chance that he might be able to live forever.

"Are you ready sir?" asked the coachman.

"Of course, I've waited a long time for this." he

laughed softly.

The carriage started through the paved streets of

the little town. It had been a while since he had been

outside of the castle walls. He had forgotten the noise of

the shouting people and barking dogs that ran free through

the streets. A few of the people stared at the carriage trying

to get a glimpse of who would be traveling in such a

luxury carriage.

They were unable to see past his curtains. All the

staring and attention made him feel proud to be above the

average man to be looked upon as something great. Soon

they would not only look upon him because of his wealth

but also because of his wisdom and immortality he would

soon gain.

Chapter 4

Alone in Desolation

There in a tall throne chair sat a creature that

looked kind of like Anubis, except made of steel and there

was a red glow from his slant eyes that stared at her from

the moment she was brought into his presence. Sharon was

resting on the floor before him and he stood up with his

large staff with a glowing blue ball at the center. A smirk

appeared on his face when he looked upon her.

She shivered with fright as he came closer to her. He patted her on the shoulder, then leaned over and whispered something into her ear. Armistice's head tilted up, alertly as she tried to hear what he was saying to the wounded angel. Whatever he had said, seemed to have made the angel uneasy and apprehensive.

"So Armistice, why have you brought this one to me?" he asked as if he didn't already know the answer. "She's not one of you."

"I agree sir," answered the iron angel, bowing slightly. "But I believe that just because of her slight difference doesn't overpower the greatness you possess."

He chuckled, softly. "Well said as always. Well said, indeed," he snarled, happily as he looked at Sharon.

Some 1,000 years later

Sunlight peeked through treetops. The grass soaking up the morning dew and the sun's warmth and there in the midst of all the silence a strange whistle blew along with the wind. Gabrial sat there in the grass, her hair blowing past her face as she held one of her arms with her hand. The wind pressed against her bareback.

Death looked upon her, she was still as peaceful but bitter as when she had first come to the place for him, keeping her as his prisoner to entertain himself since nothing in his dimension made him happy. She had wondered why her life hadn't ended like it was supposed to like everyone else? He sighed. He had to tell her the news, whether she responded or not.

"Gabrial, daughter of Uri. I have come to retrieve you from your affliction, I had a vision last night." his tone was disappointed for this meant he would be alone with only the fun of toying with those he had already broken.

Her head slowly turned to see a tall beast that looked like he was half reaper and beast, girded with armor and a sword, which was pressed inside of his halter, he had wings dark as night. The scales on his hands glinted the light of the sun. She didn't smile, she just turned back around and stared at the grass. She wanted to be left alone and disturbed no more.

"I will admit that we cannot change the past, nor what has happened, but I know we can forget it and let it be and restart everything if you are willing to leave it just as that…" he bit his lip… "the past and the world will give you another chance if you are willing to deny who you are along with forgetting. If you choose not to… well you can stay here and live as a prisoner for the world can be very unforgiving"

Gabrial looked up at him again. "And is that all? Forget who and what I am so I can live once more in a world of desolation without truth, love, faith, and hope. Is living in a world like that not death?"

He nodded his head slightly. "I suppose it is all in how you look at it." answered the winged beast. "Anything is better than being in my prison for fun, after all, you've been here for three whole years. Isn't that good enough? I mean I could live with you staying here."

The girl looked down at a river that was now flowing through the grass at her reflection. All she could see was blankness and despair written throughout her past, maybe it was time to forget it all and even surrender what she was to become something again. "Fine, maybe I will try again," she said, she knew what it meant for him when he let a soul free, it was another bone for him along with losing his biggest bone.

He smiled, then said. "You will not regret this." The winged man threw a raggedy dress at her. "I will grant you new apparel and we can do away with your old ones. Though they may not be much better, they are something besides that and I will take you away from this place."

Gabrial hurried and put on a new raggedy dress and clipped a broach that was shaped like wings. The winged beast lifted her from the ground and he flapped his dark wings, leaving behind the place she once rested, he arrived at a gateway, where he set her down on a crystal floor. He kissed her hand with curtsy.

"I will indeed miss you Gabrial and if there was any way I could convince the visions to go away so I could keep you, I would," he smirked a little revealing his razor-sharp teeth that looked like that of a shark.

Above she could hear the chant of all those that died before her that had been taken as his permanent prisoners. They were a fiery bunch like dragons, their eyes were lit with a green fire like emeralds. They were angry that he was letting her free and the floor shook from their stomping, but there was no way for them to get loose unless he set them free from their bondage like he had done for her. If they were free, they would have most certainly tried to devour her, jealous of the life she was given. Her eyes turned away from them as she directed her attention to Death, who was speaking to her.

"Now I must warn you before you go, that you can tell no and I mean no one about what you are. If they find out on their own, there will be no consequence, but if otherwise, it will be the day you die. A life for a life, remember that," he stated. "Also you will remember none of this nor what has happened before only the words I speak and your identity with some exceptions of what had occurred to you as far as your father."

She shook her head in agreement, then she put one of her feet into the gateway, then a smile suddenly crept onto her face. "Thank you, Death!"

He looked at her for a long moment, she hadn't spoken anything to him the past three years. Her words had taken him by surprise. "You're welcome," he finally replied.

She was suddenly enclosed by a light that was as bright as the sun, then she vanished. Death stared into the gateway in somewhat of a daydream, when he came out of it he turned then flapped his wings and left the place where the gateway was, leaving behind the angry group of dead beings that were trying to reach to grab at him as he flew by.

****

She was like a phantom, a dream not even real now. All his dreams had been broken and lost with her, but he knew one thing. If he were given a second chance he wouldn't become that bonded with her for the sake of his heart. No. He would only be her protector and see to it that no one ever harmed her again and he wouldn't be this beast or monster that he had now become. His eyes reopened to show the darkness and instincts that had now taken the place of where love and beauty were all once present and he had learned to accept what and who he was.

Gabrial had fallen and so had his whole world so why not just become what they always proclaim you to be, there's nothing for you to be for anyone, but that since that is all they see when you come around. They scream. Yes. They torture what is not understood, before ever taking a deeper look to try and understand it. They treat you as if everything you say is foreign to them because they are afraid to look upon you.

So since that one person who saw you for something else that you thought would be there with you forever has now vanished, withered away like all flowers in their seasons, become what everyone says you should be or what they see you as. A monster.

A tear slipped from the lion's eye, but that would be the last tear he ever shed because he had become what they had called him all the time he was what he is now. It was a burden to carry and a heavy one at that but no one was going to do it for him and that was for certain. Innocence has died and now evilness has replaced it.

Rain poured on top of Gabrial's face as she lay in the muddy water on the road. Lightening crossed the sky shedding light upon her face. Damien looked out his window only to feel the water pour down onto his damp face. He growled. He had been up and down this road like a million times and had searched this forest and there was never any sign of the angel. A dark kitten ran off into the street; he took one look at Gabrial's face, then tapped it with one of his paws curiously. When she didn't wake up, he tapped her again.

She opened her eyes only to see the little kitten staring into her eyes with his spellbound eyes. Death had perished and she was now back on earth. A smile appeared on her face, he was so cute and innocent her heart could have melted. Then she heard the sound of horseshoes from the carriage grow louder. It slowed as it approached her.

"WHOOOO EEE! THERE!" yelled the driver as his grip on the reins tightened as he stopped the horses.

"Why have you stopped Fernan?" demanded prince Damien, annoyedly.

"I think I found something." he looked down the dark road.

"It better be worth the stop." he shoved open the door and got out.

He looked down at Gabrial who was playing with the kitten. If she were the angel he was looking for, where were her wings? She stared at him as she held the kitten in her hands, then she slipped him in her pocket afraid that the prince was coming to take it away from her as he came closer to her.

His boots swished in the muddy water, his eyes focused on her. Then again, perhaps she was the one since no one in their right normal would be sitting in the rain. He kicked some mud at her as his cold blue eyes stared at her as if searching for weakness. She was dressed like a peasant in a brown raggedy dress.

"Are you Sharon?" he asked, his voice bellowing as the rain poured.

She looked at him, who was he and why did he call her by that name? She didn't answer, she stood up from the ground onto her bare feet. Something was unsettling about his spirit, it felt dark and evil, it made her want to run from him although she didn't know where to.

"I asked you, are you Sharon? Do you not know who I am?" he questioned, angrily.

Gabrial fell silent as she watched as he drew his sword from his halter and he moved a little quicker towards her. Before anything could happen she darted off into the dark forest of oak trees. Wet sticks and leaves swiping against her face as she pushed past, she held the kitten inside her pocket. Unfortunately, she came to another road, where the prince was standing with a lantern and a rope in his hand.

"Seen this place about as many times, you learn that every shortcut leads to the same place." he chuckled, tossing the rope at her.

She tried to run back into the forest but tripped when her foot got caught in his rope. He laughed as he watched her struggle helplessly as her hands slipped as she tried to pull one rope off and found another one. The kitten scurried from out of her pocket and attempted to help, but it was hopeless. As soon as Damien came in closer the kitten leaped back into her pocket to hide from him.

The young man placed his sword slowly beneath her chin, the sharper end pointed at her neck. "I am Prince Damien of Ascedia! Now is your name Sharon?"

She could feel the sword growing more and more dangerously close to her neck and she said. "My name is Gabrial."

A smirk appeared on his face as the sword moved away from her neck. He secured her wrist wrapping the ropes around them again and again until it looked like her arms were covered in wrist bands. She looked down at the muddy ground that was flooded in water, the cat moving closer to her as he pulled on the ropes to help her.

"Meow?"

"I've tried, but they won't loosen." she cried looking at the ropes.

The kitten crawled up onto her and got back inside her pocket. Damien grabbed her by the arm and led her to the carriage for so long he had waited for this moment and now it had finally come his trek was complete and he could finally return home.

"You will come with me!" he announced, swinging his cape. "And you will become my soon be wedded wife, but until then, you will remain hidden from the world, wearing a silver cloak, and when our day of marriage comes you shall take the vow to be in submission to me for the rest of your life or if not you can remain my prisoner for all I care."

Gabrial remained under all his commands and orders, living in a cold tower that was up a staircase that could go on forever. She was forced to scrub the stone floors, clean dishes, sweep anything that he required. Her hands grew tired but there were never any blisters or sores on them. A dish dropped onto the floor and Gabrial's cat jumped out of the way.

"Oh no." she cried, getting down onto her knees to clean up the mess until a foot stepped onto her hand, pushing it down into the floor as if hoping to break it.

She looked up as she pulled her hand loose to meet a tall older man's hazel eyes, he was smiling at her. "Clumsy little peasant." he laughed, kicking the glass around then moving his foot near her.

"Stop!" cried Gabrial trying to push his foot away from her.

His laughter came to a stop when he heard a woman yell from behind him. "Sir Gilliot leave the poor maid alone, it profits your name little to be found doing such a thing."

He moved his foot away, then walked out of the kitchen. The woman ran inside to help Gabrial, who had started picking up the glass. She crouched down beside her and helped.

"I can take care of this if you'd like?"

"No. No, I can take care of it. Thanks for asking." she smiled at her.

"You're welcome. I'm Maid A'key by the way, I've seen you working here for quite some time now. Are you new? Asked the maid picking up some of the glass.

"Yes. My name is Gabrial."

"Gabrial. Hmmm. Sounds like I've heard that name, anyway, I don't mean to intrude but why are you here? You look like…" Maid A'key looked at Gabrial and although she was dressed like a peasant there was something about her that still seemed to stand out from the other maids in the palace "…Like you've been taken care of by someone who loves and cares about you."

Gabrial frowned when a piece of glass cut the tip of her finger. "Ouch!" she cried. "I don't remember much of my past. The only thing I remember happening was being found by Prince Damien who took me as his captive after he found me in the street."

"Oh. That's strange Prince Damien would never bother to take someone as captive yet alone bring someone he found back to the palace to make them a maid. I guess he hasn't been the same and has been acting strangely since…." she stopped herself, no one else needed to know of the tragedy that had occurred in the royal family, she had probably already said too much.

"Since what Made A Key?" Gabrial questioned, perhaps whatever maid A'key had to say would tie in with a lot of the actions he was taking now.

****

Esmeralda looked at the girl's face covered by a hood, she was like her, evil and dark. Of course, she wasn't here in search of her, she was here searching for the one that Gabrial may have been close to. The dust in the arena picked up as the girl stepped forward, slowly a smile appearing on her face, then she pulled her hood off to reveal her long bluish-gray hair that blew in the breeze.

She bit her lip, annoyedly as she watched the girl go parading around the circular arena going on about her triumphs over those that had dared to fight her. The crowd went wild and then she stopped and stared, raising her finger slowly to point at Esmeralda with a scornful laugh.

"Lift your eyes for today this one shall also fall before my feet like those before her with a thud of death they never expected." her knives clanged together as she pulled it out of her pocket.

"I shall not fall before you for I am greater than those you challenged before." snapped Esmeralda as her look of weakness vanished from her face revealing the dangerous masked behind it. "I will slay you making you choke on the words you have spoken," she chuckled.

The crowd shouted at her with disgust and anger. "Snowflare will lay you down! You will pay!" some of them yelled.

The flag was lifted and the two of them circled the arena, eying each other like wolves.

"Is that all you're going to do and think that will kill me!" Snowflare laughed.

Esmeralda stopped, along with Snowflare who suddenly lunged her body forward at her. Only to find herself colliding with Esmeralda, who tackled her to the ground.

She pushed her knives towards the girl with dark hair, but

she was so strong. Her laughter was so evil, it was as if she

were trying to scare her into being still. Snowflare's knives

were forced out of her hand and sent flying into the air.

Her eyes widened, no one had ever done that to her. The

crowd fell silent looking at their winner being taken down.

"Get off me!" she yelled, squirming beneath

Esmeralda.

Her head slammed into the ground and it felt like blood

was rushing from all over and up her head. It was slammed

into the hard ground, again and again. This girl showed no

restraint and now Snowflare wished she hadn't said so

much. A few tears of frustration and pain fell from her

eyes as she growled trying to shove Esmeralda off.

"Stop!" she choked.

For a moment Esmeralda stopped and let her have

a breather, slowly standing up onto her bare feet.

Snowflares perfect face had so many scratches and marks on it, she yelled angrily. The girl had stripped her of her looks along with her title in one day. She leaped up from the ground, then ran at Esmeralda. Her hair was suddenly grasped tightly in Esmeralda's grip.

"Urgh!" she screamed in fury. "Release me now!"!

The girl was thrown so far back, sometimes hitting the ground as she skidded across until she hit a solid wall. She took one last look at Esmeralda, now standing triumphantly, then she collapsed letting her eyes shut. Everyone in the crowd gasped, she was down something they never thought would happen.

"NO ONE HAS NOTHING TO SAY!" she laughed. "I AM ESMERALDA AND I HAVE COME TO SLAY THE ONE WHO SEEKS TO STEAL MY PLACE!"

Chapter 5

The Girl Beneath the Silver Hood

Armistice walked closer to Sharon, her arms

stretched out as she stood in the center of a circular

doorway. She laid her head on her arm, uncomfortably

until the angel touched her face lightly and made her look

her way.

"What's happening?" she whispered, worriedly.

The angel set a silver piece on top of her head. "It's alright Sharon, our master knows what he's doing. You have to trust me."

As much as she wanted to, she longed to go home and be within her soul mate's arms again. Even in her pain, she would hardly be conscious of it with him. Suddenly, she felt something painful like a sword strike through her back. She gulped for air looking at Armistice's light brown cobra eyes staring at her.

Waves of golden threads began to make their way around her, wrapping her in light. The other iron angels closed their eyes, along with Armistice. Sharon felt as if her heart might stop or that all this power would overwhelm her and make her blow into a million pieces of dust.

It was so painful she couldn't even scream. A tear appeared in the corner of her eye, not once in her life had she experienced pain this intense. A pain that had done *something that never would have occurred made her shed*

tears.

Some 1,000 years later

There were so many secrets that lurked within the

castle walls, but of course, to every question there had to

be answers. Gabrial wandered around the palace for weeks,

ever since Maid A'Key had struggled to answer her

question. What could she possibly be hiding? Knights

marched through the hallways, holding poles with the

kingdom's flag.

A winged lion and a crown upon his head. It caught

her eye, the lion reminded her of Emmanuel. Emmanuel,

she still remembered him, but how? She thought her

memory was erased when she came back. Still, there was

something that she found very interesting about the flag.

Why would a lion need a crown, when he was so great

already? Sure everyone knows that the lion was the king of

the wilderness. Could it have possibly had some other kind of significance? She would have followed the knights secretly if Maid A'Key hadn't stopped her.

"Gabrial darling, I've been looking all over for you." she declared. "Prince Damien wants to meet with you and he says it is urgent. He has all his guards searching the palace for you." her eyes rolled with worry. "Oh my. My. My. There is no telling what he would have done if he saw that you were missing."

"What do you mean?" questioned Gabrial.

"There is no time to explain now. We must go!" She pulled Gabrial along with her along the hallway that was covered with red carpet.

Prince Damien was seated in a chair, moving wooden figures across a map, when the guard of the door opened it so Gabrial and Maid A'Key. He beckoned for them to come forward, his face full of anger.

"Leave us Maid A'Key," he ordered her as he swatted.

Maid A'Key gave Gabrial a cautious look before she was escorted out. After the door had closed there was an awkward silence that filled the atmosphere. He was staring at her a long, quiet moment, almost so quiet you could hear a pebble hit the floor.

****

Queen Eliza looked into her mirror as she put on her makeup. She loved herself more than anything in the world and she never liked a single hair out of place and wrinkles on her face were like having boils to her.

"My lady I hate to disturb you but there is someone who would like to speak with you." said a guard almost hysterical as he shoved the door open.

"Who thinks they can charge into the queen's time like…."

106

"It is Snowflare." laughed a young woman, stepping into her room.

Shock and terror-filled her both at the same time. "How did you…"

"Survive?" she answered. "Oh cousin I may have been a little naive at least in your sight, but I'm not unaware of your schemes especially when you set me up with some girl like that in the arena. You knew what she was capable of before you put her in there. Besides, I'm the same way." she threw a knife she had pulled out of her pocket at the queen's mirror, shattering it.

"What do you want?" asked Queen Eliza, letting go of her ears.

"Don't worry, it's not much." she walked over, then sat down beside her cousin and whispered. "I want my powers back. I need to get my revenge."

"Snowflare have you gone mad? Those powers are dangerous, I don't even know what happened to them.

After you left to fight as a career in the arena I saw no reason for those powers to be around." she explained.

"Come now Eliza, you and I both know that you wouldn't get rid of anything like that at least not without gaining something yourself." Snowflare began to laugh. "Keep hiding them, I'll be sure you meet with someone very special in due time if you refuse." her knife grew dangerously close to the queen's neck.

"Fine. Fine. I gave those powers to a witch in return for my youth."

"What witch? Where does she live?" questioned Snowflare.

"She calls herself the mother of nature and she lives in the depths of Wails Lake, but no one ever dares to go there. The place is surrounded by bones that come alive and seek to drag the living into their graves to join them."

Snowflare stood up quickly heading for the door. "You better not be lying to me, believe me, life has a way of getting us back with some of our own medicine." she wiped her finger up her knife as if giving her a message. "Watch out for the apocalypse that may take place right before your eyes."

****

Prince Damien looked out the window, then began to laugh, suddenly turning and pointing at Gabrial. "You think you can keep your identity hidden from me. Well, I'm sorry to blow it for you, but I and others already kind of know of it."

She looked down at the floor trying not to show how uneasy she was feeling now. He tapped her on the head to make sure she was paying attention.

"I've also decided to marry you by tomorrow so this secretive thing will be ending and I will make sure of it." he declared.

"I will never marry you," she said looking up at him. "Not ever."

He chuckled softly. "We'll see about that, anyway you have no choice. I'm making you."

"Then it's not marriage and I will not disgrace the tradition of marriage, it's dishonest." Gabrial walked away from him toward the door only to find that it was locked. The prince pressed his hand into the door, smiling at her like a clown of something evil. "You think it would be that easy to escape me, not until you tell me the truth." he pushed her hand off the knob.

"I'm not marrying you and I won't say a word if you try and make me."

He put his finger at the bottom of her chin and made her look at him. "No one and I mean no one ever gets away with something that I want, not even themselves. You are my possession, do you not understand that." he wrapped his hands around hers and squeezed them. "I will have everything I want from you."

She struggled to pull her hands away from him, his eyes burning into hers. Then he finally let her go and opened the door. Gabrial ran out but stopped in the hallway to turn when she heard him say something.

"You can try and run away from what you are, but remember you can never escape the shadow that defines you." he laughed as he closed the door. "I always get what I want."

Although he may have appeared to be mad at times, what he said always made sense and it was always somehow haunting. She walked down the halls alone, hugging herself. Some gargoyles seemed to be glaring down at her as if they knew what she was. There had to be a way to escape this place, she couldn't stay here, not when he was trying to make her marry him against her will. There was no telling what he would do next and that frightened her.

She found Maid A'Key sweeping in the kitchen, along with other maids who were hard at work. The expression on her face seemed as if she was uncomfortable for some reason.

"Are you alright Gabrial?" she asked as she watched Gabrial starting to dry dishes.

"Of course," answered Gabrial, briskly.

"It's him, isn't it? He's forcing you into marriage," said Maid A'Key.

Gabrial shook her head, but how did she know? A few of the other maid's heads perked up at the word marriage waiting to listen to what was happening. She noticed them and decided not to say anything else about it.

"Can I ask you a question, privately?" she whispered to Maid A'Key.

Maid A'Key shook her head in agreement, noticing the nosy maids also. The two of them walked out of the kitchen and into the pantry, where there was nobody in sight.

"Oh Gabrial I can't imagine you with him, he's an animal or beyond that, he's evil." she cried. "He could seriously hurt you, he's done it before."

"Done it before, what did he do?" asked Gabrial.

"That's not important it's in the past and we can't change it, but there is one thing I can do is make sure it doesn't happen again." she looked at Gabrial. "I know a way out of here..."

The pantry was so dark that they hadn't noticed one of the nosy maids, eavesdropping on them.

"...It's a long dark tunnel built beneath the tunnel, it was once used for the knights and soldiers as a way to get in and out secretly during the war. The tunnel will take you to the docks and well I guess you'll be leaving." she broke into tears and hugged Gabrial. "I'll miss you, you've been my best friend since you've been here."

“I’ll miss you too.” cried Gabrial, hugging her back. Maid A’Key was like the mother Gabrial had never had, always there to help and talk to.

The maid that had been eavesdropping on them giggled as she thought of how Prince Damien would like to hear of this news.

✳✳✳✳✳✳✳✳✳✳✳

The doors of Damien’s room opened and the maid ran in like a desperate rat for cheese. He stood up quickly and yelled at the guard. “Why has this peasant been sent before my presence?”

“I come with a message sir that is urgent.” She was breathing heavily. “Gabrial is planning to leave the palace at this very moment, through some tunnels beneath the palace.”

He stared down at the maid, who bowed before him for a long moment. “Gabrial, leave the palace? This very moment? Fin.” he called the guard inside. “Rally up all

114

members of the palace guard and tell them I want them to go into the tunnels beneath the palace, and send others to the docks where the tunnel ends. Bring back the girl Gabrial.”

“Yes sir,” he said, saluting him then racing off.

The maid was still on the floor, chuckling deceitfully. “And what are you expecting? A bone or two as your payment for bringing me such bad news.” He slouched in his chair, annoyedly, then he threw a couple of coins onto the floor at her. “There, now get out of my sight.”

She scurried out of the room after picking up the coins like a starving dog making him feel disgusted toward her and wished he hadn’t even given her that. She hadn’t done that much to feel that good or like she was going to be honored at least not to him. For him, it only added to his irritation.

Maid A'Key smiled at Gabrial as she vanished into the dark tunnels with only her lantern that reflected off her silver cloak.

"Good luck," she whispered.

Gabrial walked for hours through the tunnel looking around and sometimes seeing shadows from chains that hung in the tunnel dancing across the walls. Sometimes she heard squeaks as she walked through the dark water. The whole place was eerie, unsettling for who knew what the darkness held ahead of her. Suddenly the whole tunnel began to shake and she heard yelling from men. She turned around only to see flashing lights that grew closer to her every moment.

She began to run, afraid that the knights or soldiers would come and take her back to Prince Damien. A place that she didn't want to be. The tunnel came to an end at the docks as Maid A'Key had told her. Boats were lined up along the dock and she knew how she was going to get away. As soon as she tried to get onto the boat her arm was grabbed and she was yanked back falling into the water, along with pulling the person that had grabbed her in.

Sir Gilliot laughed as he watched her struggle to keep her head above water. She couldn't swim and she waved her arms like a struggling fish out of water. She screamed with terror afraid that she was going to drown. The knight approached her, his laughter sounding muffled. His face was like seeing a shark that was coming to attack. She didn't want to be taken back, but at the same time, she wasn't willing to drown. More knights jumped in to help him pull her back onto the boardwalk.

"So we have a fugitive that is afraid of water?" laughed Sir Pelacio as he and the other knights dragged her onto the old wooden boardwalk.

Their laughter filled the air all around her, but she was too exhausted and cold to say a thing. She was going back whether she liked it or not. She shivered all the way they took her back. What was going to happen to her? Had Maid A'Key been also caught? She let her eyes close so all the worries vanished from her mind.

∗∗∗∗∗∗∗∗∗∗∗∗

Darkness hovered over the palace, there was a storm on the rise. Queen Eliza looked out a window watching as the knight fought to try to drag Gabrial back into the palace. She didn't understand her son, surely there were fairer women in the world, why would he chose to marry a peasant? A frown made its way onto her face, something was up and she was going to find out what it was.

"Eliza, my queen," chuckled King Charles, surprising her.

"Charles," she replied in almost shock, she didn't want him to know that she was spying on the knights. "I was just looking at how dark the sky has become so quickly."

"Amazing, huh?" he looked out the window and up at the sky.

Everything he did annoyed her, it always had and now more than ever. He was always so laid-back, patient and his kindness towards everyone disgusted her. It was a wonder why he had lived so long, anyone could have attempted by now to kill him and he probably wouldn't have known until it happened. She would have done it herself if she didn't have Damien's threat hanging over her head.

"Care to sit? You look tired," she asked, pushing a chair up behind him.

He groaned as he sat down. "You know I find it amazing how I look these days and how you haven't changed a bit, it's like you discovered a little magic of your own."

She smiled a little as she poured tea into a cup for him. "We all learn a little magic of our own. I guess it comes with age."

King Charles nodded his head, then took a sip of his tea. "That is true. Oh, what do you think of Damien's bride?"

"You mean that peasant," snapped Queen Eliza, almost showing her true colors.

"I wouldn't say that, but I don't think Damien's the right person for her. I look at how he's treated her for the past few months. He doesn't love her and that's apparent, so I don't understand why he is trying so hard to marry her." He ran his fingers through his long brass beard.

"Damien never loves anyone," she muttered, thinking of how much she couldn't stand Charles, she was the same way. She had only married him for his kingdom and to escape the rules of her father. "I wouldn't let his marriage disrupt my mind that much, he's a grown man now and I can't even say young, because he is thirty-two years of age."

"Exactly my point," King Charles set his teacup down quickly. "That maiden is too young, not even an adult, only about seventeen or sixteen at least and you know what he's capable of."

"Charles it doesn't matter, he has his reasons and we have to go along with his reasons," she sipped on her tea casually, sometimes glaring at Charles.

The two of them sat near the window in silence, sipping on their tea listening to the rain outside. It always fell silent whenever the two of them couldn't agree on something and to avoid arguing they both would fall silent. Candle lights that hung above on a chandelier flickered, whenever a soft breeze blew in.

Gabrial looked up at the ceiling that was decorated with a bunch of little angels with bows that shot heart arrows, Damien's voice echoing throughout the room as he yelled at her angrily. Her silver hood hanging over her head as if to hide her shame.

"What do you have to say for yourself?" he lifted her by the front of her cloak where her broach kept it connected. The ropes tighten around her wrist while she tried to get her hands loose.

"Morals are more important to me than what you think or do," she replied.

He dropped her to the floor, tearing the broach off. His hands pushed back his hair that was in a wreck from aggravation and a soft chuckle came from him after he turned his back. He yelled in his anger loud enough to shake the palace. Both King Charles and Queen Eliza looked at each other, what had happened?

"You know," he chuckled. "Until tomorrow you can remain in your room, because at least then I won't have to look at your pathetic face and suffer from your abominable speeches or quotes." he waved a finger, signaling a knight to come in and get her.

Sir Fin helped Gabrial from off the floor. "What do you…"

"Take her and lock her in the highest tower in this castle and guard it," he growled.

She looked back at Prince Damien standing with his hands behind his back in front of his father's throne.

Chapter 6

Love

Heknew it was wrong and that if he were

seen, he would be in grave danger. But he had to know

where she was. If she was still alive his heart couldn't bear

the heaviness of being lost in the abyss. He should have

gone with her and the others too if there had been a world

down there like theirs? Was that why she hadn't come

*back? If so, why did angels fear it so much? Why could
they only take possession of beings and not walk among
them as themselves? His shoulders burned as energy
pressed through them making the veins glow with blinding
light.*

*The glory of his wings showed as they unfurled
behind them. Their rims lined with gold, some of it falling
from it like snowflakes. If he left now and came back some
time, no one would ever know. He could hear a voice
inside his mind, speaking to him, enticing him to go now
and that no one would ever know.*

*The angel took a step on the glassy floors with
water flowing off the edges. He dove off the edge, the wind
blowing in his face like little blades until he let his wings
loose, catching like a parachute and he took to the dark
skies of stars that were scattered abroad like diamonds on
a black dress. He was coming and he was going to find her
no matter what danger lie ahead.*

Some 1,000 years later

The weeks were countless now. Esmeralda spent her time fighting and watching fights in the arena. One of the challengers interested her the most, it was a lion and perhaps the one that Gabrial had been close to. His name was Emmanuel, but he didn't seem at all like the villagers had told her. He was cruel, dirty and there was a wildness in his eyes that said he was dangerous. Many of the people who came to watch fights in the arena said that he was the most dangerous and evil creature they had ever seen. Regardless of his tendencies, she had chosen to fight up against him and was going to put him down once and for all just like she had done Snowflare, but this time it was personal.

The door to Gabrial's room slowly opened, Maid A'Key walked inside holding a plate and a glass. She didn't see Gabrial anywhere in the room when she looked around, then she noticed the door to the balcony was open. Outside on the balcony, she saw Gabrial sitting on the ledge looking down at the busy village of people below. Her silver cloak hung over the edge.

"Gabrial?" she said, slowly.

She opened her eyes and stared at Maid A'Key, a sudden smile creeping onto her face. "Hello Maid A'Key, I didn't expect to see you," replied Gabrial. "How are you?"

"I brought you this," Maid A'Key handed her the plate quickly. "I'm sorry but I can't stay."

She bolted inside the room leaving the plate on Gabrial's lap. She felt confused, what was wrong with Maid A'Key? Why couldn't she stay longer? Then her question was answered, when the prince entered the room. A crooked smirk passed on his face, while his dark cape blew behind him. He threw a dark dress at her when he was close enough.

"Do you like it?" he inquired, pretending to be interested in what she thought about the dress.

She shook her head, slipping off the ledge and onto her feet walking past him as she handed him back the dress then entered her room. He glared at her as he watched her drop down into her bed.

"Today is our wedding day, I thought you would like an early gift," he chuckled softly.

She sat up and looked at him. "I haven't forgotten and that gift won't make me change my mind about it. I'm not saying a word when it's our time to take vows. You can lie all you like."

He scratched his head, frustratedly. "You know at this point I've tried everything to try and convince you to do this nicely, but I see you won't do so, at least not without force. I'm sick of this attitude Gabrial!" he yelled.

She turned away ignoring him, she could care-less about how sick he was, it still wouldn't make her say a thing. She didn't love him and she wasn't about to take a vow of lies to make him stop torturing her. He hadn't stopped and there was no way he was about to.

"Can't you see…" his voice softened along with his eyes "… I love you and I want you to be the most perfect wife ever." He nearly choked when the words came from his mouth. He never loved anyone and he didn't love her.

"No, you don't." Listening to him say such a thing made her beyond sick and repulsed. "And I don't love you and I never will."

His eyes burned into hers, angrily. "Kiss me and then say that," he ordered, pulling her closer to him.

She tried to push him away, struggling to get him off of her.

"Listen here I'll make you a sweet deal. You marry me and your friend Maid A'Key doesn't get hurt," he laughed.

"You wouldn't dare harm her," she cried, looking away from him.

"Then marry me," Damien snarled, rubbing her arms. "Look at me when I'm talking to you."

"Fine I will, but I will never submit to you."

A crooked smirk appeared on his face as he stared at her. He didn't need any permission from her for anything, not even for the marriage. All he wanted was to make it look normal so he wouldn't be embarrassed when all the hosts watched and wondered what happened to her saying her part of the vows. He rested his hand on her waist, her pale eyes staring at him. What had she done?

Prince Damien walked out of the room, along with Gabrial who was walking alongside him with her eyes closed. Sir Fin stared for a long moment, he couldn't

figure out what Damien had done to keep her so calm at

least with him. She had avoided having as little dealings

with the prince as possible.

"Ready the coach for us," he ordered Sir Fin.

"Of course sir. Right away sir." he moved down the

hallway quickly.

The fresh air made her feel somewhat better,

although she couldn't shake off the disgust she felt for

Prince Damien. He was beyond even bad, he was

completely taken by evil. Nothing mattered to him, it was

as if he had lost all his morals, his conscience. Everything

that made a person think before they said or did anything.

✶✶✶✶✶✶✶✶✶✶✶

They sat in the arena's gallery, where they waited

for the show to start. Gabrial looked over, she could feel

that someone was in danger somewhere.

"Emmanuelle!" she cried, when she saw her lion

friend below, roaring as he tried to fight off people who

were trying to stab him.

She ran down the steps of the arena stairs, she

wasn't about to let anything happen to her friend.

"HEY! Get back here!" he yelled, standing up to

chase after her, "Guards! Guards! seize her!"

The guards chased after her, but they were unable

to catch up with her. Emmanuelle was chased out into the

center of the arena, where a girl with long black hair stood.

She was armed with all kinds of knives, swords, and

smaller weapons that could take down a massive beast like

him. "Come at me beast!" ordered Esmeralda, dangerously.

His eyes grew dangerous and wild with every

second. His massive mouth opened as if he was ready to

come and just swallow her. The lion charged at her like an

animal plagued in the mind, but he was unable to catch

her. She had leaped onto his back before he knew it. She stabbed knives into his back all at once. He roared with pain, then swatted and tossed himself all over the place trying to get her off of him. The crowd of people laughing in the background was even more patronizing.

Gabrial leaped down from the top of the seating area, hitting the ground, but there was no time for being sore right now; her friend's life was at stake. She ran out into the center of the arena where the fight was happening.

"STOP!" she yelled.

The girl was thrown off his back, flying a long way until she finally hit a brick wall that cracked from her impact. Emmanuelle took one look at Gabrial then at his enemy growling. He was still angry at the girl for making him look like a clown in front of the audience and ran at her although she was still down. He was furious by what she had done to him.

Gabrial stepped out into the middle to stop him, pulling down her hood to reveal her long flowing bluish-gray hair. Her heart pumped faster and it felt as if it were going to run out of her chest when she saw him racing toward her. Even though she was afraid, she stood her ground and he came to a sudden stop like a dog in front of its master.

Still, his eyes were full of rage and anger. He opened his massive mouth and roared, lifting his giant head in the air as if to intimidate her with his size. She stood there before the angry, roaring lion. His sound was louder and greater than anything in the world and the ground vibrated and there was an absolute silence across the entire arena as if heaven had opened, but she was unmoved by his behavior.

"It's alright, no one is going to harm you," she said calmly raising her hand to calm him as he raised his paw in the air as if to hit her. "Look at me! No one is going to

harm you!"

Even though she stood right before the beast and he

could easily smite her away with his claws like a ball of

paper, but for some reason, she knew he wouldn't do that.

A grin appeared on her face and she reached her hand out

to touch the surface of his nose.

"It's alright, you're not that evil monster they're

trying to make you think you are," she said with a

consoling tone as little white snowflakes landed on her

gentle face.

His left eye stared at her, along with the other one,

although it was nearly closed, it had been so messed up. It

was as if he were trying to remember her or as if he were

searching her soul and he suddenly knelt and bowed

himself before her. The king of all beasts was even

humbled to something so small. A human. Her forehead

bumped with his nose as she hugged it with her eyes closed.

"I remember you Emmanuelle. I remember you warmed my broken heart. I remember your heart was as pure as a crystal lake and you were the prince of love. The prince that everyone thought was a monster, but I loved you, and behold I still do," she whispered.

That name, the way she said it, he remembered her and his eyes began to show the innocence, where instincts and evil had once replaced. He let out a soft snort and the air from his nostrils blew across the dusty ground, creating small waves of sand.

Esmerelda pushed herself up by her elbows and angrily as she stared at her sister with the lion. How could Gabrial choose that beast over her, it was as if she hadn't remembered all the time they had spent together? She opened her large mouth like an angry dragon and shrieked, shaking the entire ground below them, but Gabrial hugged her friend and he remained at peace and his heartbeat was calm on the inside.

Suddenly a woman dressed in a bunch of red with patterns of animals and wildlife appeared out of the dust of the arena. She raised her hands and men appeared all around them out of the dust with drums. Their earlobes were long, paintings were marked all over them as their necklaces made out of bones jiggled together. The woman let out a loud sound that was as if singing.

Gabrial's eyes opened from all the commotion and she saw that the lion had begun to glow. Vocals surrounded the whole arena in complete harmony.

Damien's eyes had widened, he couldn't understand what was taking place. The woman was suddenly accompanied by an older man that looked like a medicine man. Light shone down upon the lion his ears moved like he was happy as he was elevated off the ground.

The woman and the medicine man sang together in harmony, along with some of the other men who were seated all around the arena. Mist swarmed all around Emmanuelle, his eyes reflecting off the sun's light.

The medicine man got down on his knees in front of the lion that was floating, he lifted his hands into the air as if giving alms, then began to sing another tune. His head shook as he spoke words from another language that no one could understand.

A few of them shook their tambourines as they sang along with the chant. It sounded like something from an old sacred African chant. They danced around as the medicine man threw dust from his bowl and at the lion. Suddenly Emmanuelle vanished into thin air.

A breeze blew past her and she looked up to the sky, realizing the lion was gone, but there in the sky, the clouds swirled creating somewhat of a lion formation. The crowd of people was silent as they looked up in awe and amazement at the great king in which they had persecuted. The vocals picked up in the chant, they were saying something that was causing more light to shine down upon the arena as they paraded around, flipping and bowing themselves.

His eyes were gentle and kind, but his face was serious and stern for having known his purpose. Birds flew past and through the cloud formation, not noticing the king, but as for all the creatures, including humans below who saw him and felt his presence all across the world, they bowed themselves with obedience for they knew exactly who he was. Never before had there been such a silence across the world and never would there be thereafter for indeed he was worthy of their praise.

Then everything stopped all the singing and chanting. The mysterious tribe of people had disappeared. Everyone looked up to see the clouds suddenly split, letting the sunlight escape into a bright beam of light before Gabrial's feet from above a young man slowly floated down to the ground inside the sun's light.

The young man was suddenly resting flat down onto the ground, the crowd of inquisitive people moved closer to the edge of the arena gallery, each of them trying to get a better look, someone from the crowd blurted. "IT'S THE PRINCE! HE LIVES!"

The young man pushed himself up with his elbows, shaking his head. Gabrial walked closer to help him, still trying to understand if the lion was a prince all along, if not where did the prince come from and where did the lion go? She took off her cloak as she approached him to cover him. She jumped back frightenedly when she heard him grunt a little. He looked up at her, a smile appearing on his face. She looked at his light brown eyes of pureness and for some strange reason, they reminded her of the lion. His hair was a light brunette that was short.

"Gabrial," he said, happily as he reached his hand out for hers.

Esmeralda watched as her sister walked closer to the odd young man, but didn't say or do anything. The girl put her cloak over him, then stepped back. Gabrial bowed to herself before him, but he took her hand and made her rise from bowing. "It is you that has saved me from my sin, you shall never bow before me nor anyone else," he announced. "I must ask you for one favor though. Will you stay with me forever?"

She looked up at him, then a smile appeared on her face, she nearly broke into tears. "Of course I will, your highness." she cried.

Emmanuelle clutched on tightly to the cloak and waved to his people. The crowd of people cheered and clapped their hands making praise for their prince had been found, all except for Prince Damien, who was more disgruntled than anything else for he knew what this meant for him. The guards ran out to go and greet their long-lost prince and the girl that had found him, flower petals were dropped from above by doves and the people that were now standing in the crowd, the flower petals looked like little flakes.

Although Prince Emmanuelle seemed to be very happy and excited his brother stared at the two of them with disgust, this was his day and he was stealing it, but there was nothing he could do right now unless he wanted to be arrested by the guards for trying to kill the prince. So he just watched and looked at them, knowing that he would get even with him one day.

All their way back to the palace people crowded the streets, cheering when they saw their lost prince riding upon a white horse, Gabrial holding onto the reins guiding the horse. Unfortunately, Emmanuelle had forgotten how to ride a horse so she had to do it for him. He held onto her waist, feeling a little uneasy. She smiled, happy that he would no longer have to suffer persecution and could finally take his rightful place in the kingdom.

"I see how horses feel about having four legs instead of two, " laughed the prince, happily.

Gabrial laughed with him, she could only imagine how it must've felt having two again. Damien stared out the window of the coach, now that he was back hardly anyone paid attention to him. He looked at Emmanuelle who was waving to everyone, kindly and laughing with joy to be finally normal.

He needed to enjoy this kind of praise while he could, though Damien thought it wasn't going to last long and he was going to make sure of that. The horse stopped in front of a large gateway that slowly opened letting them enter into the palace courtyard. There were wedding decorations everywhere, even a wedding carriage. What had been taking place while he was gone? He wondered as he looked around. Nothing seemed familiar, except for the marble stairs before the entrance of the palace.

"Was today someone's wedding day or something? I hope my appearance hasn't messed things up too badly," he asked Gabrial.

"Yes, but don't worry I'm sure they won't be too disappointed." She was happy that this had all occurred, otherwise, she would be standing there with Damien by sunset.

The two of them got off the horse when they were close enough to the palace entrance. Before they reached the doors Emmanuelle came to a stop and just stared around at the whole palace, tears filling his eyes as he remembered how long it had been since he had been home. Gabrial noticed that he was missing, then looked back, when she saw the tears in his eyes as he was on his knees before the palace, she quickly ran back to see what was wrong.

"Are you alright?" she asked, touching him lightly on the shoulder.

"Alas, it has been so long since I have set foot near the place in which I called home. It has been so long I forgot that I even had a place that I called home," he chuckled softly. "I wonder if my parents will still remember me."

She smiled knowing exactly how he felt, then she took him by the hand gently. "I'm sure they will."

He smiled as she took his hand, helping him stand back on his feet. The guards pushed open the massive palace doors as they walked inside. Emmanuelle looked around as if lost or confused, but he didn't say a word until they came to the throne room, where the king and queen were seated. The king had a beard that was the color of the petals of sunflowers, a few parts of it were braided like a Viking. He eyed Emmanuelle from the moment he entered the room, along with his wife.

"Who is this dirty boy in which you bring before the majesties presents?" she snapped, standing up.

Emmanuelle let go of Gabrial's hand and walked forward, then bowed himself before them. "Can't you remember me father, mother? I am your son," he cried, looking down at the floor.

Everything fell silent after those last few words. It couldn't be true, he was dead, slain by a lion or so they had believed.

Chapter 7

From Hell to Glory

Sharon's heavy eyelids opened. Her body felt

like it was mounted with dozens of bricks. There was

nothing in sight, besides a blinding light. When she stood

up, she felt like something was tagging along on her back.

She looked behind herself to see a pair of newly restored

wings. They were white as a horse's mane. As vivid as glass. What had they done to her?

"Welcome back," said a gentle voice, from the light.

She walked into it curiously to see who was speaking to her. On the other side, there were angels from her homeland. They were flying around, playing music near the banks of Keydron. She was nearly brought to tears, this was all too good to be true. She thought she had lost this place.

"Gabrial," laughed someone from behind her, touching her on the shoulder.

She knew who it was without even turning around, there was only one person who called her that. It was him, the one she thought she'd never see again. His soft brown eyes glowing in the sun's light.

His broad shoulders and muscular built body was shining since he had just come from out of the water. Sharon embraced him, feeling his smooth skin beneath her hands. This was where she should have been and a place she should have never left. It hadn't been her time and now she didn't know what would happen.

"I love you," she whispered into his ear.

"I love you too," she heard him say in his gentle, but stern voice.

She felt him run his hand through her hair before he vanished back into thin air.

Some 1,000 years later

The King and Queen looked in astonishment at the crying young man. Her eyes softened as she realized that he was telling the truth and she was compelled to embrace him. She ran down from the throne and knelt in front of him and hugged him.

"Emmanuelle, it's you?" she cried, wiping the tears from his eyes.

"It is me, mommy. I'm alive," he answered.

Prince Damien watched from behind all the guards and knights that were in the room. He spit down on the floor, feeling the contempt with his brother rise in him. It didn't make sense, she treated him like her only son, never in his life had she ever consoled him although he couldn't remember a time when he needed any. Still, it hurt him to see her do such a thing.

His father had come over to hug him also.

"If you weren't killed by the lion, then where have you been all these years?" she cried, cupping his face in her hands so he was looking at her.

"I wasn't killed by the lion's mother, I was cursed to become the lion for the rest of my life," Emmanuelle explained. "If no one had been ever scared of me I would have come back to tell you and father, but I could never come near the palace not without nearly being killed so I left for a wasteland. Where I have lived for all these years."

"No. It can't be," spatted King Charles feeling guilty. "I nearly killed my son."

"I understand, it wasn't your fault. You were only doing what you thought was right, you didn't know I was the lion, but thanks to Gabrial I'm here now," he declared, happily, as he turned to look at her with a grin. "She saved me."

King Charles looked up searching for Gabrial and noticed her standing with the guards.

"The peasant girl?" chuckled Queen Eliza.

"Gabrial come. Please," said the king, beckoning to her.

She walked over to them, looking at Emmanuelle smiling at her.

"I'm in your debts Gabrial for saving our son," said King Charles taking her hand. "To show my gratitude and happiness we shall prepare a ball in three nights for the return of my son."

"Thank you, your highness," she said.

Damien's eyes showed the anger he was feeling, this was his wedding day there was no way he could just think he could turn this day around for Emmanuelle. He walked over quickly. Moving some of the guards out of his way so he was able to get to his father. "But father, today is my wedding day." he snapped, angrily.

"I'm aware of that, but today is the day your brother has returned and that is just as important. Aren't you happy to know that your brother is alive after these long fourteen years?"

That was just it. He wasn't happy to see that Emmanuelle had survived. His face twitched showing some of his anger as he stared at his brother. He stormed out of the room before he did anything he would get in

trouble for. At this point, he wanted to strangle his brother

and make sure he died this time, right before his eyes.

Emmanuelle watched his brother leave and wondered why

he was so angry with him, had he wanted him to die?

****

Damien knocked on the secret doorway, where all

his fellow knights were. The doors opened slowly and he

walked in. Torches were lit all around the room, but there

was a hush of silence that had fallen upon the room, unlike

all the other times. Sir Gilliot was staring at him from the

moment he entered the room.

"Well, what do you have to say?" he snapped

angrily, glaring at all of them. "He wasn't dead, which was

supposed to happen years ago! Gabrial goes out and saves

that bastard's life and everyone welcomes him home with

open arms! The wedding is canceled for his stupid party!

153

And you know what, I managed not to kill him since he is still so vulnerable! I should have! I will!"

The knights stared at him, it seemed as if he had let Emmanuelle's appearance get him riled up. Of course, it never took much to get him there, he was always such a hot-headed person anyway.

"He better be looking over his shoulder, because one of these days I'm going to come and slaughter him when he least expects it," he muttered, taking a seat that he had pulled out for himself.

"So that's it for The Disciples of Blood+Cross?" Sir Belont, the younger and zealous knight.

"No," Damien suddenly began to chuckle. "No, not at all, but there is an oath that you all must take in order to still be a part of the clan."

He stood up from his chair and walked over to a bookshelf, where he pulled a massive dark book off the shelf. It was thrown onto the table before all the knights.

"The book of Jahosafats Notes, but aren't those notes forbidden to be…"

"Does it matter?" answered Damien rudely as he threw the kingdom's flag into a fireplace to be devoured. "Each of us will burn ourselves with the Sword and Cross sign showing our allegiance to the Clan. We will never serve under the rule of my father nor my brother and we will kill ourselves if we are forced to do so. It is better for us to perish than to bow before the enemy. Those who agree, say the following words…" Two of his fingers were put together on his right hand, then he did the same to his left then crossed his heart making an X and the knights did the same "… I solemnly swear to forbid myself from falling before the sword of sin."

✻✻✻✻✻✻✻✻✻✻✻

Gabrial and Maid A'Key strolled down the hallway holding towels, it was almost impossible to stop Maid A'Key from breaking into tears whenever she said a word about the missing prince being found. She still said nothing about what had happened to cause it all to happen, no one had.

"He was the kindest one compared to his brother, who had nearly killed him three times when they were little boys," she chuckled, softly. "Or that's what his mother was convinced of, it was always strange how even though he had done so many awful things to the poor boy, Emmanuelle never let anything happen to him." Maid A'Key turned a corner. "I'll see you in a little while."

"I'll see you…" Gabrial stopped when she noticed the door slowly opened and he emerged drying his hair with his shirt. "Emmanuelle?"

His eyes looked up from the floor and at her. "Yes. Oh."

She smiled as she handed him a towel.

"Seems like I hit my head harder than I thought," he chuckled softly, feeling a little embarrassed as he took the towel. "It's been so long since I've been here, you know the strange thing is Damien hasn't spoken to me for a long time I mean how could he if…" he stopped his expression seemed troubled or something "… I guess it's been so long I don't even remember that."

"Is something wrong?" she asked, noticing how silent he had gone after mentioning Damien.

"No, just a little tired," he pulled on his shirt, then started walking down the hallway.

She watched him as he went on tiredly. It must have been worse than she could ever imagine being separated from his family for that long and knowing that if he returned he would be killed by them. If they had killed him, they wouldn't have ever known it was their son, which would have been awful.

Emmanuelle's eyes gleamed on a tapestry that hung in a grand hallway. It was him with his parents and Damien when they had been both little boys. The funny thing about the tapestry was that it showed the two of them on each side of their parents. He was near his dad and Damien was on the side of his mom with his arms crossed.

Back in those days, when he used to cross his arms it either meant he wanted something Emmanuelle had or he was upset with their dad and was just too afraid to express it. He chuckled softly thinking of those days. He and his brother had been kind of close back then, but never so close as to sit near one another or share secrets with one another.

They had never trusted one another like that.

"I thought I'd find you here," said King Charles, groaning as he made his way up the steps and into the little area.

Emmanuelle smiled, thinking of the many times his dad had come to this place when he was looking for him, trying to find a peaceful area or wanted to talk to him in private. His dad had given him great council, the thing was when he was that age he had hardly paid any attention. Now that he was older and had lost so many years with him, he wished he had cherished that time he had with him and listened more attentively.

"Still your favorite place is it dad?" he chuckled, running his fingers across an old piece of wood.

"Oh yes," he answered, sighing with relief as he sat down in a chair. "I see you still love this place also."

The two of them fell silent for a moment. Emmanuelle stared at the tapestry, while his father studied him just thinking of all the things he had been through. Even right after his birth and somehow he always turned out alright. It was as if he were protected by some fortress of miracles. He saw Emmanuelle's hand run across the crown that was made of thorns and sticks on his head and a cross that was hardly visible behind him.

"There are so many…" they both started at the same time, then stopped not wanting to cut off the other.

"I see that hasn't changed either," chuckled the king.

Emmanuelle nodded his head looking at the floor as he smiled. "I guess not. You first."

"What I wanted to say was that there are so many things I see in you that I don't think I noticed before," he finished.

"I have grown up a bit, father," chuckled Emmanuelle.

"I don't mean like that Emmanuelle," declared the king, shaking his head. "And I don't believe it came from either me or your mother."

He didn't know how to answer his father. Both of his parents were the best people he had ever known. Everything about him had come from them. Their ups and downs. If there was something different about him, it could have just been his true self blossoming in a later season. The prince heard footsteps coming up the stairs and when he looked he saw his mother.

"A men's meeting," she laughed, staring at her son standing near the tapestry. "I hope you two don't mind me joining."

When she sat down, she noticed that Emmanuelle was right near the crown of thorns on his head in the tapestry. She hoped he hadn't seen it for she had been the one who had made the tapestry. The crown had been just to put a little more emphasis on who was the prince who would be king, but he may have seen it as another way.

"Could you tell me what it was like being that monster?" she asked, insensitively.

"Eliza," whispered the king to her.

"He doesn't mind. He's an honest young man," argued Eliza.

Emmanuelle didn't answer her. The memory of being poked, burned, and stabbed without restraint was so awful it was a part of his life he wished to delete from his memory. The people he had encountered were roofless and unkind, they had burned him in the eye once with fire after throwing hot tar on him. The only memory he had that was pleasant was when he had encountered Gabrial and she became his friend.

She had been different from the others. When they had first met, she didn't scream or try to harm him. She had spoken to him like a being and helped him remember that he was still something outside of the creature he was trapped inside. That had been just a holding place concealing what he had been and somehow she had seen past it and became his best friend.

"It was an experience I have most definitely learned from," he finally replied.

"Oh," the queen looked at her husband, "and what did you learn exactly?"

"Fear cannot overcome faith," he chuckled, looking over at his father, smiling at him, proudly.

The queen smiled at him as if happy, but she despised how even through all that he had become a better person. If that had never happened to him, he would have still been in the left-field where he had been more blind than a bat with a blindfold.

✳✳✳✳✳✳✳✳✳✳✳

Bumps made the covered wagon shake like a toy car and she was suddenly awakened from her long sleep.

She woke up screaming out her sister's name, after having a dream about them being together. But when she looked around all she saw was a bunch of trash and old ragged clothes stacked up. Immediately, her heart sank like a ship in the midst of a hurricane. It was just another dream or an illusion.

Of course, her sister wasn't with her, she didn't have a clue what was wrong with her. Still there felt like a large empty hole in her heart that couldn't be filled with just anything, except for her sister she so longed for. Suddenly, the wagon stopped and she was thrown forward, hitting her head against something wooden that knocked her unconscious. The shades of the wagon were moved and three men stared at Esmeralda lying there like a broken lamb in all the trash.

"I'd say we just dump her here," offered one of the men, "I mean she'll either be eaten by the sun or found by the…" he took a pause and looked around as if to make sure no one else was around "...you know who."

One of the other men shrugged. "I mean at least then we'll know our camels will make it to the next destination with less weight."

"Let's dump her, then," said the last man.

They moved some of the stuff out of the way and one of them climbed into the back of the wagon and picked her up. He threw her to one of the other men that was standing outside. Esmeralda was tossed in the hot sand outside, left to die and as for the men they rode off in their wagon to a place they hoped to rest their camels.

Chapter 8

The Rekindling

His face rested in the cold snow, below the

blizzard. The sound of children giggling woke him up.

When he sat up his sight was blurred and the only thing he

could see was a little light moving away in the distance.

The angel climbed to his feet, standing upright in the snow.

He wondered if this had been the place where the previous angels had started their trek. A trail of footprints followed as he walked through the snow with his bare feet.

It was as if he were numb, the wind swept past him and he didn't shiver or feel the coldness even though he wasn't wearing a shirt or shoes. For a moment he thought he heard Sharon's laughter and stopped. To his disappointment, it had been only in his imagination or so he had thought. He heard it again and this time it sounded as if it were coming from the bushes covered in snow.

He ran towards one and searched behind it, but she wasn't there. Then he heard the laughter again, this time catching a glimpse of her long flaming colored hair that ran loosely down her back. The angel chased after her, laughing, convinced that he had found her. There she sat on a stone with her long light blue toga.

"What's the matter?" she asked, giggling. "Afraid to catch me, Emmanuel? Afraid I'll hurt you?"

The angel charged at her, laughing happily that he had found her at long last. He grabbed hold of her in his arms so she wouldn't get away from him. Only to find out that he had made a terrible mistake.

"Who...Who are you?" he asked.

Some 1,000 years later

The sun's light could hardly wake him. It had been so long since he had laid in his bed or a bed at all. Suddenly he felt something warm against his shoulder. His eyes slowly opened and he saw someone standing right beside him smiling.

"Gabrial?" he asked, looking at her as she moved closer to him.

She didn't answer him, but she looked much happier than normal, but he didn't know why. She kissed him on the forehead, then ran her fingers through his hair.

He couldn't ever recall her touching him, except for when he was a lion. Her hands felt soft and warm against his skin as if restoring him.

"How did you…"

"Shush," she told him, moving over onto the bed with him.

He felt her reach her hand into his shirt, her eyes were focused. When she leaned closer to his lips. Emmanuelle immediately sat up in his bed, nearly falling onto the floor with his blankets. He looked around his bedroom, but she was nowhere in sight. He touched his head, wondering how that could have ever ended up in his mind. She had never even been in his room and she had never touched him in such a strange way.

The prince leaped out of his bed, it was about time he started his day. Emmanuelle looked into a mirror as he buttoned his shirt. Somehow he looked a little different than before. Perhaps he had lost some weight over those years, then again it looked like it had nothing to do with his weight at all. It looked more like his skin was becoming snowflakes. There was a knock on his opened door. He hurried and buttoned his shirt so his skin was covered, then turned around to see his dad standing there, watching him.

"It's been a long time, I'm not sure if you still like horseback riding," he chuckled, smiling at him.

Emmanuelle smiled, then met his dad's eyes. "I think I would still like it if I could only remember how to ride," answered the prince. "The last time I tried to ride one, I nearly fell off because I had forgotten how it worked.

The king clapped his hands down on his son's shoulders. He couldn't remember a time when Emmanuelle had been willing to say he couldn't remember or knew how to do anything. Back then he had

always thought he was the best or needed to be the best.
His eyes were brighter so that he was able to tell the color
of them. They had always thought his eyes were black. He
even smiled, laughed with happiness. Something had
changed with him, besides his personality.

"No need to worry about that, I'll help you with
that," declared the king, walking toward the door. "I'll
meet you out there."

"Of course," said Emmanuelle, tucking his shirt in.
"I won't be long."

Before long the king was gone and he was left to
himself to get dressed. He stepped out of his room,
colliding with Gabrial and falling to the floor. He caught
himself from falling on top of her. Their eyes met and he
could hardly take his eyes off her as he helped her from the
floor.

"I'm sorry," he said, holding her hand.

"It's okay," Gabrial answered.

Emmanuelle's eyes darted to the end of the hallway as he thought of his dad waiting for him outside. The only thing was, that he didn't want to leave her for some strange reason. Her hands felt as soft and warm as cotton. They also made him feel relief and a kind of energy that empowered him. For that moment he thought he saw her as someone else, besides the girl that had rescued him. It was like someone had lit a candle shining light onto a dark pathway he didn't even know existed.

She smiled at him, bashfully when his eyes were so still as they stared at her. It was a little awkward since she didn't know what he was thinking.

"I should be going," the prince said, slowly, releasing her hands.

Even as he left down the hallway, a few times he looked back at her as she stood there looking down the hallway at something. He noticed a dark cat pounce into her arms and he heard her laughing as she held it. Gabrial walked the opposite way of him with her cat. It seemed as if she were pretty close to it from the way she was playing with it. Part of him wished he were that close to her like that cat.

The king was already on top of his horse outside, waiting for his son. He chuckled when he saw him walk down the steps.

"Took you long enough," he chuckled, watching as the prince got onto the horse, nearly falling back over the saddle.

"I guess I got a little sidetracked," Emmanuelle admitted as he struggled to get on.

"Hmmmm. I wonder with what."

Emmanuelle sighed, deeply when he was finally on the horse. He held on tight with both his hands and arms to the horse's neck, afraid to fall off. His dad laughed at him since he had never seen him so afraid in his life. Eventually, the prince sat upright. His hands were clenched tightly to the reins and for once in a long time, he felt the excitement of riding a horse again and this time on his own.

The first time Emmanuel moved the reins the horse took off leaving the king to chase after him.

"Good luck, you're highness," said Sir Kelvin, stepping away from the king's horse.

"Thanks. I think I'll need a lot of that right now," laughed King Charles, whacking the horse's reins.

****

Gabrial looked at the tapestry that Emmanuelle's mother had made. There was something dark about the way it had been created. She couldn't help noticing how she had placed her sons on the sides of them, instead of in the middle. Then there was a crown made of thorns on Emmanuelle's head. She didn't know who would ever put that on their son's head. Sure the crown meant greatness as far as royalty.

"And what are you doing here?" questioned Queen Eliza, staring at the broom that had been leaning against the wall. "Doesn't at all look like you're cleaning to me."

"I was, I just was looking at..."

"The tapestry? Of course," snapped the queen, walking closer to her.

The queen's heels on her slippers were so high, it made her look like a dinosaur compared to Gabrial. Her nails were as long as pencils and red as blood. A few times she snarled, eyeing Gabrial with envy. She had everything she had always wanted and that she now had but because she had used magic to get it. Her skin was perfectly soft without any blemishes. She had eyes that were the palest blue and Eliza's were brown without using some kind of magic water.

She wondered why did this girl think that she could stop working when she felt like it? She wasn't supposed to stop until she told her to. She may have felt like she didn't have to just because she saved her son and all, but that didn't change anything.

"Well what do you think of it?" she asked, touching the end of the tapestry.

She frowned as if sick. "It appears to be dreadful and sad. The two sons are separated and you put thorns on the other's head."

"Oh, I hope that's not your way of complimenting, because it is awful," Queen Eliza snapped, dropping the end of the tapestry.

"I don't know what is complimenting if you don't want the truth," Gabrial replied, picking up the broom.

For some reason, she didn't feel like she should stay anywhere near the queen right now. Eliza felt like smacking Gabrial for being rude. She could have said something better than the word dreadful. She didn't understand the works of artists, that was what it was. No matter, her words had overcome the queen's lying thoughts and she tore down the tapestry with her own hands, screaming with fury.

Gabrial turned around when she heard her screaming. Something was wrong with her for her to be screaming like a little girl at her parents when she couldn't have her way. The only thing she could do right now was stay away from her. Eliza finally stopped screaming, glaring down the steps the girl had walked down. How could Damien have ever brought such an annoyance to the palace? One of these days she was going to take one step too far and Eliza knew she was going to get her and she was going to go as far as she could to make sure she remembered who was the best in the kingdom.

The forest was so lush green and full of wildlife it was like a place from someone's imagination. Emmanuelle had finally learned to control his horse and was following behind his dad. They stopped near a small pond, where they sat down to relax. His dad put his hands behind his head and leaned back a little way.

"So what's on your mind, Emmanuelle?" he asked as he looked at the prince stared at the lake.

"I don't quite know," he answered. "Or I kind of do, I just don't know how to explain it."

King Charles, smiled at him, thinking of when he was that age and looked to have been carrying the world. "I know exactly how you feel. I felt the same way when I was your age."

"You did?" he asked, looking at his dad.

He nodded his head in agreement. "Marriage was probably one of the reasons why and then of course the kingdom. Your granddad died when I was only seventeen so I had started running the kingdom."

"I thought grandfather hadn't passed until you were at least twenty-five," explained Emmanuelle, realizing how little he knew.

"No," gasped King Charles. "And that was just one of my problems. Your mom or then the princess of Dalmenar was there at a ball on my eighteenth birthday, then there was another girl I had cared about. The problem was she wasn't royalty and we couldn't be married unless I wanted to disgrace the kingdom and I was not willing to sacrifice anything for that."

Emmanuelle's head felt like a bunch of wires were in his head. He couldn't even think about marriage right now, there were so many other things he wanted to do before that. But from what his dad was telling him, it sounded like he had married his mother for the kingdom's happiness and honor more than anything else. He wondered if his dad had ever been content with that kind of marriage or rather a lie.

That was worse to him than marrying someone who was not royalty. If he had married that girl then at least their marriage and vows wouldn't have been a lie and to him, that was more important than any kingdom or honor.

If he had married his mother for the kingdom's sake had he

loved her?

"You'll make the right choices in that time, I know

you will," the king patted his hand against his shoulder.

"Even if it means sacrificing something so dear to you."

His dad dozed off slowly into a slumber.

Emmanuelle looked at the lake and his blank reflection.

He didn't know if he could sacrifice all that for a kingdom.

If he did that he would be lying and if he didn't he would

live the rest of his life in dishonor and his kingdom would

hate him for it since he'd be leading a bad example for his

successors.

There had to be a way to quench both of the fires.

He couldn't think about that now, lucky for him he had no

feelings for anyone, or did he?

****

The little venture with his dad had been nice and at the same time illuminating. Maid A'Key caught Gabrial looking down from the balcony, watching as the prince entered the palace.

"What are you thinking about?" she asked, startling her.

Gabrial smiled when she realized it was just her, but she didn't answer.

"Gabrial?" she asked, looking at her as she smiled. It was the first time she had ever seen her smile and it seemed strange. Whatever she was thinking about sure seemed to be making her happy.

"I don't know how to answer that," Gabrial said, finally turning and walking to her bed. "I feel strange, I've never felt such an awkward kind of happiness. It feels like my stomach is churning but it feels like there's a bunch of air."

The maid stared at her, complacently. She didn't

know what to say, she had never felt that before. It made

her wonder if maybe Gabrial was coming down sick or

something. After all, she had said it felt churning which

normally meant someone was sick. There was also a

strange glow in her eyes that had never been there before.

"Are you feeling well?" inquired the maid,

touching her lightly on the shoulder. "You don't feel like

you're going to fall out do you?"

"No," laughed Gabrial, happily. "I just feel odd."

"Oh, okay," Maid A'Key sighed with relief. "I'll

see you sometime later or in the morning."

"It is morning," laughed Gabrial, laying on her bed.

The maid smiled, it was early morning, how could

she have forgotten? She walked to the exit of the room,

then took one last look at her friend. She wished she knew

what was wrong with her. It kind of made her feel bad that

she didn't know what every feeling meant. The door

closed behind Maid A'Key as she left. Gabrial noticed that she had left behind her change purse. She couldn't let her leave it behind, otherwise, she'd be wondering where she had left it and be scared out of her wits.

The hallways were dark outside her bedroom with only a little light from the windows across. She took the candle from her room and left the room. There was no telling which way the maid had gone so she took the way she thought she may have gone. As she walked across the upper floor. Below was a large room, lit up by a chandelier above them. She could see Damien and a few of the knights laughing as they talked among one another, playing their game of chess.

"I see we have a cheater," he snapped, knocking over Sir Gilliot's piece.

The knight scoffed at how he had lost the game again. No one was able to beat the prince in the game. He cheated as if a part of the rules and when they played by the rules he called it cheating. There was no use in trying to talk to him.

Gabrial turned a corner into another hallway, where she was grabbed by a knight. He chuckled, softly.

"Spying on us?" he snapped.

"I'm not, I wanted to return this to a friend," she explained, quickly.

He looked at the little sack. "You're not allowed to wander around after midnight," snapped the knight, snatching the bag.

"Give that back," she ordered him, trying to grab the sack from him.

"Give what back? Your marriage," he teased, then he took her by the arm. "I think Damien would like to hear how his future wife was spying on his fellow knights."

He dragged Gabrial along with him, down the steps, and into the room where they had been playing chess. Sir Belont's eyes narrowed when he saw her, what had she been doing here?

"I found her spying on you, sir," declared the knight.

"Really?" he chuckled. "Ready to submit yourself to Prince Damien?"

"No," she answered, turning away from the knights.

The knight grinned deviously, then smacked her in the face knocking her to the floor. Sir Gilliot stepped on her back, shoving his foot against her as if trying to push her further into the brick floor. Gabrial screamed with pain when she felt a few of the knights kick her and Gilliot's foot digging into her back. Sir Belont bent over down to her level, then looked at her as she struggled to breathe.

"I don't know what you're thinking about, but just because Prince Damien's dad has postponed the wedding doesn't mean that he can't make it happen," he declared. "And until your wedding day, you are still under anyone's rule, which means you're not allowed to spy on me or do anything without my permission. Our prince saved you out there."

"No he didn't," cried Gabrial, gasping for air. "Your prince brought me here for his interest."

"And how do you know?" chuckled the knight, standing upright once more.

The knights began to laugh at how she had fallen silent as if afraid of him. She didn't want to say anything since they may have found a way to turn it against her. Suddenly, the door to the room squeaked as it opened and she saw shadows in the hallway. Emmanuelle shook his dad's hand, happily, then walked into the room. For a long moment, he stared at them in confusion about why they had been pinning her down like a criminal. Sir Belont snarled a little, then chuckled, approaching the prince.

"Sir Belont, why are the knights pinning her down like that?" demanded Emmanuelle, charging past him.

"Because I can, why else, little prince?" he

explained, bitterly as his teeth clenched tighter together.

"Well, I don't like it."

"No one cares what you like," snapped Sir Belont,

pushing him forward as if to make him fall.

Emmanuelle glared at him but refused to be drawn

into whatever he was trying to do. He had had enough of

fighting with him from before and he wasn't trying to

relive that all over again."You'll kill her," he snapped,

pushing the knights off of her, then crouched down next to

her.

He felt the knights lay hands on him and pulled

him away from her. They pulled him back into a wall. It

was happening all over in his mind, he was going to lose

her again just like when he was a lion. The prince fought

to break away from them, but they had his arms restrained

and he could only watch as Sir Belont approached her with

a knife.

"I need what you have bad, but I don't believe I don't need it that badly," he stabbed the knife through her side and he listened to her yell with pain until she finally fell silent.

Emmanuelle broke free from the knights, desperately. Then tackled Sir Belont into the floor, he held his fist just above his knight's face as he laughed, sinisterly.

"Do it," he laughed.

As much as it ached to hurt him just as much as he had done to him, he couldn't. Then he heard Gabrial's voice, which was almost in a whisper as she tried to talk to him. When he looked over, he saw that she was still alive and his anger turned into tenderness when he looked at her. He released Sir Belont, then ran over to her as quickly as possible.

"Gabrial," he cried as he looked at her.

"I want to tell you..."

"Shuuuusssshhh," he whispered to her as he picked her up. "You can tell me when you're well."

Sir Belont watched as the prince carried her away. She should have been dead after that, but then he remembered why she probably wasn't.

Chapter 9

Le Petit Prince

This was worse than a nightmare, she couldn't

go home and she would never see him again. What would

he think? He would have thought she had died like all the

others and probably blamed himself. She couldn't live with

that. He had never done anything wrong, if anything she

had been the one in the wrong forever-ever letting their

friendship get too far out of hand.

*There would be no more being chased by him as
they would run along the brooks of Keydron. No more days
when he would take her across the universe to look at the
stars up close. No more playing with him in the garden of
Gath, where he had first discovered her hiding from them
when she thought they were someone else. There would be
no more of any of that. It would only be her staring into a
reflection always missing part of it.*

*Armistice touched her lightly on the shoulder as
Sharon looked into the endless brightness of the light. She
longed to go home and return to him, but they wouldn't let
her because of what they had made her into. That burned
more than anything and she could feel a blob swell up into
her neck and she broke into tears.*

*The iron angel let one of her wings wrap around
her and she drew the angel closer to her and hugged her,
compassionately. She knew how she must have felt for she
had felt the same way when she realized she could never*

return to the others. The only thing was that no one had been there for her. To wipe the tears and hug her. That was part of the reason why she did it for her because she didn't have that but whatever she didn't have she made sure the next person got to have it.

"You'll learn to love this place," she whispered, consolingly. "I promise."

Sharon wiped her tearful eyes, that was just it. She didn't want to learn to love this place, she wanted to go home where she knew she already knew she loved it and had found love.

Some 1,000 years later

Water ran from out of the rag and into the bowl of water. Her silver cloak was hung over a chair. It would have to be cleaned from the blood before she would be able to wear it again. The prince cleaned off her side that had been bleeding. He didn't know much about doctoring, but he had to try and do something for her, besides watch her suffer.

"I sent Sir Kelvin to get the nurse, she should be here soon," said Emmanuelle, wiping off the area Damien had stabbed her.

"Thank you for everything," she said, as she rested one of her hands on his hand that was on her side. "Can you stay with me when she arrives?"

He looked at her, uncertainly. A smile appeared on his face and he set the rag on her side and put his hand over hers. He couldn't leave her when she needed him most, she hadn't done that to him and he wouldn't do it to her.

"Of course I will, there is no place I'd rather be right now," answered the prince.

Gabrial smiled at him, he was so kind and considerate. It was as if he were less human than anything else. The door opened and a nurse entered, a knight following behind her. The first thing the maid noticed was how the prince had completely failed at helping her, she should have been dead since it looked like she had lost a lot of blood. She glared at him, quickly. He should have never attempted to help since he didn't know what he was doing.

"Your highness can you and the knight please give me some space," she asked, trying to sound polite. "It'll take a little while.

The prince looked at her, he didn't want her to think he wanted to leave her alone with the nurse. But he didn't have much of a choice if he wanted her to help her. He gave her an assured look as he let go of her hand.

"I'll come to visit you as soon as they say it is okay," he told her. "Okay?"

Gabrial nodded her head. "Of course," she answered him in almost a whisper.

Her understanding made the heaviness of his conscious lift and he followed behind the knight into the hallway. The nurse took no time with closing the door and shutting them out. The two of them stayed in the hallway without moving anywhere until night had fallen.

Emmanuelle frowned, he had wanted to stay with her to be sure she would be alright. Sure, he kind of trusted the nurse, but it would have made him feel better to have been there right by her side to be sure of that. His heart ached on the inside and his mind swirled with thoughts of worries. There had to be something he could do to make her feel better or make her feel welcomed when she was healed or even now.

"She'll be alright, your highness," assured the knight, standing beside him. "I know no one would want you staying up this late, it's not good for you."

"Thanks for the consideration, but I'm not all tired. I wish I could believe that Sir Hamilton," he cried as the worst of his nightmares flashed through his memory. How could he have let them poke and burn at her without fighting back? Now he was standing outside the door when she was near death again and he was just standing out here waiting like a vegetable. He didn't even know how he had just let Damien harm her without stopping him.

"Then don't wish, just believe, sir," said Sir Hamilton. "I learned on my ventures that belief goes a long way."

The prince turned towards a wall and banged his fist against it. If she died, it would be his fault for not staying in there with her. He heard the door open just when he was thinking of going back inside. The nurse stood in the doorway wiping her hands and looking at the prince whose eyes were full of both worry and hope.

"Is she alright?" he asked as he tried to look through the doorway.

"Settle down, your highness," she snapped. "Of course she is, but she needs rest and doesn't need anyone to disturb her."

"Did she tell you to tell me that?" Emmanuelle inquired, narrowing his eyes at her.

The nurse shrugged, then looked at Sir Hamilton. "It's a necessary precaution we are supposed to take, besides you need to be in bed yourself, sir."

"Not at a time like this. I have to see her first," he declared, taking a step forward only to be blocked by the nurse.

"Sir Hamilton, could you please escort Prince Emmanuelle to his quarters?" she asked, desperately.

The prince looked into the room, where he saw her sleeping. There was no need to make a matter this small into something big. He didn't feel like it after what had happened that early morning. Emmanuelle left the

bedroom and down the hallway without the knight
accompanying him.

✳✳✳✳✳✳✳✳✳✳✳

Emmanuelle looked down from the balcony and
Gabrial as she sat on some steps. Her long hair blowing
loosely from her ponytail. She hadn't spoken much after
the incident and he didn't know quite why. If there was
only some way he could get her to spend more time with
him. That way she could get to know him better and he
could do the same. He needed to find a way to escape his
duties and be with her.

There were so many things he wanted to tell her,
express to her. He didn't know why but he felt as if they
were once close like that. Perhaps if he decorated a room
for her.

She stood up on the stairs and he realized what he
could do that might help him along. If he brought her a
dress so she could come from out of the dark pants, white

200

shirt, and silver cape. She would have to want to be with

him more or he could at least spark her interest in him.

He didn't know what color she would like or if she

would wear it at all. He did know one thing, she looked

magnificent in a soft blue. That's what he would do, he

would find the right dress for her and then maybe get a few

other things for her.

The idea of doing that for her made him smile. She

would never expect it and that's what made it all the

better. Guards marched up and down the hallways when he

exited his room.

"Prince Emmanuelle," said Sir Mercer.

"Good evening," the prince greeted.

"Where are you off to this late evening?" asked the

knight, watching as the prince hurried away.

"To town, I'll be back before nightfall," answered

Emmanuelle

The knight nodded, then continued walking to where he was going. Gabrial looked behind her when she heard the doors open. She saw Emmanuelle heading her way and he seemed to be in a rush. He saw her turn his way and his heart nearly felt as if it had dropped when he saw her.

"Your highness," she said, standing up.

"Emmanuelle. Please," he told her, moving a little closer to her.

He couldn't help imagining her in a beautiful gown, the thought of it made his eyes look away from her. It was like he thought she was able to read his thoughts.

"Okay," Gabrial answered as her hair blew past her face. "If I may ask, where are you going?"

"Just to town, I have a few things to get from there," he chuckled, clapping his hands down on her shoulders. "I'll be back soon."

The prince walked past her and started down the stairs. She watched him as he walked away. Her heart felt so heavy after he had touched her, he had left some kind of feeling with her. It wasn't bad, but it felt like she might be sick. She was so filled with some kind of nervous excitement.

****

The dressmaker walked around the room, hardly noticing him even after the bell had rung. His eyes looked around the place, he saw gowns both elegant and normal. But none of them looked like they would fit the image he had come up with in his mind. The place was filled with the sound of women talking from another room and customers purchasing things.

"Excuse me," Emmanuelle said to a woman bending over a basket of needles and thread.

"If you're looking for the…" when she saw that he was the prince, she caught herself "… What can I do for you, your highness?"

A grin appeared on his face when he saw that he had gotten her attention. "I was wondering if you'd have any kind of dress that a princess might wear."

"Of course," she answered, briskly. "Right this way."

She led him to a room in the back of the store. When they entered he was surprised by all the magnificent dresses he saw. Some vividly pink with crimps, others lavender-purple that were made of satin. No matter how beautiful they looked, he kept in mind that he was looking for a color that would match Gabrial. Not one that looked extremely beautiful but didn't fit her at all.

"These gowns are magnificent," he said in astonishment as he looked through them one by one.

"We do our best," she answered.

"Abby, a customer needs you at the checkout," said a young girl, peering in at them.

"Okay, I'll be right there. Excuse me, your highness," Abby hurried out.

He continued to look through the dresses until he saw something that interested him. The prince pulled it down from off the pole and looked over it. It was the palest blue he had ever seen and sparkled like diamonds when it was in the sunlight. The only thing was it had no sleeves and the back of it was open. He didn't know if she would be too pleased since she had always kept herself covered by the silver cloak. That was only the just of his problems, he didn't know if it would fit her. As far as he could tell, it was too large for her.

"Are you finding everything, alright your highness," asked the dressmaker, walking in. "Oh, that is a glorious dress for a princess." She ran over to touch it with her hands feeling the fibers beneath her hand. "It was made from the finest satin, lace and took months to complete the designs like these crimps and embed these gems.”

The woman was great at convincing and even made him rethink leaving it. If it were a little too big, he could bring it back and get it altered for her. Now he just needed to find some slippers and hair clips.

“Do you also sell things like slippers and hair clips?” he asked, smiling at the lady.

“I’m sorry, sir, but we do not,” she answered. “But there is a place not too far down the road that does. I’ll take that for you and get it all packaged up so you can be on your merry way in no time.”

“Thank you,” Emmanuelle said, following her to the front of the store.

****

“She’s an angel. What do you expect,” chuckled the Black Knight, leaning against a wall. “If she knows she'll be killed then she's not just going to throw herself out there like that."

"I don't expect her to, I just don't know what to do anymore," laughed Damien. "My brother has come home and she's been under his protection, I can hardly get in a few feet of her without him being there."

The Black Knight nodded his head, thinking of his life before this had happened to him. "What's your reason for wanting this angel? To kill her so you can find happiness in vengeance?"

The prince shook his head, laughing. "No, it's more like getting the power of immortality, to control, rule this world. So that our kingdom can outshine the others or better yet take every kingdom and make it one with mine. I want to rule this world."

"I was like that once. Of course, that was when I was the young King Arthur, legendary for taking the sword from the stone, defeating Morgana, rescuing the young maiden Guinevere," he sighed, woefully. "This is where I ended up, in the forgotten books closed for good, I blame the angels for all this."

"Speaking of angels, how would I know for certain that she is one," he asked. "I know her back is bruised with bloody streaks, but she doesn't act like one."

"You still believe that I'm lying about this whole thing, don't you?"

The prince chuckled. "I've known people to lie to themselves and others."

"If there are two markings of blood on her back, then you know that she is one for certain," he answered. "I've seen it in my day when angels were punished and their wings were cut from them. Really a tragic story, but that was how things were then."

Damien's cold blue eyes looked at him, he couldn't believe that this savage was the king that was known worldwide as everyone's hero. The great king who ruled

Camelot. If his story was true then why was he here acting like an insane man? The Black Knight curled into a corner causing the chains to rattle as he tried to find comfort.

"I'll see you soon, good prince," he chuckled before he fell into a deep sleep.

As he headed for the exit, he could hear the moaning of the prisoners as they slept. His belief that Gabrial was an angel grew almost every day and after talking with the Black Knight about the streaks on her back, there was no doubt in his mind that she was one. He had seen one of them once when she was sleeping and it explained why she normally wore a cloak over herself. There was always a way to squeeze the truth out of someone.

Gabrial looked up into the sky at the doves flying above her. Their little wings looked like soft, white petals of a rose. In a way it always made her feel free and spirited away into the soothing air. She caught a glimpse of

Emmanuelle riding on his horse into the courtyard and he had at least about twelve packages mounted on the horse. It appeared that he hadn't just gone to town for normal things.

He hadn't noticed her as he walked into the palace while one of the guards took his horseback to the stables. A few of the others helped him carry the items. They had come to a stop in the hallway near his bedroom door.

"Thanks for the help," said Emmanuelle. "I can take it from here."

"Of course," said Sir Hamilton, wiping his hand across his forehead.

He pushed open his door when the guards and Sir Hamilton had left. Now the only thing he had to do was find Gabrial and get her to come with him. She was on her bed looking to be asleep when he entered her room. Then he saw her cat playing with her hair with his paw and she moved a little as if playing with him.

"Emmanuelle?" she said in surprise, she hadn't expected to see him.

"Sorry for the intrusion, I just wanted to do something with you," the prince answered. "It'll only be a little while inside the parlor."

"It's fine," Gabrial smiled at her cat as she stepped out of her bed.

He took her by the hand as she let Knight slip from her grasp. She had left her gray cloak lying on her bed and hadn't realized it. When they had made it to his room the prince stood there, staring at her for a long moment as he took something from out of his pocket.

"Do you mind if I blindfold you?" Emmanuelle asked.

She shook her head and he moved closer to her, carefully tying the blindfold around. He felt her breathing deepen as he did so, it was as if she were nervous. The door to his room slowly opened and he led her inside. Gabrial felt him brush past her shoulder.

"Emmanuelle?" she said.

"I'm still here," he answered as he reached a red rose with a few purple petals out towards her. "Can you tell me what this is?"

It was a long while before she was able to figure out that he was holding something in front of her. When she was finally able to touch it with the tips of her fingers she was able to tell what it was. The strange part was why would he blindfold her so she couldn't see the rose he was trying to give her?

"It's a rose," she answered, happily. "But is there something I need to know about it?"

"Of course there is," he chuckled as he couldn't help but feel the side of her face. "But I'll leave that up for you to discover."

Emmanuelle took the blindfold off from her eyes. When she was able to see everything clearly again, she realized she was inside his bedroom. Nowhere near the parlor room.

"This is for you," he told her as he approached her with a bunch of packages. "I wasn't sure if you would like them, but I had to show my appreciation."

She looked at the things he had brought her in astonishment and was brought to tears. "Emmanuelle, they're beautiful," she cried, leaping onto him and giving him a tight hug. "I don't know what to say. Thank you."

"You're welcome," Emmanuelle answered, smiling at her as he hugged her back. "Well, are you going to try them on?"

She shook her head in agreement, but before she went to change she kissed him on the cheek. Suddenly, he felt his heart race with excitement as he watched her head for the changing area. He smiled, he knew he may have had a chance now. The prince sat down on his bed and waited for her.

"Do you like it?" she asked, walking slowly into his room.

He rubbed his eyes thinking that he was dreaming, she looked so amazing in the soft blue satin dress. If she looked that amazing in that one then she would look like a dream in the other one he had brought her with the lace. Gabrial felt a little awkward when he didn't say a word as he stood staring at her.

"It's beyond my wildest dreams how beautiful you look," he finally said.

Her face began to turn red as she felt the nervous and abash feeling rise. She looked down at the floor in the long dress so she wouldn't have to meet his still eyes that were staring at her.

"Thank you," Gabrial answered, smiling.

"There are really no words to describe how amazingly beautiful you look," the prince slowly walked over to her, then seemed to be looking at what was still missing from it.

"Please stop, Emmanuelle, you're making me feel so… bashful," she laughed, feeling as if there were butterflies in her stomach.

There was a box on a shelf that he had pulled down. He opened it, then reached his fingers inside, pulling out a necklace with two crosses on it. It made him happy when he saw that it was still in the same condition he had left it in. Gabrial looked at the necklace as he untwisted the chain. Slowly he made his way around her neck with the necklace. She moved her hair out of the way so he was able to clip it together.

He frowned when he saw the blood on her back and he wondered what happened to her? The idea of someone ever harming her made him sick and angry. Her hair fell

back onto her back down when she let go.

"It's beautiful," she said, happily.

His eyes could hardly move from where he had

seen the blood. If someone had done something so awful to

her why hadn't she said something? He lifted his head

when he heard her giggling happily. He couldn't kill her

joy and he didn't ask her.

Chapter 10

False Hopes

The thing that had pretended to be Sharon

vanished beneath him and turned into a dark shadow that

went across the ground and into an even greater being.

Birds flew from out of the trees, chirping as if angry and

the wind picked up. Emmanuel was thrown back, staring

up at the dark beast. He remembered the creature or he remembered the being that had become it.

"What have you done with Sharon?" he yelled at the dark creature.

It kind of resembled a man, but it was covered in bloody red as if he had been burned. Its teeth looked like little pricks of ice and behind him hung his dark wings that had formed from the crows that had gathered together. There was a golden ring where the color of his eye was supposed to be and the rest of his eye was black.

"I took back what was mine," he snapped, his voice sounding like a million screams or wails. "You don't think there would be an angel-like Sharon for you? She's my possession and will stay that way."

"No. She's not like you. She's better," cried Emmanuel, flapping his wings. "Release her at once, wherever you have taken her. I will do anything."

The creature cocked an eyebrow, that was what he wanted to hear. The angel was heading straight into his trap just like he had expected. "An angel is worth more than just anything, especially because of who she is. If anything is that including giving everything you hold dear, including yourself?"

He was asking for too much, he couldn't do that. If he did the world would be at stake, not to mention how he would live. He couldn't sacrifice his love for her and he couldn't sacrifice what he was, if he did he would soon have more than just his life on the line.

Some 1,000 years later

Papers were thrown everywhere, he couldn't be more frustrated with the knight's decision. Even he wouldn't have pulled such a bold move. Zealous or not, he needed to shut the lad down before he became the end of his name. Sir Belont was brought into the room, by Sir

Gilliot and Sir Chester. He gasped in worry, when he saw the look on Damien's face, it was glowing with anger.

"Sir, you asked to speak with me?" he asked, nervously as he put his hands behind his back.

The prince chuckled, angrily. "And I wondered who told you that much. I thought I made it clear to you and the other knights not to do anything out of presumption," he scowled as he pushed the knight lightly in the chest. "I don't like it when my orders are not carried out and you, you completely went against them."

"For a reason, my lord," he pointed out, cocking an eyebrow.

"Oh, and it better be a good one, otherwise I'm taking you out from the clan," Damien laughed as he picked up a little dagger. "A wise person once said, if thy right eye offends thee, pluck it out," he stabbed the dagger into an apple, letting juice spill out from it. The knight watched, gulping, thinking his stomach may just give way.

"And you, my brother, I find very offensive."

Damien took a bite of the green apple, from off his knife, then tossed it onto his desk. Sir Belont tried to hide the sickened look on his face and stood more upright. "She overheard us talking about what you plan to do with the royal family and I didn't want her to tell anyone so I decided we should kill her."

"And what if she didn't hear you fools at all and you just raised everyone's suspicions about us? Huh? What about that?" snarled the prince, his voice deepened.

There was nothing he thought he could say, besides that he had messed up. And that was the one thing he hated most. He never wanted to mess up in the prince's sight. He was the only person he had ever looked to as a shining light, his guide to getting self-righteousness; without him, he'd be nothing.

"How can I gain your forgiveness, your highness?"

he asked, kneeling, before the prince.

A grin appeared on the prince's face, this was the

kind of revenge he liked," Damien said.

"You're highness!" yelled a guard, charging

through the door almost breathlessly.

The two of them turned from each other and looked

at the guard, wondering why he was acting so nervous and

scared half out of his mind.

"What is it? Can't you see I'm in the middle of

something?" snapped the prince.

The guard leaned one of his hands against the

doorpost for support. "I can, sir. But it's your father, he has

fallen ill and wishes to speak with you," he announced,

breathing heavily.

It was as if he was unmoved by what the guard had

just told him, he shrugged. "Take me to him," he ordered,

plainly.

"Of course, sir," the guard headed out the door leading the way.

Before they left, the prince stopped in the doorway and looked at Sir Belont. "Give me a day and I'll think about whether you are worthy or not to be a part of the clan," Damien answered, finally as he closed the door.

"Whatever you believe is right, sir," Sir Belont replied, still on his knees.

The door closed and the knight was left to think about his mistake that could've tarnished his whole entire career of being one of the most highly recognized knights. He had been noticed by the most powerful person, how could he have messed that up?

****

Gabrial found Emmanuelle outside at the stables, where she saw him in the corral trying to perform tricks with two white horses. The horses galloped with such poise. She realized he must have been trying to regain some of the talents he had lost.

"Faster Perseus and Aristaeus," he cheered, standing up slowly on the saddle of the horse.

He looked over at her once but kept his eyes focused forward. She was here. This was his moment to show her what he could do. His heart felt on fire with such excitement. Perseus and Aristaeus began to pick up the pace, circling the corral. She watched, it amazed her how talented he was, she had never seen anything like it and it brought excitement to her. From above his mother watched through a window. She looked at Gabrial who had been laughing. Queen Eliza was still trying to figure out what Gabrial was hiding from all of them. The girl didn't behave like normal ones in their kingdom. She wasn't dark, gloomy in a way she was like her son.

"Emmanuelle no!" yelled Gabrial as he reached one of his hands out to grab a pole.

The horses galloped faster than before and just when he reached out his left foot slipped off the saddle and he fell between the horses. He was still hanging onto the reins, but eventually, let go. She ran inside to make sure he was alright.

"Emmanuelle?"

He was lying on his face, then he arose. He instantly began to laugh. "That was the most fun I've had, besides my head feeling a little dizzy in the mind," he answered, sitting up. "Urgh." He reached the back of his neck, when he looked at his hand there was a little blood on it. "Maybe it's a little more serious than I thought."

She helped him to his feet and took him back to the palace. He limped a little on his left. The prince still hadn't stopped laughing about how silly it was for him to try a stunt like that after regaining control over the horses.

✳✳✳✳✳✳✳✳✳

None of the gowns looked like the ones that would catch the prince's attention. Gabrial held a dress in front of herself as she looked at herself in the mirror. She wondered which one he would have liked to see her in. It was hard to tell with him since he said he liked her in every one of them.

"If you ask me, I think you look better in the one that's on your bed," admitted Emmanuelle, standing in the doorway, startling her.

She smiled bashfully, he had already seen her in that one and he acted as if he hadn't. But she had been wondering which one he'd like better and she had him tell her in person which was better than just depending on her guess on what he may have liked. He would have walked into her room if he hadn't heard someone calling for him.

He looked down the hallway where he saw a guard heading his way, seeming to be in a hurry.

"Your highness, you must come quick, it is your father who is ill," declared the guard quickly.

The prince looked at Gabrial as she picked up the dress he had thought was right for her. He had something to ask her, but he thought about his father's health, which came first before anything else. After he went to check up on him, he could come back and tell her what he wanted to do, that was what he was going to do.

When she turned back around, she noticed that he was gone. Although she didn't know where to go. She thought he would have at least said something before he had left. It seemed a little strange considering he normally would. Gabrial tossed the dress back onto her bed, there was no need for her to wear something like that if she was going to be working in dirty places anyway. It made her wonder what she had been thinking about.

Esmeralda lay in the hot desert sand, she had passed out. After losing the battle in the ring, no one cared about what happened to her and she was kicked out. The sound of horseshoes was what woke her up. Her green eyes stared as she slowly pushed herself up by her elbows. There was a multitude of men with wrappings all around her, their faces with only their eyes showing. A few of them rode horses with bags, while others walked with camels.

One of them stepped down from his horse and approached her. She watched him carefully, she had learned through her time in this world that no human was trustworthy ever. When she saw him take out his knife, she immediately leaped onto her feet and kicked the knife out of his hand. The men smiled, when they saw what she could do. Some of them having teeth as dark as the bark of trees.

She held the knife at the man's neck as she eyed him for a long moment. He began to grin when it got a little closer as he grew nervous that she would kill him.

"I am Achmed Ubduh and we seek you no harm," he said, quickly. "Only to be sure you were alright. We are camel drivers and only seek to get home and take these goods to our family. Well, I myself is sort of a guardian guide for these guys."

Esmeralda chuckled, sinisterly. "And like I'm supposed to believe you," she laughed.

"It's the truth, you may see for yourself," Achmed told her, looking back at the camels.

She eyed him for a long while, then withdrew the knife and walked around, checking the bags. It turned out that he hadn't been lying after all. She saw spices, roots, vegetables, and other kinds of things. When she turned around, he was watching her closely.

"Your destination is it nice and has water?" she inquired.

He nodded his head slightly. "Water is not a question there. Our city is built on an ocean of it," he replied, walking closer to her. "We can give you a ride there if you'd like. We're heading there anyway."

It was a little strange for anyone to be so kind to someone they didn't even know. She was a stranger that they had come across out here. Certainly, they had to have some kind of suspicion. Achmed and the others waited for an answer from her, which they kind of knew what she would probably say. Esmeralda nodded her head in agreement, squinting her eyes from the sun's light.

"You may ride on my horse. And here," he said, wrapping a large piece of cloth around her head and neck. "It'll keep you cool and protected from the sun."

✱✱✱✱✱✱✱✱✱✱

Days had passed and although she saw him at times, she had seemed to become like a phantom in his sight. He would speak a little to her, but never like how they had done before. She came to a hallway with a broom, when she noticed a line of young ladies outside the throne room in beautifully designed gowns that had so many vivid colors.

They were princesses from far and wide, who had come to meet the prince, she had realized when she saw a few of them with tiaras. He stood on a platform. His brother and father watched the prince from a place above them. Emmanuelle bowed before every one of them as his father's advisor announced their names. Each of the girls smiled at him and he returned the smile, although he wished this could have been over.

One of the girls walking before him, who wore a dark pink dress, accidentally dropped her handkerchief on his shoe.

"Oh dear," she said, trying to sound worried as she looked down.

The prince picked it up for her, smiling at her. "Here you are," he replied as she stared at him with a bashful smile.

"Thank you, it seems that you are as kind as everyone says you are," the princess complimented looking at his soft brown eyes. "I'm Princess Arabella." she reached her hand out that had a white glove covering it.

"A pleasure to meet you," he said, slowly.

Emmanuelle had noticed Gabrial near the doorway. He felt pierced to the heart that she had seen him. It wasn't what it seemed, but how would she know that? She petted her black cat as she looked at the young ladies in their elegant gowns. They were in the same league as him, she would never be fit for him, that was a false conception she had almost convinced herself of. She had seen the look in his eyes when he had handed the girl back her handkerchief. It was obvious.

"Damien look over there," whispered Sir Gilliot, tugging on his sleeve and pointing to the corner where he had noticed her.

A devious smirk appeared on his face when he saw that she was looking disappointed. "Things just keep on getting better," he chuckled.

Eventually, Gabrial turned her back and walked away, disappearing around the corner. Emmanuelle took a step forward when he saw her leave, then remembered he couldn't. His heart ached to run after her, but he knew he couldn't do that. The kingdom depended on him now to make the right choice.

Gabrial left the broom in the hallway, running off to a place far from the throne room. She had been so frustrated by what she had seen. In the kitchen, she saw Maid A'Key and the other maid hard at work. This was where she was supposed to be. Where she belonged in the first place with those like her. Not with the prince. Not near the throne room or even dressing like she was more than what she was.

Maid A'Key starred up from the floor, where suds of soap were bubbling. She noticed Gabrial hunched over the sink with her hands plunged into the water. Her long ponytail was hanging in a wreck and she was shaking as if cold, although it wasn't. It made the maid wonder what was wrong with her. She touched Gabrial on the shoulder consolingly, holding the mop with her other hand. The girl reached her hand onto her shoulder where the maid was and petted it, gently.

"Gabrial, what is wrong?" asked the maid. "You seem troubled."

She shook her head and turned around, her cat was on the floor playing with her cloak. "Everything," she cried. "I embarrassed myself and I want to just leave this place so I won't have to remember all the things I can't bear to think of. I feel like a fool."

The maid leaned the broom against the counter when she saw that she had begun to shed tears. She embraced her so she wouldn't feel like she was alone.

"Oh A'Key," she cried, closing her eyes.

"There, now, it couldn't have been all that bad," assured the maid. "See."

A few of the other women looked at her trying to figure out what was happening. Gabrial felt as if she would break into a million pieces. He had to know how she felt about him, how she had been convinced that they shared the same background and understanding. Emmanuelle had been the only one she felt that she could confide in with anything without him judging or saying something. For the most part, he was very good at making it so he never said anything that might make someone feel worse.

The night had fallen upon the kingdom. Gabrial watched from above on her balcony Emmanuelle and the princess. The two of them had seemed to have had a lot in common from how long they had talked to one another. Which shouldn't have been that much of a surprise to her since he was a prince. If she cared about him, she knew she had to leave him to be happy.

Her balcony outside her bedroom was peaceful and she could hear herself think. Doves flew over her, off to someplace outside of this building. Maybe it was time for her to leave or move on to some other place. Outside of the palace. She wasn't royalty, she wasn't even a part of their family. There was no need for her to be here or any reason for her to want to be here. She pulled on her cloak, then let her hood drape over her head.

She heard her cat as he walked over to her and rubbed the side of her leg as if trying to comfort her. A grin slowly began to appear on her face and she picked him up, raising him in front of her.

"I have to go, there is no reason for me to be here," Gabrial told him as if he understood. "You take care of yourself, I'm sure we'll see each other again."

The cat was set down on the floor and she petted him gently on the head. As she headed out the door to the balcony, she heard him. She knew he would miss her just as much as she would miss him, but she couldn't take him along since she had no idea of where she was going or what would happen along the way. It would kill her if something were to happen to him. Gabrial tossed a rope she had made from a bunch of sheets over the banister climbed down. Her cat leaped onto the banister watching her leave, sadly.

Her feet finally touched the ground and she knew that there was no going back now. The little town outside the castle was deserted with the lights from a few lamps that had been lit up. In a few windows, she saw candle

lights with flowers beneath them. She didn't know which

way was the way to the end of the kingdom so she

followed a long road that went on into a dense darkness.

In the Dead of Night

Chapter 11

Another World

Chains surrounded her and she was in a place

that was gray with swirling lights as if the northern lights

and it was empty with only laughter like those of witches

and evil beings that thrived off one's misery. He called to

her a few times, but it was as if she couldn't hear him as

she pulled herself closer together. Her head was facing the glass floor as she hugged herself trying to fight away the pain of her wings that were tearing through her back like bloody knives.

He heard a sound that was like the tearing of a tree branch, she began to cry covering her eyes so she wouldn't have to see her shame. He gasped when he saw what had emerged from her back. They weren't wings, they were more like the bloody skeletal parts of wings that used to be there. A few feathers hung from the tips of them.

"Go back," he heard her whisper to him, faintly. "Go back. Don't save me."

Emmanuel yelled as he banged his arms against the field trying to get to her, only finding his arms bruised afterward. But nothing had happened to the strange field. He could hear Darcel laughing at him making him even more frustrated. He had done this to him on purpose. He wanted him to see how Gabrial would suffer if he didn't cooperate.

"Had enough?" he asked.

"This isn't her right now is it?" inquired

Emmanuel, angrily.

The field vanished and the dark figure hung over

him once more. He shrugged. "It could be, but you can

save her."

"How?" the angel asked, eagerly.

"As I said before, give me yourself and I'll set her

free and you can have her back," chuckled Darcel,

narrowing his deep red eyes at him.

"Fine, just don't torture her anymore and give her

back to me," ordered Emmanuel.

"I'm proud that you made the right decision. Just

remember if you slip up and try to get away somehow, I'm

coming after her and you can kiss this entire world

goodbye," snarled Darcel, stretching out his dark wings,

some of his feathers flying off and becoming dark ravens.

"She's more valuable than you think."

Emmanuelle had searched the entire palace, but he could not find her anywhere, it was as if she had turned into a phantom and left the place. The only place he hadn't checked was her room and that was because the door had been locked. Even then he had knocked, but there was no answer. He thought to give it another try, maybe she had been asleep or out wandering across the balcony like she normally did.

"Excuse me, sir, but do you think the king would prefer danishes or bread at his conference?" asked a chef in the kitchen.

"I think he'd prefer danishes," answered the prince. "By the way you haven't seen a girl?"

The chef chuckled. "We have a lot of those," he pointed to women cooks and maids that looked discombobulated as they worked around in the noisy kitchen. "Choose the right one."

It came to him that he hadn't been specific and there had to be at least about a dozen girls in this place. "Her name is Gabrial. Pale blue eyes. Tall. A kind of… how would you say…" he had to think for a moment "…kind of a bluish-gray kind of hair," he explained, smiling as he felt a little silly for not explaining in the first place.

"I'm sorry but I haven't seen her lately," he answered, shaking his head.

There was no use, she wasn't anywhere to be found. "Thanks," Emmanuelle said, then headed for the exit.

He nearly bumped into Sir Kelvin, who gasped for air in surprise.

"Excuse me," said the prince.

"Oh, and what's the hurry?" he asked, cocking an eyebrow.

"I'm looking for Gabrial. She forgot this in my room the other day," Emmanuelle showed the knight her necklace. "It seems like she has disappeared."

"I'm sorry, sir, but I haven't," answered Sir Kelvin, briskly as he rushed past him. "If I do, I'll tell her you've been looking for her, you're highness."

The prince shook the necklace in his hand, thinking of all the places she could have been. But every place he thought of, he had already checked. Then it came to him what he had told her earlier on during the day. He rested one of his hands on his forehead and sighed, deeply. What had he done? There was a chance she could have been there at the pavilion.

Now he had to get inside her room and get this cleared up. Emmanuelle started down the hallway in a hurry. Sometimes he wished things were for him, not against him all the time. When he reached her room, he knocked on the door.

"Gabrial," he called. "I want to speak with you, please."

The door opened slowly to reveal that the room was left all alone without anyone in sight. The curtains to her balcony blew as a soft breeze blew in from outside. Emmanuelle walked inside, looking around the room carefully for any signs of her. Her dresses were still in the closet when he looked, everything was there except for the silver cloak. If she wasn't here, where could she have gone? His eyes caught a glimpse of something dark on the banister of the balcony.

He thought she may have left it there as some clue of where she was. To his disappointment, it was Knight, sleeping, and then he saw something else tied to the banister where the cat had been lounging around. The prince pulled on it, bringing it up onto the balcony where he could figure out what it was. Knight awakened when he felt part of the sheets rubbed against his fur.

"Meow," went the cat, leaping down from the banister.

Emmanuelle pulled a big bunch of sheets tied together to make a rope over the banister. It surprised him, when he realized that Gabrial may not have been at the palace at all, but somewhere else. Which meant she was trying to escape him. Gabrial had to know what kind of dangers lie outside of the palace.

If only he had explained things to her. Things may have seemed a certain way, but appearances could be deceiving. He didn't feel anything for the princess, at least nothing compared to what he felt for her. What he felt for Gabrial always made him think he was going to lose his heart. He couldn't lose that.

****

The prince searched the entire kingdom for her, but everyone he came across had told him they hadn't seen anyone. His hopes of finding her began to dwindle.

Someone had to see her and know what direction she was heading in.

She may have been good at escaping the palace of knights and guards, but getting past these people without anyone noticing her seemed as if they had all been put under a forgetting spell or something. Emmanuelle climbed onto his horse and decided to search further towards the end of the kingdom.

He had to find her and tell her the truth. It would almost kill him to think of her thinking thoughts of him that were not true. Even if she didn't want to be bothered by him, she would have to at least let him explain, and then he would leave her alone.

"Your highness," he heard a man yell.

A man stood in the street on the side of his horse. His hair was medium length and wavy and the color of a reddish-brown. He had a mustache which made him look as if he were a prince himself. He wore a black wool coat that covered the rest of his clothes. The only thing that was

noticeable from his black outfit was his copper-brown

boots.

"I heard you were looking for someone that I may

have seen," he declared, quickly. "A girl with a silver

cloak?"

"Yes, do you know where I might find her?"

inquired Emmanuelle, stepping down from his horse.

"I can't say that I know where her destination is,

but she was heading in that direction," he pointed to the

long road that led to the end of their kingdom and the

forest.

It made his heart feel like it skipped a beat when he

thought of her being out there. There were bandits,

warriors, witches, wild animals, and all kinds of other

things. He had to find her before either of those did,

especially before witches did. They had to be the most

dangerous thing out there since they were clever and

pretend to be nice. You would never know if you ran across one until you were inside their house.

His father had told him some stories he would never want to happen to her. That is before he banished all of them to the Dark Forest, which was outside the kingdom that separated them from the Southern Kingdom.

Nothing was going to happen to her, he wouldn't allow it to. Emmanuelle was going to have to find her before either of those did. If she was on foot, she couldn't have gotten far. If only she hadn't seen him with that princess. The prince climbed onto his horse in a hurry, grabbing hold of the reins.

"Thanks for the help," Emmanuelle said, happily.

The man cocked an eyebrow. "It is not everyday you are asked by a prince to be of service," he replied.

Emmanuelle smiled, then whacked his horse's reins, setting off for the dark forest in hopes of finding Gabrial. He held onto the cross necklace, tightly. It was as if he hoped by holding on tighter to it, it would prevent anything from happening to her.

****

Sir Belont had been walking on pins and needles afraid to lose his entire life. There had to be a way for him to regain the prince's trust. Sir Gilliot sure had his trust and he hardly had to move a finger. He had to do more just to be considered one of them. There was no doubt that Sir Gilliot had made many mistakes during his career and Prince Damien had probably never threatened to cut him from the clan. It just didn't seem fair how harshly he was treated.

His ears grew attentive when he heard the sound of the prince's voice. He sounded frustrated for some reason and that wasn't the only voice he heard. He peeked around

the corner into the library and saw Damien and Sir Gilliot.
They seemed to be pinned against one another right now.

"And you just let her escape?" snapped Damien, slapping his fist against the table. "This isn't going accordingly at all and it is all your fault."

Sir Gilliot stood there like a statue. "I take full responsibility for it, sir," he chuckled. "But what did you expect to happen?"

The prince stared up at the tall, older knight and sighed with annoyance. "What I always expect you to do. Your job."

Sir Belont smiled, craftily as he watched the two of them go back and forth with one another. Then it looked like Sir Gilliot had given up and stormed down the staircase without any other words. He slowly crept in as the prince stared down at a table of a bunch of papers that looked like maps or graphs, part of it was covered by books.

"Prince Damien, sir," he greeted, nervously.

Damien took one glance over at him, then was suddenly hit in the head by a book that seemed to fall from out of the sky. He growled, annoyedly looking up to see who had thrown a book at his head. But no one was one the upper part of the library.

"Are you alright, your highness?" asked the knight, approaching him more swiftly.

"And you have the nerve to ask me if…" his eyes noticed something on one of the pages of the book that caught his attention.

"What is it, sir?" inquired Sir Belont, hovering over the table where the book had landed.

On the pages, he saw angels fighting a much greater being. Then on the other page, he saw two halves of two angels being placed in the center of a lotus flower. The writing was so small he couldn't make out all the words, but part of it said. *'Out of the darkness came the light and from the shadows reveals what is to come that has not reached, not what is.'* The prince chuckled, lightly and the knight thought he must have read the same passage. Damien turned to the knight with a smile, then he patted him on the shoulder. Sir Belont smiled back but felt as if there was some kind of motive for why he had changed his whole attitude towards him so quickly.

"I have a proposition for you that may just earn you back your place," he said, calmly.

His heart spun with excitement and it felt like his skin wanted to run away from his skeleton. He would have cheered, but he knew better than to do that in the prince's presence. "Of course, sir," answered Sir Belont, hiding the excitement he was feeling.

"Find that little tramp and return her to me," Damien ordered, but unlike the other times his voice was calmer. "I have a feeling that she may be able to read the rest of this."

"Consider it done, sir," replied the knight, happily.

The knight exited the library, quicker than someone snapping their fingers. Damien looked over the pictures closely as if hoping to understand the meaning of the words by just staring at them. There had to be a reason why he had never run across this book all the other times he was in this old place. As a boy, he had probably read every book about ancient times and mythology in the library, but he couldn't recall a single time when he had seen one with this kind of language or pictures.

"*Ekeínoi tou fotós kai tou skotadioú,*" he heard a dead, raspy voice whisper.

Damien turned around, quickly but no one was behind him or anywhere in the room.

****

Emmanuelle began to feel like he was riding in a circle even in the broad daylight. The forest was lush green, some water fell from the leaves. It was a wonder why this forest had been called the dark forest, it was so beautiful and full of light. His head tilted up when he thought he heard someone's voice. Then it went away and he thought that it could've been an echo in his head. He was tired after all, which played a role in the reason for him hearing things.

A few sounds of laughter or singing made him rethink that thought. This time he was sure he heard someone. He looked over at a bunch of bushes that were on the side of the dirt trail. The talking and singing may have been coming from behind them. They were too tall to look over so he was forced to get off his horse and walk it towards the bush. He wasn't sure what or who he was going to find, but he hoped it was her or maybe someone who had seen where she was going.

The prince peered through the bush and the singing grew louder. For some reason, he thought he remembered that song, although he couldn't recall ever hearing it. The song took him back, somewhere far back, maybe even before he had become a prince. This entire moment seemed memorable like it had happened already. He saw Gabrial standing in a crystal blue lake with her back turned as she played with a few fishes that were the color of the sun and white as sheep's fur.

Her bluish-gray hair hanging loosely over her shoulders and down her back. He felt as if his heart on the inside had escaped from him when he saw her. He thought he couldn't catch his breath at one moment, but he couldn't figure out why. He had been with her and near her a lot of times, but never before had he felt such a strong urge from the inside to be with her.

Gabrial cupped her hands, then poured some of the water over her head. Her grey shirt hung over her like a dress that looked like she was wearing a mirror. The prince couldn't bear to stare at her any longer and he walked out from behind the bush leaving his horse.

"Gabrial," he called.

She turned around as if frightened when she heard his voice and noticed him walking across the beach. How had he found her? Was he angry at her for leaving? There was something he didn't understand, she hadn't left because she wanted to, but she didn't want to be a hindrance in his marriage. Currents ran against her when he stepped into the water, approaching her slowly.

When he was close enough she felt one of his hands move up her left side while his other hand moved gently against her face, he missed so dearly. He had nearly lost her for a second time and that would have taken its toll on his heart. He looked down at her, the soft golden brown glowing in the sunlight. A breeze blew past her face carrying small particles and her eyes closed as if giving him permission. His lips touched hers lightly, before he kissed her, deeply.

"Emmanuelle, I'm sorry for leaving you, I didn't want to make things difficult for you," she whispered in his ear.

"That was my fault, I should have explained things to you before doing what I did," he told her. "I'm sorry for not being honest with you. Sure I have a duty to my kingdom, but I have a duty to myself and that is being with the one I was with in the beginning. With you, Gabrial."

His arms wrapped around her as he held her close to him. Nothing was going to get between them. Not even his thoughts, what he had with her was irreplaceable. Gabrial felt his hand rub her back up and down as if he were trying to console her. Her skin was so smooth beneath his hand, it felt almost like the petals of a rose.

She didn't know why but for some strange reason the Emmanuelle she had remembered as a lion was somehow different from the one she was with right now. This one was more affectionate, although he was still very understanding and loved to do fun things. Such as horseback riding.

His eyes looked at her as he held one of her hands, he moved it across the surface of his shirt, his eyes still focused on hers. Slowly the zipper began to move as he helped her move it down. Part of his chest was revealed, then she looked up at him growing hesitant. He was a prince, he couldn't marry her and it would be wrong of her. Emmanuelle's eyes stared at her lips, his heart ached to kiss her just once more just to feel them against his.

"Emmanuelle, I don't feel..." She didn't want to say anything to him, although she thought he was taking things a little far. It wasn't that she didn't want to be this close to him, she just didn't feel like all of her was going along with the other part of her.

It suddenly began to rain and the two of them looked up to see lightning flashing across the sky. He took her by the hand and led her out of the water.

"Gabrial, come back with me, we can ride back to the palace before this storm gets…"

Lightning struck a tree causing it to fall nearly on top of the horse if it hadn't runoff.

"No!" yelled Emmanuelle, watching as his horse ran off into the forest.

That was the only way they could have escaped the storm and now it was gone. The storm seemed to have started to pick up and he knew if they stayed any longer in this rain that they were going to be extremely cold and wet.

"Come with me," she told him as she led him into a bunch of thick trees. They came to a thicket of bushes that wasn't too far. "We can stay in here until the storm clears up and it'll keep us dry."

He watched as she entered into the little place covered with leaves and vines that were tangled together. Once she was far enough in, he went inside also. The little place was drier than he had expected and he noticed her silver cloak on the ground. It appeared that she must have hidden in this place for the past few nights she had been out there. She had a mat of leaves laid across the ground that she had slept on.

"I guess we'll be staying here for the night," he said, sitting down.

She nodded her head in agreement as she laid down the opposite way of him. Emmanuelle did the same facing her back, noticing that the streaks on her back were gone.

265

Chapter 12

The Unhealed and Forgotten

Sharon stepped onto the small stones, her armor

reflecting the light. Her eyes were blindfolded with a black

wrapping. The sapphire necklace Emmanuel had given her

just before she left was still hanging from her neck.

Armistice and the other women watched as she emerged from the doorway that had luminous, blinding light flowing from it. She had forgotten her past life, she had hoped just like all the rest of them. When she was close enough Armistice approached her, then stopped and whispered something into her ear.

"What is your name?" she asked her.

The angel took a soft deep breath, then answered. "Arsonist."

Armistice smiled, happy to see that she didn't remember a thing of her past. The blindfold was removed from her eyes. She felt like they were going to tear up from all the light. Arsonist let her wings unfurl behind her, they were large and white, the ends of them sparkled since they had gold. They were different from the other iron angels, who had iron wings with only the feather parts at the ends and glowed from the inside whenever there was darkness.

She looked at her friend, then chuckled, softly.

"What is our mission?" she inquired.

The angels looked at their leader as if waiting for her to answer the question.

"Save the world and our fellow friends," answered Armistice, beckoning for the others to come near. "Evil has no place in the new world and neither do the average angels."

Some 1,000 Years Later

Guards flooded the prison cell, where the Black Knight was being kept. He had grown restless for some reason and they were afraid he was going to get out. The shackles that had been put around his ankles were broken, ground by some of the loose bricks that had been in the cell. For so long he had been quiet and they thought he'd remain in that state of dormant, but he hadn't. The knight sounded to be talking out of his head, some of it they couldn't even understand.

There were strange pictures drawn into the wall, along with an odd kind of writing. The only words they could understand were a few names he had thrown out such as *'Damien and Sharon'* then after that the rest of it seemed to be just gibberish.

"O destino do mundo reside en quen e' Deus esta connosco," said the Black Knight, confusing the knights even more.

Damien pushed past all the guards that had been trying to retain the knight. He had the book he had found in his coat so that it was concealed from everyone around him. The prince beckoned for the guards to go away, some of them were hesitant to leave him alone with the knight that appeared to be crazy. But they couldn't disobey him, even if it was for a good cause. When they were all finally gone he crouched down in front of the cell.

"What's wrong, Old Timer?" inquired the prince, smiling.

The knight stopped drawing and saying the same things and turned when he heard Damien. He looked at him for a long, quiet, stale moment. He knew he would come, although he had noticed a kind of change in the way he had addressed him. The Black Knight shook it off like it was nothing after all he was beyond old at this point he was more like ancient.

"Why have you come," snarled the knight, playing with a few rocks.

The prince leaned forward, closer to the cell. "I heard you were losing it down here. Speaking things that no one could understand. Do you know what any of it might mean? Or do you remember any of it at all?"

The Black Knight chuckled, softly as he turned his head to look at the wall he had drawn all over. Of course, he knew what he had been saying all along, otherwise, he wouldn't have been saying it if he didn't understand himself. To him, the prince needed more help than he did, but he wasn't about to say that. A piece of rock fell from the ceiling, barely missing him.

"This place is very old," he observed, trying to annoy the prince.

"Is that all you said?" Damien inquired, knowing that he was messing around. "They told me you said something more like 'destano mundo' or something like that."

The knight leaned against the wall. "I'm an Old Timer, how should I recall what I said?"

This game or whatever the knight wanted to call it was starting to anger him. He knew that the knight knew he needed him and as long as he knew that he would continue to play with him like his little mouse in a trap.

"Okay. Okay. What do you want?" asked the prince.

The Black Knight turned almost immediately, his deep blue eyes that looked like the sea, standing out from the rags that covered his face.

"I want that angel, Sharon," he snapped, bitterly.

"More like Gabrial," chuckled Damien, thinking of how she had invented a name like that as a disguise for her true name. It wasn't at all very clever, the name was so close to her actual name. If it had been him he would have tried a name more like David, Dirk, or...Darcel.

He grunted a little as he set himself more upright. "Gabrial? You say? Awful attempt to try and conceal her identity."

"I thought the same thing," announced the prince. "What do you want with her anyway? You never asked for her before."

The knight shrugged. "For my use, I owe her a little something."

"Hmm. It can't happen. At least not now."

"Why not?"

"She's run off somewhere, I can't find her."

✳✳✳✳✳✳✳✳✳✳✳✳

Both Emmanuelle and Gabrial lay under the trees that had covered them from the storm. His eyelids slowly opened and he noticed that his horse had not come back. He moved his arm from around her, careful not to wake her. It all somehow reminded him of when he was a lion and when he had fallen asleep and when she had slept right with him. In those days it had been just the two of them and she depended on him just like he had depended on her to always be there or to be the one person who always understood.

He tossed his cape off of him so that more of it covered her. The wind began to pick up outside, it was fresh after the storm and kind of cool. It was quite some ways back to the palace, but he knew of a town somewhere down the long road. Gabrial sat up from the leaf pad she had created. The storm had passed over and the little place had kept her almost completely dry.

She walked out of the little place and noticed Emmanuelle looking at a plant that looked like a bird with its blazing red petals. He touched the petals of the flower gently, he had never seen one like it before and thought it was remarkable the way the colors changed with the more or less sunlight it got.

"Gabrial," he said as he stood up, not realizing a yellow kind of dew from the flower that quickly soaked into his hand. "I just remembered that there is not a town too far from here that I may be able to get another horse from."

"That's great," she replied, looking at the flower that looked to be breathing.

"You can come with me, I'd like that much better than going alone," the prince admitted. "From there we can go back to Ascedia, the ball is only five days away and I'd like you to be there with me."

She looked back at the little place. She had been content here, there was no kind of trouble or chaos, it was just peaceful and simple. Although she did miss him when she was here. Going back to that place would be like returning to the place where she was unwanted and always a target for Damien.

"Please, Gabrial," Emmanuelle begged, his soft brown eyes looking like a lost newborn pup. "Come back with me."

Gabrial nodded her head, slightly. He had done so much for her. "I will come with you," she finally answered.

He smiled at her, happily. She was going to be happy she came back with him. There would be no misunderstandings or anything like that or so he was going to try and make sure of. It was easy to think you could accomplish such things, but it wasn't that easy. Gabrial went inside the little place to get her cloak, after she found it, the two of them set off for the town.

The two of them were silent for a long while, but questions continued to flood his head about her. He had wondered who her parents were or had she been an orphan since she never spoke of them. He wondered about the blood on her back that sometimes went away and the list of things could go on from there. She didn't say much about anything, not even about her life at the palace before she saved him.

"So, how are your parents?" he blurted, then suddenly wished he hadn't asked that.

"My father?" she asked, looking up at him as he kept his eyes focused on the road ahead.

He nodded his head, noticing that she had only said her father, which either meant she had lost her mother or she had left her with her father. "Yes."

It took her a while, she couldn't remember her father for some reason. The only thing she could remember was Death releasing her, but he was not her father. She grew somewhat frustrated that she couldn't remember so she could answer his question. Her mind was blank, as empty as a slate.

"I don't know, it's like I can't remember him," Gabrial answered, feeling a little daft.

"I understand," he told her.

"Why do you ask?" she inquired, sensing that he wasn't just asking to have a simple conversation.

Emmanuelle sighed, deeply. "I thought-- it can wait."

She watched the sky closely as it swirled above her making formations. For a long moment she stopped, there was something high in the sky and it looked to be staring in her direction, but she couldn't make out what it was. The prince asked her nothing else. He began to slow as they approached an entrance, where a few men that wore hoods covered themselves. One of them looked like a shadow since he was dressed in all black. They glared and scowled at him as he walked past them. He could recall running across men like them as a lion, a few times he was attacked by them since they got a thrill out of tormenting someone or anything.

Gabrial drew near to the entrance, she couldn't figure out where he had gone in such a short time. It was like he had gone through the entrance and vanished. She thought that she may have been able to find him if she went inside, that he may have been waiting on the other side of the tall wall. As she approached it she saw some children struggling to get by the men. They laughed and pushed them around like their toys.

How could they have been so cruel to pick with children? She couldn't allow it to happen, it made her feel sick just looking at them. Inside of her, she could remember feeling like that and being treated the same way at that age.

"Stop," she yelled, racing over and stepping in front of the children as if to protect them. "What gives you the right to treat them like this?"

A man smiled at her, showing his nastily rotted out teeth, although his face was covered by black wrappings and his hood. "They're orphans without parents, robbers, that means they belong to everyone in this place," he chuckled. "And what are you, some kind of guardian angel for low lives."

The children stood frightenedly behind her, one of them hanging on to the end of her cloak as he sucked his thumb.

"Gifts from heaven that should've never been given to those who are unable to receive them," she said, backing the children into the entryway of the town so they could escape. "You people are wearing blindfolds. You don't believe in anything anymore like children," Gabrial felt the children scurry off behind her to someplace away from the men. " The only reason you attack them is because it hurts you to see that they still believe in themselves and you don't."

"Listen to this little peasant girl talk," chuckled the man.

She tried to go through the entrance as the children had done, but two of the men shut the gate so she was unable to enter. They laughed at her, she couldn't escape them now and they were going to make her pay for the words she said. No one talked to them in any kind of way, especially not a young girl. Gabrial watched as they approached her with their weapons, sometimes the right thing was not always appreciated and neither was honesty.

****

The men grabbed Gabrial then tossed her in the center of them with a few of the other men. She looked at them. They laughed, but that wasn't all she heard laughing. Something else was laughing deep inside of them, the very same thing she heard or felt whenever Damien had come too close to her.

"What's your name?" asked the one with the dark hood.

There was no answer from her and she focused her eyes away from his face. She felt one of the men knee her in her back and it felt like a stone being thrown at it. She bit her lower lip to keep from screaming with pain.

"I know you understand me," he snarled, walking closer to her.

They grew frustrated when she refused to answer them and pretend that she didn't have a voice. Her cloak was suddenly snatched from off of her, by a man behind her.

"Give that back," she cried trying to break free from their grip as the man handed it to the man with the black hood.

"So you can talk," he chuckled, holding her cloak.

She noticed he took a knife out of his pocket.

"Such a pity such beautiful apparel is going to waste like this," he began to cut it.

"Stop," Gabrial told him, wishing she could do something as he cut the cloak in half.

"Stop having fun? I'm just getting started," teased the man.

Gabrial felt something sting like the tip of a blade into one of the spots on her back. One of the men laughed, then rubbed her blood on his fingers.

"Hey, boss, she's bleeding," he said, pushing her onto the ground.

She caught herself by her hands before hitting the ground. She gasped as her eyes grew focused on the ground beneath her. The voices of the men talking were so loud and sounded more like a bunch of squabbling birds.

"So having problems with uncontrolled bleeding?" asked one of them. "We can help with that."

He took a sizzling knife from the fire. Two of the men pulled her up from the ground and held her still as the man neared her with the fiery knife. If anything he was going to cause her more pain, not help her. She wouldn't let him even get near her with that knife or she would try not to.

"Or there are other ways you could get that healed," he laughed, holding the knife so close to her shoulder it could have burned her. He stared at her face and eyes, they were mesmerizing to him and so clear he could have seen into all her thoughts. "I can be very reasonable at times as long as you're cooperative."

She shook her head in disagreement as he reached his hand out to touch the side of her face. Gabrial frowned, she couldn't deal with this and she kicked him as hard as she could in his large stomach. It knocked him back and he lost his breath. The pain inside his stomach felt like a fire was burning on the inside.

"You little wretch," he insulted, pulling her free from the other men.

He threw her into the gates brick wall and she felt more pain sting through her back like electricity striking her. The man pulled off his dark hood revealing his scarred face. Some looked to have been sewed up while others looked to have been melted skin. His eyes were the color of algae and most of his hair looked to have fallen out with only a few blotches of hair.

"Look at me, when I'm talking to you," he growled, angrily as he shook her.

For some reason, she couldn't do that. When she looked at him it was like seeing his entire history, sad and bitter, a path of unfulfilled dreams that turned him into the thorn bush he was today. He slapped her on the side of her face so hard the handprint could have been visible.

"Look at me!" he yelled.

"I can't," she cried.

"Why not!" the man snarled, shaking her again as if to get her to speak. "Why not!"

Gabrial didn't answer him and his anger only began to burn even more. He picked up the knife he had dropped, it was still sizzling with the heat. He began to laugh at her, she could keep playing this game of silence, but it would only get her further into the trench. She began to scream when she couldn't break away from his grip and the knife grew near to her back.

"Stop," she yelled.

"You're going to feel exactly what I felt," he chuckled until he was suddenly knocked over.

"Gabrial," called a familiar voice.

287

Chapter 13

In the Midst of Ashes

Emmanuel could hardly catch his breath. Smoke

burned his lungs as he soared through the dark clouds of

ash. There had to be a way out of this forsaken place. His

white wings were the only thing bright, besides the molten

red lava below. He had made a deal with Darcel and he

knew where to find her, but if he could only find a way

through this ash he may have been able to still get away

with his life and her.

Thunder boomed through the dark clouds and

sometimes lightning flashed nearly blinding him. He

clenched on tightly to a string around his neck that had a

cross attached to it. It was his only guidance to escape this

place. Hail slipped off the tips of his wings and fell like

little droplets of frozen tears from the angels that he chose

to make such a bad decision.

He had been given one of the most honorable

positions as the protector of the world and he was risking it

for love. Nothing should have ever meant that much to an

angel. The only thing that should have concerned him was

his position that he was completely throwing away.

Emmanuel was created to keep balance and to put

everything before his own heart. His own emotions and

feelings.

Yet, he was doing the complete opposite. Another flash of lightning came and this time it struck him in the middle of his back, where his spine was. He yelled and was forced to crash onto the ground below him. His wings disappeared and he was left standing and looking around at the desolate place, searching for a way to escape it. But there wasn't a place that looked to be an exit.

The cracked ground with lava bubbling went on for miles and some mountains compassed the place. He didn't have a clue how he was going to get out of the place, but he started to walk, deciding to start somewhere, although flying was over. He had been struck one too many times by that kind of lightning that had nearly put him out.

Some 1,000 Years Later

Gabrial looked up as the dust cleared; she saw Emmanuelle and she had never been happier to see his face. The other men came over to avenge their leader. One of them attempted to stab Gabrial with their sword, but it was met by the prince's. The man's sword flew out of his hand like a bent fork.

"Stay behind me," he ordered her as the men surrounded them.

Each of them charged at him with their weapons and he fought each of them off. Some of them were kicked away when they attempted to tackle him. She had never seen him fight the way he had. She had thought he had only enjoyed playing with swords as something to do, but she never knew he was able to fight with one.

Eventually, their boss stood up and tried to attack him, that is until he felt the prince's sword so close to his neck he thought he might kill him. He stopped almost immediately, glaring at her. The only reason she wasn't half-dead right now was because the hero boy had to show up and ruin his fun.

"I think you've worn out your welcome," chuckled the man. "Don't think this is the last you've seen of us, little lady. We will be back and we won't be so nice."

A grin showed on the prince's face and he withdrew his sword. The man stuck to what he said and he beckoned for his men to follow him as he headed for their horses. Emmanuelle turned and looked at her, the side of her face had a gash and her clothes were wrecked and torn.

"I was looking everywhere for you," he declared as he embraced her, warmly. "I thought I had left you, although I was sure you had been right beside me."

Even though she felt like something was stabbing into her back, she couldn't help but smile. His voice was comforting in such a strange place. He gasped when he noticed blood on his hand after hugging her.

"Gabrial, you're bleeding," Emmanuelle said, feeling startled.

"Oh no."

The prince took off his cloak and gave it to her since the blood had gotten into her shirt so no one would see it. "I think I know a place we can take you and stop it," he told her, taking her by the hand and leading her into the town. "Keep the cape over yourself until we get there. Okay?"

She nodded her head in agreement. The town was busy with people selling things and hard at work. Her eyes couldn't help but wander around everywhere she heard noise. This was her first time being in a town during the day and it seemed so much more different than at night. There were so many smells of freshly baked goods and then there was the smell of trash when it was dumped through windows out of nowhere.

Some of the trash had nearly fallen on her when she had been walking too close to the cottages. Horse-drawn buggies raided through the streets as if they were driven by madmen. What caught her attention was a cage with a dove. It was so beautiful, but it made her sad to see it locked up the way it was. Every creature deserved to be free and living on its own. She let one of her fingers reach through the little bars and petted their soft, white feathers.

"You're so pretty," she said as the bird's head tilted up and down as if it understood what she was saying. "Do you have a name?"

The bird lifted its feathers, revealing the gold speckles beneath them. Gabrial smiled at the bird.

"Serenity is a beautiful name," she told the bird. "You want me to tell Sharon that you will return to her? Who's…"

"Gabrial, watch out!" yelled Emmanuelle, running over to her as a wagon that was pulled by oxen that got out of control and headed her way.

She was shoved out of the way by him and into the ground. The cage was run over and the wagon fell, spilling dozens of fruits and vegetables into the street. The oxen had stopped when the wagon had fallen over. A man shouted at his ox, angrily for ruining his business. Emmanuelle stared at Gabrial as she leaned over on his arm.

"Thank you Emmanuelle," she said, breathing heavily. She stood up quickly and ran over to the cage where the dove had been when she heard a faint sound.

The only thing that was left was a bent cage and a bunch of feathers. There was no sign of the dove. She broke into tears when she saw traces of blood across the ground. It wasn't long before the prince had come over to see why she had her head bowed. When he noticed tears were streaming down her face and she was praying he touched her on the shoulder. He wasn't for certain where she had come from, but she had to know the rules.

"Gabrial, you can't do that here," he whispered.

Her eyes opened and she stared at him as if confused. "But I have to pray for…"

"Shush," Emmanuelle said, he didn't like stopping her from doing anything she thought was right, but he didn't want her to end up hurt over it. "I promise I'll let you do it when we get to a more sacred place."

She didn't understand what he meant, but she trusted him. He took her away from the place the incident occurred so they wouldn't be asked any questions about what had happened. There were a lot of things he didn't understand about her, but that had to be one he didn't understand. Gabrial had to know that praying was an abomination to the people if you were not in church and even then people didn't want anyone to attend those sessions. When they reached a place to stay he was going to have to talk to her and maybe get a better understanding of her and tell her about the things people hated most and would even kill for.

****

Water was carried in a mist when blown in the wind. Esmeralda's eyes looked around, this whole place's existence seemed to have been impossible. There was water everywhere she looked and the people were dressed in some kind of clothing that looked similar to the chitons she and Gabrial had worn when they were at home. The buildings looked to be made of glass and at the tops of each building were some kind of crystals that made light. Achmed and his men took off the coverings that had been around them and breathed in the fresh air.

"Beautiful place, isn't it?" he asked her.

"I'm not sure," she answered, touching one of the solid marble pillars. "Familiar, yes, but beautiful, I don't know."

297

He knew what she meant, everyone that was ever brought to this place always said the same thing. They started down the paved roads, she was startled when she saw people that had pets that were tigers and other exotic beasts.

"It is a tradition for anyone in these parts to have any kind of pet of their heart's desire. They believe that whatever animal you choose is choosing you as a way to see into yourself," he explained as they walked by a woman with a monkey hanging around her neck.

"And I take it that your mirror is that camel," chuckled Esmeralda.

"No. No," he laughed along with a few of the other men. "We are not from this place so our traditions are somewhat different. I just know from being through here a lot."

A devious smirk appeared on her face when she looked over at him and the others. She thought for a moment that maybe she could learn to enjoy this place. It was kind of like home but maybe better since she wouldn't be under her father's rule.

"How long do you intend to stay at this place?" she inquired.

"We usually stay no longer than a month, but I have a friend who would be more than happy to have you stay at his place," Achmed told her, pulling on the rope of the camel to get it to walk again.

She frowned at the ground, she would have rather stayed with them and their convoy than stay at someplace with one of his friends. If she had stayed with them she thought she may have had a better chance at finding her sister and taking her back to their true home. This world was not their world and they didn't belong here.

****

Darkness had fallen upon the little town and the place Emmanuelle had thought of taking her turned out to be closed and they were forced to continue wandering through the streets. There were fewer people out now, there were a few that slept on the streets. A man shivered terribly with discomfort beneath a little paper-thin blanket. Gabrial approached him slowly when Emmanuelle wasn't looking and touched the man's forehead.

His breathing softened and he stopped shivering. A grin appeared on his face as he suddenly felt warmth travel through him. She felt as if a great weight had been lifted from her when she saw him no longer shivering.

"Gabrial," whispered the prince, wondering what she had been doing.

"Over here," yelled a woman from across the street, the light from the monastery flooding into the street, chasing away the shadows.

She followed behind the prince as he headed for the entrance of the monastery. Before she entered the cottage she took one last look back at the place where so many people had been sleeping in the streets, shivering and struggling to sleep comfortably. They were unsettled on the inside and it was causing them to be unsettled on the outside. She wished she could have helped them all at one time. Then she felt Emmanuelle touch her lightly and helped her along into the building.

The woman shut the door quickly, startling them. "Oh dear, you're lucky I saw you," she told them, seeming to lose her breath. "Those streets are dangerous after dark."

The prince looked at her, seeming to be just as confused as she was. The woman was dressed in an all-black dress, her head was covered by a large black hood-looking thing. She smiled at them, happily.

"Father Benedict," she called up the stairs. "Father Benedict, we have guests. You two must be tired."

He smiled a little, then said. "We are much obliged to you for taking us in. Is there any way we can repay you?”

“Yes, thank you,” said Gabrial to the woman.

“Oh no,” she chuckled. “We take in people all the time. I’m Sister Laura.”

“A pleasure to meet you. I’m Gabrial and this is Emmanuelle,” she explained, happily.

The woman smiled. “Likewise. I suppose the brothers and sisters must be asleep. Come with me, I’ll take you to one of the guest rooms,” she told them, taking Gabrial by the hand and leading her down a hallway.

As she took them through the place, it started to look more like a cathedral than a monastery. There was stained glass with so many colors that looked to be telling a story. The ceilings were higher in some places than others. They came to a staircase, where the woman took a torch and started up the long staircase.

"Here you are," Sister Laura told them as she opened the door. "A room for the lady and I will show you to your room, young sir."

Gabrial smiled at Emmanuelle, she could tell he would have preferred to have stayed with her in this strange place and she would have preferred that also. It wasn't that she didn't trust the sister, but they were strangers here.

"Good night," she told the prince.

He nodded his head. "Good night," he replied. The sister took him by the hand as if telling him to follow her. He watched as Gabrial's door closed. The hall was kind of dim since there weren't many torches that were lined throughout it. There were a few other doorways that looked like niches between every torch.

"Do you have any water?" asked Emmanuelle as she led him down the hallway.

"Of course, but the well is outside in the courtyard," she explained. "It's not safe at this time."

He stared at her complacently. "Is that the only place?" he inquired.

****

Learning of activities happening in the kingdom didn't take long to reach anyone since there were so many people, who were always talking. Even those from far away lands, merchants brought stories back in no time. The knight had not come back with news about whether or not he had found her. Still, that wasn't about to stop him. If there was one thing he had learned during his life was that you couldn't depend on people to get things done every time you told them to jump or do something.

They'd carry out his orders like any person beneath the prince, but sometimes the task proved to be too difficult for even them to perform. Damien eyed a man performing dangerous stunts on his horse. His father clapped with excitement, but he leaned against his balled

fist that rested on the armrest of his chair, unamused. If the

horseman wanted to amuse him he would have to perform

some tricks more risky than flipping and doing handstands

while the horse trotted along in a cantar dance.

He didn't have time for this, not when he could've

been studying that book he found and the words the knight

had spoken. The prince stood up from his chair and went to

the doors so he could leave this kind of misery behind.

"Damien," called his father.

The doors closed as if he hadn't heard a word he

had said.

Chapter 14

Torn in Two

Through the ashes of the burning city that had

turned day into night, their glowing wings could be seen

flashing like lightning in the desperate people's eyes. Their

angels were coming to save the world, they hadn't

abandoned them like they had been almost left to believe.

Armistice pulled her spear out from behind her and waved

it high above her head, clearing the smoke and the sun's light beamed upon her making her appear to be an entity of light. Her short golden colored hair looked like glowing brass and her sea-blue eyes looked like that of the darkest sea. The golden halo made of iron looked as if it were her crown of loyalty to the human race.

She came down onto the ground, smashing the bottom of the spear into the ground, cracking it. As she stood up, her army of warriors appeared behind her from the dark ashes as if telling the evil ones that they were coming to avenge the world and give the righteous back what belonged to them.

"I am Armistice leader of the iron angels of war and we ask you to lay down your weapons and to set the others free," she declared. "We seek you no harm, but if war is what you're asking for, war is what we will give you. This must all end."

Gabrial held a wet rag near her back that was bleeding. It seemed almost impossible to stop the bleeding no matter what she did. The mirror made her feel no better, it made the places that were bleeding look larger or further away than they were. She winced whenever she felt the rag touch part of her back, it felt like needles poking at her for some reason. By now the places should have healed, although they hadn't.

"You'll never believe what I just… sorry," said Emmanuelle, noticing that he had been intruding. He was just about to leave the room when he noticed how it looked like she had been struggling. "Do you need help?" The prince slowly walked over to her, then crept up behind her. He took the rag from her hand.

She looked in the mirror, noticing his reflection behind her. "Thanks for asking, but I can…"

"Let me help you," he said as he turned her his way.

There was a glow in his eyes when he said those words, but he had helped her enough. She didn't want to be a burden to him. They were good friends and she didn't want to mess that up by always having him do something for her.

"Please," Emmanuelle asked, smiling at her. "If you're worried about me pressing too hard, then I'd like to let you know that I had practice being gentle with the petals of flowers."

She laughed a little, she wasn't worried about that at all. "Okay."

The prince led her over to a mattress near a window, where the sun's light had been pouring in like a river flooding the room with light. She sat down slowly leaning forward so she could rest on her stomach on the mattress as he hovered above her. Emmanuelle submerged his hand with the rag into the bucket of water. The places on her back had slowed with bleeding, but not completely.

"Emmanuelle, I don't want to sound ungrateful, but why did you travel so far away from the kingdom to look for me?" Gabrial inquired, looking up at him, slightly.

"I felt like it was the right thing to do," he answered, quickly when he felt her back tense up. "Sorry."

"It's okay," she said, trying to smile.

"I don't regret doing it either. That's what friends do for one another or…" Emmanuelle paused for a moment taking a deep breath. He wasn't sure how she might react if he finished what he was going to say.

She kind of knew what he was going to say because she had felt the same way. What also gave it away was how he always wanted to be near her. He had gone out his way so many times to impress her. All she wished he would have done was just tell her, she wasn't going to bite him as a viper would.

"What is it, Emmanuelle?" she asked him.

She felt the surface of his warm palm touch her. When the rag slipped from beneath his hand. It was like he had grown nervous with just those few words. Gabrial slowly sat up, letting the rag slip off her back. Their eyes met and he looked to have been mesmerized by her eyes. He wished he could have grabbed his heart; it was pumping so fast it felt like it wanted to jump out without control.

"I have something to tell you that I have been wanting to say for the longest," the prince admitted moving closer to her. "It seems to be complicated in my mouth but in my heart, I want to say…"

A flash of lightning seemed to strike her in the eyes because she was suddenly blinded and it was like her hearing had also blanked out. She could no longer hear his voice, but there was a lingering excruciating pain in her back like something had been pulled from it. There were trees all around her that blossomed with early spring buds that were the color of cherries. The grass was so high she couldn't even see her feet.

This couldn't still be the monastery, but she didn't know how she had come to be here either. For a long while, she thought she may have heard a faint sound of laughter of happiness and some voices. She took a few steps forward to try and go to the place where the laughter was coming from, then there was a breeze that carried dust blew past her eyes, blinding her. The forest grew distant as it seemed to disappear.

"Gabrial," she heard Emmanuelle yell.

She found herself screaming and crying for him to stop whatever it was he had done. He was above her, seeming to have attempted to restrain her when her sight came back. In one of his hands there looked to be a rag with something wrapped in it. When he saw that she had finally calmed down, he released her.

"I'm sorry," Emmanuelle told her as he moved from off of her.

Gabrial stared at him, confusedly. She couldn't figure out what he had done to put her in such pain. The prince sighed deeply, then handed her the rag. When she unwrapped it she saw something that looked like a piece of a blade, although it was red as a ruby. She smiled at him, happily, he may have stopped the reason her back bled so much, even though he put her through a lot of pain.

"I think it may have been the cause of why you were bleeding so…"

The door squeaked as it opened and a man wearing a white robe stepped inside. Immediately, Emmanuelle stood up from the bed and removed his hand from her back, although he stayed close to her. Before the man seemed to notice the prince his attention was quickly drawn to her. When he noticed her eyes, she glanced over at him for a quick moment, before she pulled the cloak over herself. There was something about her eyes that looked different from any person he had encountered.

"Good evening," he greeted, kneeling in front of her. "I am Father Benedict. Sister Laura told me about you and someone else," the man spoke, calmly as if trying to put someone to sleep. "Your name is Gabrial, am I correct?"

"Yes," she replied.

"Such a historical name, not at all used," he chuckled, grinning. "And you are Emmanuelle or a prince as it has come to my knowledge."

"Emmanuelle is fine," the prince replied, chuckling a little.

The father shook his head. "Such a secretive age we live in," he muttered, putting his hand on one of hers that was resting on her lap. "Tell me, my child, why were you crying out in pain?"

Gabrial wasn't sure if she should have answered his question and the prince shook his head at her, disapprovingly. He didn't know what he might think if she were to tell him why. The man smiled at her, staring into her eyes as if searching through her soul for something.

"Could you leave the two of us for a little while, I feel that I and Gabrial have much to talk about," he declared, keeping his eyes on hers as she looked up at Emmanuelle as if begging him to stay. He noticed the expression on his face and he knew he wasn't about to just leave her with him. "I need to help this child and I don't believe you'd want to interfere with that."

There was something about when Emmanuelle looked at him that made his limbs feel tired and he thought he might fall. She was going to be alright if he left her for just a moment alone with the man. After all, he was a part of the church, which meant he was a good man. Gabrial watched as he left the room looking to have been about to collapse at any moment. The door closed behind him and she was left alone with the father.

"He is a troubled young soul and has many dreams of his past," chuckled Father Benedict. "Don't let him hinder you Gabrial from being so much more."

She didn't know what he meant by that and she didn't know how he thought he knew so much about Emmanuelle. He had just met them and through his tightly clenched teeth that made a smile, there was a strange motive behind it all.

****

The light was so dim in the library he could hardly read the small writing on the pages of the book. A few times Damien pinched the middle of his nose, whenever he thought he was starting to grow a headache. There was something about the book that made it almost impossible for him to stop looking through it.

It went back to the history of when angels were first seen on the surface of the Earth. He came to a part of the book, where he noticed four pages were torn out and the page behind the row was ruined from water damage. He banged his palm against the table, annoyedly. The prince pushed his hair back wondering why someone would ever tear the most important pages of a book out. It always seemed to happen that way.

"You're highness, are you alright?" asked Sir Begum, appearing in the doorway.

"The reason you're here better be because you have news of that little tramp's whereabouts," he snapped, leaning over on the table with one of his hands. "I prefer not to hear the same rhetoric about how my father is doing. He's ill and I know that."

The knight scratched his curly caramel hair, nervously. "Actually, sir, it is concerning neither of those,

but about a king who wishes to speak with you, privately,"
explained the knight.

Damien chuckled, softly. "Does this king have a
name or is it just king?"

"Why no of course not--I mean of course he does
have a name, sir," stammered Sir Begum. "King Caesar of
the kingdom of Gercion."

The prince sat down in a chair, then pulled his feet
up and rested them on the table. This king he was talking
about must have thought he was great to think he could
just request to speak with him, unannounced or anything.
He didn't deal with people that thought they were better
than him and that was one of his first rules.

"He'd better have a good alibi for bringing himself
here, unannounced," snapped Damien, looking at his
fingers. "I don't like unexpected company."

"He says he won't be staying very long at all, sir,

he just came to talk with you and I think he'll be on his way," Sir Begum told him, taking off his helmet.

The king better not have been about to talk about something that didn't interest him or he was going to have to pay a price for wasting his precious time. Damien played with the end of his feathered pin near his lip, thinking.

"Fine, I will speak with him," he answered, acting like it was such a burden as he walked towards the exit of the library. He touched the knight on one of his armored shoulders. "Oh, I'd like you to keep this place guarded against my mother. I'd hate to have her snooping through my things."

"Of course, you're highness," he replied briskly.

The prince grinned, then patted his shoulder. "Good." He walked down the hallway, whistling a haunting song that even made the knight turn around. The prince whistled a lot of strange toons, but the one he was whistling right now had to be one of the most disturbing

since it was different and in a way, creepy. The prince did

a few spins, then walked kind of in a zigzag way as if he

were dancing with some invisible person. Sir Begum shook

his head, then put his helmet back on trying to act like he

hadn't seen anything.

****

The prince had nearly cut his fingers a few times

when he helped Sister Laura and a few others cut potatoes.

It was his first time and already he was messing up. She

looked over at him as he struggled, then smiled.

"Ouch," he said, swinging his finger a little to

shake off the pain.

"Here, let me help you," she insisted, taking the

knife and potato from him. He watched as she slowly

peeled the skins from off the potato. "You have to take

your time and watch your fingers. See?"

He nodded his head, watching her closely.

"Now you try," Sister Laura said, handing the potato and knife back to him.

At first, he was a little hesitant, afraid to cut his finger again, but he did what she did and took his time. Her face glowed with a smile when she saw how he had mastered using the knife. It was clear that he was a very fast learner, along with being very observant. The peels slipped over the white little potato and the prince felt as if he was good at something outside of using a sword or horseback riding.

"Are you going to the festival tonight?" she asked, nearly making him drop his potato.

"A festival?" Emmanuelle inquired, excitedly as thoughts filled his head.

She shook her head in agreement. "It's going to be going on throughout the entire town. There's going to be food, performances, games, sports, and dancing," Sister

Laura set the potato down on the counter. "I'm sure you'll have a lot of fun if you go."

"Aren't you going?" the Prince inquired.

"No," she answered, keeping her bright smile on her face. "I don't have much of an interest in festivals."

"I'm not sure if I should go, to be honest," Emmanuelle declared, looking at her. "It'll be kind of strange."

"You should go with her," blurted Sister Laura, setting her knife in the sink. The prince turned around, wondering who she was talking about. "The girl that came with you, Gabrial."

Emmanuelle smiled, taking his glance from off of her feeling a little bashful. "She's very nice, but…"

He noticed Gabrial standing near the staircase. She wore a long gown that had a black, thick rope that was tied across as if to make the letter x three times. Sister Laura noticed how the prince had tried to remain silent and keep his glance on the potato he was cutting, but she could tell he had grown tense. She slowly came down the stairs and he noticed she wasn't wearing any shoes.

"Father Benedict thought that I should wear something else," Gabrial explained, noticing his expression. She thought he may not have liked the way she was dressed and it made her feel a little nervous.

He smiled at her so she would know that he wasn't thinking any bad thoughts about it. The dress was nice, but it just wasn't what he would have preferred for her to wear. She deserved better if he could help it. Emmanuelle wished he had brought something with him from the palace, either way, she was still just as beautiful to him.

"See I told you she would be perfect to take with you to the festival," chuckled Sister Laura, happily as she looked at Gabrial.

The prince coughed a little, uncomfortably. "Excuse me," he said, walking past her.

Sister Laura stared at Gabrial wondering what could have caused him to leave. The woman eventually turned around and began to peel potatoes again without saying anything. Gabrial looked at the corridor he had left through, she wondered if she should have gone after him and tried to figure out what was wrong. She went through the corridor after him only to enter a hall with a bunch of other corridors. He could have gone through any of them and she didn't know which one was the right one.

Emmanuelle sat on a banister outside looking at the vast sea below the bridge. Birds flew past him like a large cloud of colorful feathers. He grabbed his head when he felt pain strike through it as if someone were throwing invisible baseballs at it, again and again.

His body shook as he shivered and he felt so terrible he collapsed onto the stone pavement, breathing heavily. Something was happening to him and he wished someone would come to stop all the aches and pains inside his body. It was as if it had a mind of its own and was trying to transform him into something else. He yelled with pain, then grabbed his head again to try and stop the banging on the inside of it.

Chapter 15

Dancers in the Twilight

His sweaty palm touched the doorway and he

chuckled happily. He was finally going to find her and they

would be united again. Emmanuel pushed the doorway

open, then covered his eyes with his hands when a light

like that of the sun poured into the dark place. It was like

he was devoured or something, when he awakened his head

was lying in the grass and the desolate world had

vanished.

The angel stood up and looked around at the world he had been brought to. Children ran around chasing one another while parents sat on some marble benches talking to one another. It was like they couldn't see him. None of them stopped what they were doing and they walked by him without noticing he was there.

He wondered if this was the world or place Gabrial had journeyed to, if so where was she now? Emmanuel walked around searching for her; his wings were folded behind him so he wouldn't hit anyone with them. Then something caught his attention.

"With King Asgard reigning every angel will be sure to be found and killed, even those who are possessed by one," gossiped a woman with light brown hair that looked like bouncing springs of brass. "I'm sure glad that I don't have one of those cursed creatures, they're bad luck just like witches and other creatures of evil that live in the Dark Forest."

"We may not be possessed by angels, because we don't believe in them anyway, but what about the children?" inquired a woman with long white hair. "They believe in those evil creatures."

The woman with hair like springs shrugged. "Too bad for them. I believe he's taking the angels captive to a prison beneath the old cathedral, but no one dares go near that place; it's drowning in blood."

The angel had heard enough of what they thought of them. They hadn't caused this war and they were doing everything to stop it. But saving an unbelieving world was just as hard as saving a stone from its old bed. He thought of Gabrial, she wouldn't give up on them so easily and maybe he shouldn't have either. Perhaps they had taken her to the cathedral the women were talking about, he sure hoped they were right. That way he would be able to save her and set the other captives free and end this war once and for all.

Some 1,000 Years Later

There was no telling how long he lay there on the stone ground. The night had fallen and the pine had made the place look even darker. He didn't know where the sea had gone or maybe he had imagined it all. He kept hearing someone whispering to him, saying. "Come dance with me, my prince of this fair night." Then it trailed off with a bunch of giggling.

His eyes caught a glimpse of something beneath one of the still streets with lights lined on the bridge. He couldn't make it out completely, but he noticed a dark feathery mask concealing the things face and a long dark gown that sparkled a little showing the blueness of it.

"Come dance with me, my prince of this fair night," the voice giggled, then the figure started to run along the bridge. "Lest you lose me forever."

The prince leaped from off the ground, then chased after it. He followed the sound of its giggling until he came to a large door made of wood. Someone tapped him on the shoulder.

"Do you have an invitation?" asked a guard, staring at him.

"No. What's going on?" inquired Emmanuelle.

"Okay, let me see if you're on the guest list," the guard said, pulling open a scroll and looking over it.

Emmanuelle looked around feeling the chilliness of the forest whip through his clothes. The thing with a feathered mask had been a young lady. She looked out from the side of the doorway at him as if waiting. Her lips were so red, they looked like they were made from rubies then pasted onto her lips to make them so red. Her eyes were a possessed green that stood out from her dark clothes.

"Prince Emmanuelle," chuckled the guard,

stepping out of his way. "You have permission to enter."

As he walked into the place, the first thing he saw

was people dancing together in a large ballroom with four

stairways. Two on one end of the room and two at the end

he was standing. A chandelier hung high, but it didn't give

the room any kind of light. The room was overcast just like

a stormy day.

He took a few steps forward-thinking to join them,

then he was suddenly caught up in a massive light that

covered him. When he came out of it, he was dressed in

something completely different. He moved his fingers near

his eyes, then realized he was wearing a mask just like

everyone else in the room.

"Thanks for joining me," whispered a voice in his

ear. "Now come, let's dance beyond the midnight hour."

He let her lead him into the ballroom where

everyone else was dancing. Her red hair was pinned up

behind her making her ruby necklace show. They swayed

one way, although the first few moments he was confused

about what kind of dance they were performing.

Eventually, he caught on and was laughing along with her

happily.

"Promise you'll stay with me so we can always

dance together," she baded him.

The prince sighed deeply. What about Gabrial? He

couldn't just drop her as if she were nothing and promise

this woman he would stay and dance with her. Surely she

knew he would have to get home, back to her.

"I'm sorry, but I can't promise," he whispered to

her, then pulled himself away getting ready to leave. "I

have to go home. I have a life with someone else."

"Oh, but you can't," cried the woman, chasing

behind him.

"Why not?" he inquired, turning around.

"Once you enter the doorway you are to dance here forever and eventually you will forget about your home," she said, happily. "This is your home and we will dance to finish the rest of our lives. If you do not dance, then eventually you will fade into non-existence."

He shook his head, none of this was true. It was just a bad dream that he would wake up soon. The prince took a deep breath and tried to reach his real self so that he would wake up, but when he opened his eyes he was still in the ballroom. Nothing had changed.

"You must dance," she told him, touching his forearms. "See you're already fading."

"Why did you bring me here? I have to get home," he argued, frustratedly.

"You are home," she answered, giggling again.

Parts of his arm had become almost transparent. His mind was going to crack. She was wrong. There had to be a way to get back. When he looked at her she was smiling still and giggling as she had done at the bridge. He should have never followed her into this place, but now that he was here, he had no choice but to dance if he wanted to continue living. She took his hand and the two of them went out to join the others in the ballroom.

****

In the midst of the birds, Gabrial stood staring at him as he looked to be in deep thought. She approached him, slowly unsure whether or not he wanted to be bothered. His head slowly turned her way for a moment she thought he was frowning, but he wasn't.

"A great place to think," he started, cocking an eyebrow at her, then slowly pushed himself up so he was standing.

"It is beautiful," she replied. "Are you feeling alright?"

He shook his head, happily. "Of course I am. I'm always alright as long as you're with me," Emmanuelle explained, moving closer to her. "Will you come closer, the sun is kind of blinding and I can't see you completely."

Gabrial walked a little closer to him, although she couldn't recall a time he ever struggled with seeing, even with the sun's light. The look on his face was closer to a scary smile, there was something strange about the atmosphere when she came closer to him. It felt like it was an entrapment of darkness, something she had never felt when she had come near him. Even the pupil in his eyes looked to have grown bigger, which could have been because of the sun's light since he was standing in its direction. They looked to have become normal when she was close, maybe she had been imagining the things about him.

The prince chuckled, softly sounding more like a snarl. He moved her hair out of her face and behind her ear so he was able to see her face better.

"What are you doing?" she inquired, when he started to move his hand around her neck. He gave her no answer and he pulled her so close to him and held her so tightly against him she thought he might squeeze the life out of her. "Stop." Gabrial pushed him off of her, she didn't know what was wrong with him, but she knew that he would never have made her feel so uncomfortable.

"I can't help it," Emmanuelle said, pushing her so close to the edge of the bridge she thought he may have pushed her off.

"Emmanuelle, please stop," Gabrial cried, trying to pull her wrist free from his grasp. "You're my best friend and I trust you or I did, but I don't know if…"

"You still do," he snapped. "Just like you did before, I just have to be honest about the way I feel about you."

"What has happened to you? You've changed," she told him.

It felt like his head was banging in the front, he immediately touched the front of his head to try and stop the pain. When he opened his eyes again, he was holding her so close to the edge he could have killed her. Panic aroused him like floodwaters in the spring and he pulled himself away from her. He looked at his hands as if they weren't even his. He didn't know how or what he had done to her but he didn't feel like it was anything that made her feel any more comfortable around him.

"Gabrial, I--I don't know what happened to me," the prince admitted. "I never would harm you. I just..." he didn't know what to say, except for that he had messed everything up with her and that hurt him worse. He had wanted to ask her to go to the festival, but after this, he didn't know what she might say or think.

She didn't know what to say for once she was speechless to him. His eyes looked at her hoping that she would forgive him for what he had almost done. The prince took a few steps closer to her, then reached his hand

out to her as if to try and ask if they were still friends. For

a long moment, she stared into his eyes that looked to have

nearly lost their glow to them and something else was

trying to come and replace it. As much as she wanted to

take his hand like she always did, she wasn't certain if it

was such a good idea.

"Maybe I should just go, I've done my share of

embarrassing myself for the day," he said, disappointedly

as he looked at the monastery.

Gabrial shook her head, it didn't feel right making

him go away even after how he made her feel. "No, I

should be the one to go, I came here and disturbed you,"

she explained, walking in the direction of the monastery.

There had to be a way to explain to her that he

wasn't in his right frame of mind, he would never hurt her.

It made him feel worse that she seemed to be rushing away

from him as she had done to his brother. She would usually

leave whenever she was nervous or uncomfortable, but he didn't want her to feel that way. Emmanuelle felt like he had made a large step backward instead of forwards with trying to say what he wanted to.

When she reached the monastery she grabbed hold of a pillar as if fainting. Her eyes looked to the ceiling above her as if looking for some kind of sign that maybe it was just an illusion or dream that he had attacked her, but she saw nothing that would make her be able to tell if it wasn't real. She didn't know what was wrong with him, she thought all the people would have an understanding of their friendship. Of course, it was more than that or so it had tried to be until he acted like that.

****

The royal family was starting to act more like savages just like all the others in her mind. There was no telling what Damien was up to since he kept her locked out of the library each and every day, even when he wasn't in there. He made it so obvious that he was doing something there. She couldn't get past his knights and the guards were very heavy in that area.

Besides him being strange, her other son had just run off to find a peasant, even though the ball was in six days. He had to know he needed someone to dance with and she didn't want just anyone. Queen Eliza tapped her long red nails on her knee as she waited for the carriage to come to a stop.

When she stepped from out of the carriage her long red dress flopped over her feet and she started up the stairs to the palace. Her head turned when a man that looked to have been dressed like Robin Hood ran up the stairs, calling to her. At first, she narrowed her eyes at him until she noticed a brown sheet of paper in one of his hands.

"What's this," she growled.

"A letter from a small town on the other side of the Dark Forest, your son has been located, your majesty," he explained, excitedly.

"And what about the girl?" she inquired, coldly. "She's not there is she?"

"I'm sorry your highness, but it says nothing of a girl," he answered.

She scoffed, then walked with her guards as if he wasn't even there. It was not her son she was worried about. She was only worried if he was with her. If he found her the queen knew he would bring her back with him and take her to the ball. He never cared what anyone thought of him and that annoyed her. Gabrial was a peasant, not fit for a prince and she should have never tried to be more than that.

"Come back when you have something I want to hear," she snarled, waving her hand for him to go.

"And what might that be, my queen?"

"Something about that little tramp's death," Queen Eliza snapped, shooting him a dead look.

The door to the palace was opened and the queen vanished behind it leaving the messenger alone on the steps.

✳✳✳✳✳✳✳✳✳✳✳✳

Gabrial pushed the door open deciding that Emmanuelle would show up when he wanted to be found. On the other side, she saw Sister Laura and a few of the other nuns walking through the halls with their veils nearly covering their faces. The woman noticed her and smiled as if she knew how she was feeling. She moved her hand as if summoning her to come into the room to join them. Gabrial walked into the room, closing the door slowly behind her. She sat down next to her and the women began to talk to her.

She hadn't noticed that Emmanuelle had followed her. He leaned against the wooden door and would have knocked if he hadn't heard what the nuns were talking to her about.

"If you'd like you can join us for a few prayers," said Sister Laura. "We enjoy having girls there, it helps them decide whether or not they want to be one of us."

"That is very kind of you, but..."

"You don't have to do anything, we just want you to get the feel of it," explained one of the other sisters.

He listened for a moment, she had to say 'no'. If she became one of them or even joined them for their ceremonies she wouldn't come back to him. "Say no," he whispered, moving his hand against the door. "Please say no, Gabrial."

To his disappointment, she accepted their invitation to their prayers. His hand slowly slipped from the door. How could she do this? He thought...then he remembered why she may have been doing this to get at him. She was probably angry at him and wanted to get back at him. Just the thought of her doing such a thing made him angry and he stormed off before he could hear the last part.

"I think I should talk it over with Emmanuelle. He may want to leave soon," she told the nuns.

"Oh," gasped Sister Laura, looking at the others. Her smile came back to her face. "Of course."

"Is there any way you could get around to speaking to him about it later?" asked another nun. "It is your decision anyway and he'll understand if you want to join us to see what it's like before you start."

"Oh, but..."

"Trust us, he'll understand," the women said together.

" Okay. Thank you," Gabrial said, happily, standing up to leave. She couldn't wait to speak with him.

Chapter 16

Forgive Us Our Sins

Never in his life could he have imagined the

place where he and other angels had walked among

humans to look so desolate, so sad, and disappointing.

They should have gone further with the help of the angels,

but it seemed like instead of going forward the clock went

backward uncontrollably. He landed on the ground with a

massive gust of dearth flying everywhere. A few people he

hadn't noticed covered their eyes, but they didn't see him.

As he walked further into the battlefield he heard

screaming and crying. People ran for their lives through

the burning streets of the village. They were being pursued

by soldiers that swung their swords, a couple of them took

out their bows then placed arrows on them.

He stood there for a moment wondering what the

soldiers were aiming at when he noticed they were aiming

at families that were trying to escape with their little

children. Surely they were not going to shoot them down or

were they?

"Nooooo!" he yelled, then let his wings emerge

from his back.

When the people turned around they didn't know

what was stopping the arrows from hitting them. All they

could see was the arrows freezing as if paused. Dogs

barked and it was almost impossible for the soldiers to

keep control of their animals. Emmanuel clenched his teeth tightly as he winced in pain. The arrows were caught in his wings and body. He wanted to yell, but at the same time, it was too painful for him to.

One of the soldiers chuckled, then let his dog loose to find the angel. The dog ran to the place where all the arrows had seemed to have been frozen. They chuckled and ran over to find him.

Emmanuel tried to flap his wings to escape until he felt more arrows being shot at him. He gasped when he got off the ground only a few feet before collapsing to the ground. He had to get up, he had to find Sharon and bring her back. The first step he took was his last step before he was stabbed in his back and fell.

Some 1,000 Years Later

Damien was seated in his chair at the top of the round table. His knights had all finally been united once more and now they could talk amongst each other to figure out what to do next. Sir Gilliot sat down with a bunch of grunting as if in pain.

"What ale's you?" chuckled the prince.

"Age, I guess," responded Sir Gilliot, smiling at the others.

"Hmph," Damien snarled. "What a coincidence since that is what we're going to be speaking about."

The knights looked at him. It was going to be a long meeting if he was just going to talk about everyone's age. Although it would probably be kind of good since none of them knew each other's ages, they just kind of pinned an age on each other from the way they spoke or acted.

"I'm sorry, sir, but you have lost me," blurted Sir Kelvin.

"When I say age I want you to think of time and not someone's time of being here," he told them. "It has been brought to my knowledge from reading a book I found that there was an age when angels lived in a world parallel to ours."

"And where are you trying to go with this, sir?" inquired Sir Gilliot, wrinkling his brown mustache with his finger.

"Their kingdom fell many, many hundreds of years later and no one ever knew exactly where it landed, but that's not all," Damien said, setting the large book on the table. The knights leaned over to see where he was pointing to on the paper. They looked at one another, then they all met his eyes that were so full of madness. "You see where I'm getting."

"You know all this could be just a nasty little fairytale someone came up with, your highness," said Sir

Belont. "I mean this map isn't even very clear and it looks to me like it fell off into the sea."

"It's no fairytale and that sea has been long dried up years before kingdoms were ever established," Damien explained, his tone growing to be defensive as he glared at them to make sure no one doubted his beliefs. "I know and my knowledge should be good enough for you and anyone else in this room who doubts it."

They shook their heads, they'd never doubt his intelligence at least not right in front of him. He smiled at them, making the dangerous frown wipe straight off his face. They didn't have a choice but to believe them if they intended to stay safe from all the charges he could punish them with even if they had never committed a crime in their life.

"I knew I had your allegiance," he chuckled.

****

Light flashed from off glass that was lined up that looked like crystals protruding through the ground. Late at night when the sun went down, they showed their glory. A few times the light blinded Esmeralda as she walked with the men into the magnificent palace. Its ceilings were as high as the heaven themselves and she couldn't help but look up, twirling around in awe as she took in the beauty of the architecture. It almost reminded her of her old home.

"This way," Achmed told her as he and his men walked around a small waterfall.

She could feel a few sprinkles of the water touch her face gently. On the other side was a couch, curtained by gold dust transparent shades. Someone was talking from the other side.

"Your honor, Fatima," all the men said, getting down on their knees.

As for Esmeralda, she stood there looking like a duck in a group of horses. She eyed them for a moment wondering if she should've done the same. Then the curtains moved and a girl emerged. She had raven black hair, just like her. Emerald, evilly green eyes like hers. She wore a bloody red covering that only covered her nose and it was transparent. At first, she looked at the men, but when she noticed Esmeralda it was like looking at herself. Immediately, she walked past the men as if they weren't even there. She looked to be in deep thought when she saw her.

"Are you me?" she inquired, pointing out her index finger toward her face as if lost.

Esmeralda's mouth dropped. "This can't be real, you look just like me."

The girl didn't even wait for her to give her permission, before she touched Esmeralda's hair, curiously and Esmeralda did the same. The men watched as the two of them scanned over each other like two lost friends that had lost each other along the line.

"We were wondering if you'd…"

"Shush, Achmed!" she ordered him, coldly. "An image of myself."

"It feels like…"

"I'm dreaming," they both said at the same time.

They both looked at each other and then broke into laughter. Achmed looked over at his men, boringly. They knew what this more than likely meant for both Esmeralda and them. So he moved his head forward as if signaling for them to go forward and leave.

"Achmed," she called when she noticed them. He stopped in his tracks, squinting his eyes shut. "You and your men will tarry with us for some time since you have found me something of such class as me. You will stay with me and you can have whatever you want. What is your name?"

"Esmeralda," she told her, excitedly, feeling as if she had found something she had been missing from her life.

"Oh, we are just going to have such fun just you and I," Fatima assured her as she put her arm around her, "I'm going to show you everything and everyone is going to know your name."

Achmed and his men didn't know what else to do so they followed Esmeralda and Fatima as she showed her around the palace as Fatima went on and on about the history of it.

****

The blanket that was over the prince went up and down as he slept. He still hadn't spoken to Gabrial after what he had heard her talking about to the nuns and he had no intent on saying anything. He would be leaving soon, this place was starting to annoy him and so was her attitude towards him.

Gabrial knocked on his door, she thought she may have finally had the courage enough to speak to him. His blanket hardly moved from off of his head, although he heard her knocking. If it was her then he didn't want to be bothered. When he heard her knock on the door again he gave up trying to keep her out.

The door to his room opened quickly and when he saw her face he thought his heart might melt. He didn't know how he was going to stay angry with her. She didn't seem to have even thought about how angry she was at him the day before. Instead, she acted as if nothing had happened.

"Good evening, sleepyhead," she teased him, noticing the dark rolls under his eyes.

"What are you doing?" he inquired. "Why are you playing this game?"

"What game?" Gabrial asked him, confusedly as she sensed the rise of frustration in his voice.

He cocked an eyebrow at her suspiciously. He didn't know why she was acting like she was happy as could be right now with him when yesterday she was ready to tear him in halves. It made him question how twisted her mind could have been behind the smile on her face. If she wanted to play as nothing had happened then that was what he was going to do also, either way, it worked at least now he may have been able to fix what he messed up.

"Never mind," Emmanuelle chuckled.

"Are you sure?" she asked him, staring at his eyes that looked so empty.

He nodded his head, then leaned his hand against the doorpost feeling a little weak. His breathing deepened as he struggled to catch his breath. Then he felt her hand touch him on the shoulder and he felt like part of his life had been restored. The weakness lifted off of him and he was able to catch his breath.

"I brought you this," Gabrial said, handing him a small basket.

It made him feel guilty for thinking anything bad about her when she was still thinking of him. For a moment he thought he could have forgotten about her decision, then something like a bunch of shadows showered over him and he thought about why she was doing it. She wasn't thinking of him, she was trying to play the guilt card on him and make him feel like his apology wasn't enough.

"Thanks, but no thanks," he snapped, turning away from her and walking back over to his bed.

She looked at him for a long moment, he had to be hungry by now, he had practically slept the whole day away. It was almost dinner time and he didn't want anything. She set the basket on a chair, then followed after him. Something was wrong with him and she was starting to see that now.

"Emmanuelle, are you feeling okay?" she inquired.

"Of course, why wouldn't I be?" Emmanuelle chuckled. "I'm good old Prince Emmanuelle, who loves to play viper and mouse."

The words that came out of his mouth were like from someone else's. Not one time had she ever heard him speak in such a sarcastic tone or come up with bad jokes since he hardly joked anyway. Then he kept on using the word *'play'* like someone was using him, but who would do that? The other question was who he was referring to as the viper and mouse?

"Can you tell me…"

"Gabrial," intruded Sister Laura, noticing the prince. "It's time."

The prince glanced at her as if hoping she wouldn't go. When she turned he didn't show his look of disappointment, instead, he smiled at her. The door closed behind her and the prince was left all alone with nothing but the sound of his coughing ever so often. Emmanuelle

pulled his blanket over himself and went back to sleep.

✳✳✳✳✳✳✳✳✳✳✳✳

Soft sounds of hymns and songs could be heard

outside the door. Gabrial wore a long gray robe with a veil

that had a golden line that curved its way along the ends. It

was the same as Sister Laura's and the other nuns. The

door was opened slowly and she saw all the other nuns

with their eyes closed as they said a prayer that was like a

whisper. She stood in the doorway as if in a daydream.

Each of the nuns held a cross in their hands that was

attached to the beaded necklace.

In front of all of them on a platform was a coffin

that was white and dressed in many flowers. Candles were

set on little plates surrounding the coffin. Two lambs were

set at each end of the floor, each of them looking to be

smiling at her. On top of it was a large cross with a person

hanging on it and it wasn't long before she realized what

361

the person represented. Sister Laura joined the others and Gabrial tried to do the same.

Her heart felt like it had been pierced through with something sharp as she bowed her head and attempted to do the same thing as the other girls. It was as if something were telling her she was wrong for trying to hide and her heart began to burn making her feel like she might have to drop the cross she was holding and grab her heart. When she looked up at the cross she thought about all the sins she had committed throughout her life just living was probably a sin. She wasn't like the others, who had wings, were looked to as glorious creations, who weren't here with a deadly purpose, beyond her attempts to do what was right.

A scratch started to show crossing the top of her nose and towards her left eye. The pale blue of her eyes vanished and was replaced with a scorching brown that glowed as if on fire. Horns began to grow from the sides of her head and curved their way backward and she began to weep, afraid to even look at her reflection in the mirror behind the coffin. She didn't want to be that person. That wasn't her, she never wanted to be something so evil.

"Forgive me," she cried in a whisper, before falling onto the steps on her knees. "Forgive me."

"You are forgiven my child," whispered a voice and she felt a hand touch her shoulder.

When Gabrial opened her eyes and turned around she noticed the room was empty and Father Benedict behind her with a smile on his face. She stood up slowly as if startled, wondering what had happened to all the nuns that had once been present in the room. The man took one of her hands in his and petted it.

"God forgives and God saves," he quoted. "Now tell me, my child, what troubles thy soul. Is it what you have done in the past or your fear of never fulfilling your soul purpose for being created?"

She didn't know how to answer his question, it seemed so strange how he knew exactly how she was feeling at this moment in time. There was something else that was strange about him; his hand, it felt like there was something else there or someone else besides who he said he was. Even when he smiled, it was like looking at an upside-down smile. She couldn't figure out what it was about him since she didn't feel any kind of eerie force when he had taken her hand or any force at all. It was like everything about him was just empty. A being with no inner self.

"I can't," she told him, slowly withdrawing her hand from him.

"Why can't you?" Father Benedict inquired, tilting his head.

"It's not right," Gabrial answered.

"To understand yourself and free yourself from these chains," he explained, taking a few steps forward. "

You must first misunderstand yourself and become bound to the chains to become free."

Emmanuelle had been trying to help the nuns with some of their duties as far as keeping the place nice. Then he heard talking from inside the room and one of the voices sounded like Gabrial. He couldn't help but take a look to see who she may have been talking to. The prince set down his bucket of water and tossed the rag into the water. He saw Father Benedict grab hold of her wrist when she started to try and walk away.

"I see a very submissive soul inside of you that wants to serve God, but you're trapped with this being," Father Benedict tilted her chin up so she was looking at him. "I don't want to lose one soul to the slaughter if I don't have to."

As he continued to talk with Gabrial, Emmanuelle watched them from behind a pillar. He couldn't hear anything Father Benedict was saying to her, but he couldn't help thinking something was going on between

the two of them just by the way he had touched her on the

shoulder. For a split second, he wanted to storm in there

and knock the man's hand off, but this was a church and he

was a monk. Fighting was not a thing to do in the church

and he knew it wouldn't make him seem very heroic

despite his intentions.

He took a few steps backward, forgetting his bucket

was behind him, and accidentally knocked it over. Both

Gabrial and Father Benedict looked over when they heard

the splashing of the water.

"Emmanuelle?" she said, confusedly.

He took one look up from the bucket of water he

had spilled on himself to meet her pale blue eyes. This was

all making him crazy and he couldn't take it, so before

they could ask him anything he ran away. without saying a

word. She wondered what he had been doing and why he

had just run off without saying anything. But that wasn't

the only thing that seemed strange, he looked scared or frustrated and she didn't have a clue why. From this point on he knew what he had to do, although it was going to be a very painful decision.

"Emmanuelle?" he heard Gabrial yell in a more aggressive voice as she came around the corner.

There were dark rolls beneath her eyes and he wondered what had the monk done to her. Her hair looked stringy and wet as if she had been in the water. As she walked closer to him, he noticed that even her walk wasn't normal. When she walked it looked more like her hips were moving from side to side like a slithering serpent.

"Gabrial, don't you think it's about time we leave?" he inquired, then was interrupted by her abrupt, sickening laughter.

"Uh-huh, I don't think so," Gabrial snapped, wrapping her arms around him. "We're going to stay right here."

"No, we can't," Emmanuelle answered as he stared into her eyes. They were a darker blue than they normally were. "What has gotten into you?"

"You know what," she released him and stood up. "You're not as much fun as Father Benedict. You care too much about how everything's going to turn out and look about you. But he...he understands me."

"Understand you?" Emmanuelle chuckled and looked up at the ceiling. "Gabrial, you hardly even know him."

"I know him better than you. He doesn't keep secrets," she laughed. "If you want to leave, then that's just fine, but as for me I'm staying I have too much…"

"Gabrial, my darling," chuckled Father Benedict with his arm stretched out for a hug.

Emmanuelle watched as she leaped to hug the monk. She giggled, deceitfully, then whispered something into his ear as she looked at the prince. The man looked old enough to be her father or even grandfather, he didn't get why she was acting like this toward him. If she wanted him to leave, then he would just do that. The only reason he had stayed around this long was that he hoped she would come back with him, but it seemed like that wasn't going to happen.

She had found someone better than him or as she had put it; 'understands her.' The prince couldn't bear to watch the one he had truly loved do this to him any longer and he turned his back and walked along the marble hallway, alone. He felt like she had split his heart in half with his sword.

✳✳✳✳✳✳✳✳✳

"So what's going to happen now, Emmanuelle? Do you still wish to go home," inquired the girl as he spun her around.

He nodded as he leaned her back as they paused for a long moment in that position. "I think I could learn to accept this place as my home," he answered, a grin appearing on his face. "Besides, there's nothing left for me back at home. Gabrial...I don't even recognize her, but you, I think I can dance with you forever and ever and never tire."

There was a sudden golden spark in her eyes that quickly came and went away so he wouldn't notice, when he said those words and she smiled at him, triumphantly. "I'm so happy you finally see things the way I do."

"So am I."

The two of them danced in the ballroom with the others. All of them were doing the same thing. Emmanuelle that this was something that would never go away or change as long as he danced. Though others may have faded away with time, while others quit they would continue this waltz beneath the light of the full moon that shone through the crystal clear glass. Letting the light from the moon in the early twilight reflect off all the maidens

that danced in the room's dresses.

Chapter 17

Slain By Their Own Sword

The battle between man and angels had been

long, but so far they had won every battle and were able to

save thousands of both their own and humans. Armistice

rode through the battlefield on her galloping horse to help

the others since they were surrounded. When she was close

enough she stood upon its back, then lunged herself into

the air. Her iron wings emerged from her back. When she

landed it was as if the world had been hit by a cannonball

and the land rolled back like the tides of the sea making

every soldier that had fought against her army fall.

When the dust cleared, the other angels smiled at

her, happily. She always seemed to show up when they

needed her most and they didn't have to say a word. The

angels flapped their wings and joined each other in the air

so they would be able to find the prison where the angels

and people were being kept.

"I believe they're being kept underground,"

declared an angel with long red hair that had a few small

braids, in one of her hands she held a spear with two sharp

ends on either end.

"I believe so too, Laonacia," replied Armistice,

looking over at Sharon who looked to have been struggling

to breathe.

Sharon felt like the inside of her was being bruised by something like a scorpion tail. The only thing was no one was hitting her with anything. Her blue necklace glowed with a bright light as if signaling something, but she didn't know why. The angel gave one last deep breath before everything just stopped and she collapsed, falling toward the ground.

"Sharon," cried Laonacia, watching as the angel fell.

She felt completely powerless as if something was holding her bound. Then her fall was broken by Armistice, who caught her by her wrist. The angel strained a little as she struggled to keep Sharon from falling. The weight of her wings was so great, it was weighing her downward. Armistice was able to make it so she landed easily on the ground like a feather. Sharon's wings lapped over her as she lay in the dirt, her friend beside her as she was left wondering what was wrong with her.

$\mathcal{E}$ven in some of the darkest moments, places,

times, if there was just a little light even if it were just a

little keyhole somehow the light always managed to bring

things you never saw to your attention. Her eyes couldn't

help but wander around at the paintings at the top of the

canopy of her bed. There was something about it that she

hadn't noticed when she had laid there the first two days,

but now she saw something.

They dove with the envelope that looked to have

been signed with blood, was flying through a battle that

had taken place. There were both angels and humans one

against another, above them, there were smaller angels that

looked like babies with wings. They were laughing and

looked to have been whispering things to one another. But

that wasn't the only thing she saw. In everyone she saw

another being's inside of the humans shining bright as the

sun, but not in the angels. The being looked to have been guiding them. Some had their swords pointed the opposite way, while others looked to have been trying to proceed on.

Gabrial sat up slowly in her bed, then looked up at the moral. In the center of it was what looked to have been a timer. Her eyes scanned from place to place on the moral, when she started to hear a faint sound of singing, from angels. It was as if they were calling to her or like she had heard the song before. Although the song didn't have words or those that anyone could understand.

When she reached her hand up towards the moral, she noticed more clocks. They were in everyone's eyes, ablaze in fire and spinning as if they had been activated by her. She didn't have a clue what was happening when it seemed like the whole moral had begun to move. Even the clouds that the baby-like angels were hiding behind and she was suddenly able to hear their laughter.

She noticed another person behind the battling men. It was a woman who looked to have been tied to a wall or something. On one side of her looked to have been winged skeletons, climbing to attack her. On the other were angels looking to have been sounding trumpets making some of the winged skeletons hide. Above the woman was a being with a hood covering their countenance so they couldn't be seen.

"Mary, mother of Christ," she whispered as she looked up, realizing who the person that was tied to the wall was supposed to represent.

"Indeed she was," she heard a voice say.

Gabrial pulled her cover up to herself, when she heard Father Benedict's voice, he had startled her. The monk welcomed himself into her room, strolling over to her bed, where he took a seat. He smiled at her when he saw the frightened expression on her face. The monk moved closer to her ear before she could go anywhere.

"I know your secret," he whispered, then broke into chuckling.

She tried not to show any kind of fear, she didn't know how he could have possibly known that. She and Emmanuelle had both noticed how he had known so many things they had never told him, but they thought it could've been just a guess. But now that he knew what she was, something that no one could have suspected seemed a little strange and it made her uncomfortable. Father Benedict took her hand and patted it as he had done before. His smile was not even comforting, it only made him look even scarier than his personality was making him out to be.

"Why don't you come and take a walk with me?" he inquired, happily. "That way both you and I can discuss more things about the spirit."

"I'm sorry, but I don't feel that I should," replied Gabrial, slowly withdrawing her hand from him.

"I know how you must feel about what you are. And I know how you must keep it a secret," he explained, watching her as she walked over to a closet. "I feel the same way because I am just like you. I'm an…"Father Benedict stopped and bit his lower lip, wondering if he should tell her his secret "...angel."

For some reason, those words caught her off guard and she slowly turned around to face him. If he was an angel then that would explain how he knew so much about the both of them. Father Benedict pushed himself from up and off of her bed and walked towards her. His eyes were now a burning brown that looked like they had been lit by a match.

"Ask me anything and I assure you I can answer it," he told her.

At first, she thought she may have had a question, but then it quickly went away and she shook her head. "I don't want to be rude, but how do I know that you are who you say you are?" inquired Gabrial, turning the opposite way of him.

He cocked an eyebrow. "I'm the glowing being in your dreams that has been calling to you since you were a girl," explained Father Benedict. "On this Earth, I am known as Father Benedict, but as an angel my name is Evian. I've been searching for you."

Gabrial felt as if everything about her was somehow known by him and with him knowing it made her feel uneasy. He didn't at all give her the feeling she had felt whenever she was near that being in her dreams.

She didn't know what kind of feeling it was he gave her, all she knew was that it was familiar.

"I…"

Sister Laura came bursting in through the room door. "It is your friend, Emmanuelle, I fear he has run into a bit of trouble and a child has told me that he wishes to see you," she exclaimed.

Father Benedict noticed how she wasted no time to go and help her friend. He wished she was just as devoted to this place as she was to Emmanuelle. Then he remembered that it would probably take time.

"Please take me to him," Gabrial said to the nun as she pulled down a navy blue cloak.

"The child. I will have the child take you to him," answered Sister Laura. "I'm afraid he has left these walls and I do not know where he is."

It made her wonder where he had been planning to go or why he had left in the first place. Emmanuelle had known that outside the monastery was a strange and busy place. Either way, she had to go find him and bring him back, unless he wanted to leave, which was her first hope. The monastery was starting to become just as strange as the world outside.

****

Outside the inn, the child had led Gabrial to was a dark horse. The child had told her that it was the horse Emmanuelle had purchased, which meant he had been inside the place. She smiled at the child and knelt in front of him.

"Thank you for bringing me here," she told him, handing him something.

"You're very welcome ma'am and thank you," he said, happily, then he raced away like a leprechaun that had been set free.

She watched the little boy for a moment as he disappeared behind a wagon. When she saw him no more, she went to the door of the building, hoping she would find the prince inside. For a moment she stopped and thought before opening the door. Her eyes were focused on the ground complacently. Then she heard a bunch of laughter from the inside and she thought she heard his voice for a moment. Immediately she pushed open the door.

The place was crowded with people, who were seated at tables, eating and drinking. Its atmosphere was kind of stuffy. As Gabrial walked through the place to look for Emmanuelle, a few people stared at her with dirty looks. Not one of them looked like him and she thought that perhaps he had exited the place. Just when she was about to turn around and leave she heard his voice again and she stopped in her tracks. Gabrial noticed him above on a landing area, strolling across. His forehead was pouring in what looked like water. He wore a blue robe that had sleeves that hung so wide they were like the mouths of giant fishes. It was girted about with a rope that looked to have been made of silky material.

"Here I be, thy savior be here this day to save every one of thy lives from the evil in which I have created," chuckled Emmanuelle, raising his hands as to signal everyone to give him a round of applause. Instead of an applause, the people broke into laughter convinced that he may have had some ill kind of problem. But in his mind,

he thought he heard them clapping proudly. "Blameless,

but not shameless to say that here be thy king and savior.

Here to save thee all, undoubtedly and dubiously from this

grave evil," the prince leaned over the banister. "How fair

it is for the young Maiden Sharon to join me this very

night," he said, reaching his hand out to Gabrial.

She looked at him confusedly, sensing that all the

people were staring at her. "Emmanuelle," she whispered,

watching him as he opened the top of his robe.

His eyes glowed like that of a dragon when he

heard her voice. It was like he had heard something he had

so longed to hear again. For some reason, he was unable to

snap out of whatever was keeping him bound in this

masquerade. He felt like he was here, but then not here.

Gabrial thought that maybe he was going to stop

completely until she heard him chuckle almost as if
coughing and she knew it hadn't stopped yet.

"Chagrin d' amour. Oh come, Sharon," he pleaded,
leaning so close to the edge as he walked along, she
thought he might fall. "If we do not go now, then I fear that
by the time we do decide our tarrying here will have
delayed our marriage and we shall not be able to do so for
my body shall be set to burn in the embers of the burdens
of this world and you will not save me nor remember."

The laughter of the people was starting to make her
feel bad that she was letting him make himself appear to
be silly. Gabrial walked towards the staircase to retrieve
him and take him back with her to the monastery. She
didn't know what was happening to him, but for some
reason nothing about him was normal. His eyes were
brighter than ever as if trying to let something from the
inside manifest.

"That's it, Sharon, come hither for if my words are not enough, then I shall offer up my body to satisfy thy…"

"Emmanuelle, I don't know who this Sharon is, but I am Gabrial," she cried, looking up at him, hopelessly."Come with me."

"Gabrial," he muttered as if he had forgotten. "I do not know of a Gabrial, only a Sharon. Never mind," chuckled the prince as the top of his robe fell from his shoulders and hung behind him. "This very night we must go because I shall be set ablaze. To wither. To die in the endless wantingness of the feel of thy lips I will forever long to be against mine own. Shall that not be death of its own accord, besides my body burning?"

"You must remember me," Gabrial whispered into his ear when she was close enough. She slowly reached for his hand and took it in hers. "I am Gabrial, there is no Sharon."

"Gabrial," Emmanuelle muttered again as starting to seem to come back to remembrance.

She looked at him for a long moment, he had to know that these people were laughing at him and that if she didn't get him away from the place he may not ever come out of whatever he was in. There was no hope in explaining his entire face looked as blank as a sheet of paper and he was left muttering her name as if in a state of shock or lost memory. As she led him through the aisleways of the tables, the customers shouted a few things at him and her, then they laughed even more.

The prince didn't seem to care or was even aware of what was happening. She pushed open the front door so they could exit the place. Emmanuelle almost shut his eyes when the sunlight beamed into his eyes, blinding him. All at once, he felt like he was being baked and someone was trying to burn his eyes with something. Gabrial noticed how he was struggling, then set one of his hands on the saddle of the horse.

"I'll manage from here," she heard him say, sounding normal.

He didn't look half as confused as when he had been inside the inn, but he still didn't seem to be completely normal either. The way he got onto the horse was as if he had been riding horses for years. Normally, he struggled to get onto a horse. It took him a few tries before he would be able to get on one. When Emmanuelle took the reins from her, he was overcome by a sudden urge to sleep and he nearly fell off the horse. Gabrial caught him before he was able to fall off and set him back upright. They were not going to make it back to the monastery with him riding the horse, he could easily fall off as tired as he seemed to get. She took the reins of the horse, seeing that he wouldn't be able to ride. The horse began to walk slowly behind her as she led it through the town.

Even in his sleep, he looked as if he were troubled with something. He continually tossed and turned in his bed like he couldn't get comforted. Gabrial couldn't bear to look at him suffer any longer in his sleep and rested her hand on his forehead and he slowly calmed down. His breathing went back to normal and he no longer moved. She couldn't figure out what was wrong with him.

When she left his room, she was so distracted by looking back into the room at the prince that she hadn't noticed Father Benedict as he crept up to her with his hands behind his back, smiling at her as he always did. His lighter brown hair that looked to have been turning white was brushed back and his beard made his smile look even bigger than what it was.

"He is ill?" he inquired, startling her.

"Ill? What…"

"Sick. Unwell. Come down with disease. Maybe even a personality change," explained Father Benedict, quickly as he moved closer to her so he was able to peek through the door also at Emmanuelle.

"Is there a way to make it leave?" Gabrial asked.

"It depends. Sometimes people recover and I've seen many do so, that is of course with the right treatment," he sighed, doubtfully. "Then there's the unfortunate, who sometimes don't make it."

Gabrial's heart sank by his words and she looked at Emmanuelle as he started to continually cough again, along with becoming restless. She thought to go in again and try to heal him this time but was stopped by Father Benedict, who gave her a look of disapproval.

"He needs me," she cried, looking at the man, sadly. "I can't let anything happen to him."

He turned her around so she was looking at him. "Do you want to help him?"

She bit her lower lip trying to fight away her tears just the thought of losing him made her feel like part of her was already gone. It was almost impossible to keep the thoughts from flooding into her mind. "Yes," Gabrial cried.

"Then join me. Become one with me," he told her. "I'm an angel and if you trust me enough like the one in your dreams, then stay here that way I can heal him. My god wants you as one of his children Gabrial and I want to help you get there, but you must believe that your friend being sick is only a sign that you must stay."

"Will he be healed if I stay?"

Emmanuelle sat up in his bed when he heard her talking with Father Benedict. He caught the last part when she said. "If it means this will all be over with then I will stay." The prince leaped out of his bed and raced for the door. He peeked out a tiny crack that she had left in the door. The first thing he saw was Father Benedict patting her on the shoulder, then Gabrial smiling. After he was through talking with her he went on down the hallway. All at once bad thoughts of her raced through his mind. There were a million things that she could've meant by that sentence and not one of them he liked. Emmanuelle boiled with anger and he couldn't bear to hide his feelings any longer.

"Emmanuelle," Gabrial said when he charged through the door.

He took a deep breath before lunging at her and wrapping his arms around her and pulled her close to kiss her. His arms held her so tight, she thought he was trying to kill her. For a moment she wanted to shove him off of herself, it made her feel so uncomfortable. Eventually, she broke free from his grip and stepped away from him.

"What's wrong with you?" she inquired, glaring at him. "You act like an animal."

"I didn't mean to catch you so off guard, I just thought that if I didn't do it now I may never get to tell you that…"

"You love me?" Gabrial chuckled, rudely. "Save your breath, I already knew, and I kind of wish I could've just let you say it. Would've made things a lot funnier."

"No, but you don't understand," he walked closer to her and attempted to take her hand.

She swiped her hand away from him so he wouldn't be able to take it. "I don't feel that at all. Not now and I don't know if ever."

Emmanuelle shook his head as he looked down at the floor. "Then I'm not the one," he cried, meeting her eyes. "I can't make you bleed your heart out for me as mine does for you. I can't change your past or what happened to you."

"It's not like that at all, Emmanuelle," Gabrial told him. "I just don't know if I'm ready to fall in love with you or if I ever will be. I'm sorry."

He was nearly brought to tears. All this time he had tried so hard to impress her. Do things that no one would dare to do. He had even stayed with her, even after he had planned to leave when he saw how much she showed interest in Father Benedict.

"You're in love with someone else?" he asked as if he had known who it may have been. "That's why you're afraid to love me."

"No, if I wanted to love someone it would be you, but I'm not so sure if I'm ready."

"I won't let this happen. Maybe you'll know after this," he let go of her and hurried away from her.

She stood there as if she could care-less if he went away. He walked past a hallway, where Gabrial noticed that he was awake and moving. The only thing was she wished she knew where he was going. He couldn't go anywhere in his condition. Right now he needed help so he wouldn't get any worse. She raced into the hall to stop him and help him get back to his room.

"Emmanuelle, where are you going," she inquired, walking beside him.

"Home to find something that will maybe change your mind about who you love," he explained as if in a trance.

"Emmanuelle no," Gabrial cried, grabbing hold of his sleeve. "You can't leave, I've found a way to help you."

"Help me?" he chuckled, thinking of how much help she needed. "Help yourself if anything." The prince pushed past her as if she were nothing and continued to the exit.

If he thought she was about to let him leave just like that, then he had more air in his head than a balloon had inside of it. She pursued after him trying to stop him from leaving, only to be dragged along with him as he went through the doors. His horse was saddled and ready for him to ride off.

"Look, Gabrial, I learned one thing from you," Emmanuelle laughed as if sore. "I should never pour my heart out and tell someone I love them because that pain of letting someone in that close feels worse than arrows to the heart. I love you, Gabrial and I probably will never stop, not even after the day I die."

"Love me?" she murmured, realizing what he had said. "Wait!"

The prince rode away, letting her chase after him. His golden eyes looked brighter than ever when he stared down at her. The light blue dress bringing out all the details about her face and eyes that he would soon miss.

"Emmanuelle, stop this. Please," she begged as she reached her hand to touch him just a little so that he might come back for a moment.

"I'm sorry, but I can't stop what has already been said," he answered, whacking the reins harder so the horse would speed up. "Goodbye, Gabrial."

Her hand grasped hold of the air and she was forced to stop chasing him once he had left the bridge and into the town. Gabrial watched as he disappeared with his flowing red cape. How could she have let him escape? Now she couldn't help him and by the time anyone found him it may have been too late. She slumped down onto the pavement of the bridge and brought her legs closer to herself.

Her head collapsed onto her knees and she no longer fought away the tears that had so longed to pour from her eyes. She had failed him, something that he would've never done to her, and the worst part was he didn't believe she loved him. If only she had the chance sooner to tell him before any of this happened that she loved him. If only she had never left the palace in the first place, then maybe he would be still alright and living. Although he was still living now, there was no telling how long that would last. This dream had gone from a bad dream to beyond a nightmare and there seemed to be no kind of silver lining in the clouds to tell her that this storm would be over soon and the sun would shine once more.

"I'm sorry, Emmanuelle," she cried into her knees, "I'm sorry I didn't see it sooner."

Chapter 18

Shape of Lies

$\mathcal{E}$mmanuel was brought back to awareness when

he heard the squabbling of people's voices. When his eyes

opened he saw people being held back or restrained by

soldiers that wore armor the color of comets. He felt out of

place like a shoe with the wrong match. The people

pointed and yelled, calling him names. A few threw things

at his wings like tomatoes and fruits, splashing and

covering the glorious and vivid white of them.

A man wearing a white tunic covered by a black vest stood upon a staircase of a palace ahead of him. The man took one look at Emmanuel when he was brought before him. One of his eyes glowed with a dazzling red wine color while the other was a stone-cold blue. The man spit into the angel's face as if he were a disgrace and he turned away.

"Guardians of the world and humans," laughed the man. "Well I tell you this much, I'm King Asgard and I am as a god to everyone even you angels and until you learn to submit yourself to me I will continue to persecute this world."

"So go ahead and try, you can only go as far as the true and living God allows you," snapped Emmanuel, feeling one of the soldiers that were restraining him pluck a feather from his wing.

"I like this one," chuckled Asgard, shaking his head. "And I will break your spirit also if I don't kill you

first with my torturing. I know who you are. Emmanuel, guardian of the world and peace. So tell me how does your God let you fall this far as great as you are? Brought this low before the filth of my shoes to eat the mud and sweat that I give you? Do you believe he will come through to end this war after all these years?"

The angel looked away from him as he listened to the man laugh sinisterly.

"Bring him to my quarters. It is there we shall keep him locked up," ordered the king as he started for the palace.

The soldiers dragged the angel up the stairs leaving behind all the angry people, who sought to kill him. He didn't understand how they could've hated them so badly, they were the ones who had tried so hard to protect them from harm. To watch over them when they slept at night and even be a friend and advisor to those who were in need of someone.

"You must dance, otherwise you will die," ordered the woman, fighting to keep hold of him.

His eyes looked desperately, something was crying out to him from outside, telling him that if he didn't go now, he would never be able to go back. Emmanuelle pulled himself loose from her grasp and immediately the dancers in the room began to fall like dominoes all around him in a spiral. The woman began to wail his name as he tried to escape the place. Suddenly from out of all the silence, he heard something that sounded worse than the tearing of a veil.

The sound was almost painful in his ears and he covered them, wincing as he fell to the ground. When he looked at his hands there was blood on them. He looked over at the woman he had been dancing with, but she looked almost unrecognizable. There was black all in her eyes with only a glowing ring where her iris was. From her back hung a pair of bat wings that were halfway torn looking like an old curtain with holes, where the wings like that of a swan had once been.

Her dress was a bloody red with black lacing and over her hands, she wore a pair of black lace gloves. The woman's lips were pursed together in their raven black. Her hair hung like black serpents that had been coiled over and over until they reached the end. She had nails that were now like claws, they looked so sharp and long.

Emmanuelle darted for the door to escape her, then she reached her hand out in front of her, shutting every opening and door there was in the place. One by one the candles went out and somewhere he could hear the laughter of people like the laughter that had been present within the room when they had been dancing. He was startled when he felt her hand rubbed across his shoulder and he felt her breath softly and whispered into his ear.

"I love you, don't you know that," she chuckled, letting her hand touch against his face. "Let's play one last game."

"I must go home," he answered, before stepping away from her. "You deceived me, I will only die if I stay here with you, but you used me to keep you living. Just like you've done all the others."

Her breathing deepened as her shoulders hunched up making her look more enormous than what she was. "How right you are, charming, but I'm afraid I just can't let you go," she laughed, then pointed a finger at him.

Suddenly Emmanuelle felt his body throw himself forward as if performing the waltz all over. The woman laughed as she spun her finger around so that he would spin. He struggled with himself to try and stop dancing the waltz they had danced for so long, but it was like his body had a mind of its own and it continued to dance. All the dancers that had once been dancing in the room became present once more, dancing with one another around him. It was like they hadn't even noticed all the darkness around them, that the ballroom was gone and they were trapped on something like an empty black sheet of paper.

"Having fun?" she inquired as she watched him struggle to try and stop.

"Stop this," Emmanuelle yelled, painfully.

She moved her finger quickly close to herself and made it so he was forced to dance with her once more. "Oh, how I would if I didn't find such a thrill with having you dance with me."

The prince leaned her over and she hung back his body feeling like every bone in it had been broken. Sweat ran over his forehead like a fountain and his feet felt so numb he didn't even know if he had them anymore. His legs staggered with weakness from all the dancing. The woman pulled him by his shirt so she was able to kiss him deeply. Immediately, dark veins began to show throughout his face as he became pale as if cold. He fell only to land on something soft like a bunch of clouds, she hovered above him.

"Sleep now and wake up tomorrow another person," she told him as she closed his eyelids so that he would sleep.

He shivered, feeling as though his lips had been turned to stone. The glow in her face had vanished and all around him, all he could see was darkness outside of the bloody red canopy that hung over wherever he had been laid down.

Rain continuously poured over Emmanuelle's head as he traveled through the forest on his horse. He didn't know why, but he felt a terrible urge to sleep or lie down. The horse he was riding upon stumbled over a bunch of branches that had been in the middle of the trail. It snorted a little but continued walking. For just a moment he thought to take a little nap, the horse would continue on the path.

Then just when he thought to go ahead and do so a streak of lightning flashed across the sky and was followed by a rumbling sound of thunder that shook the ground. The horse was sent on the run, waking him up immediately.

"Herod, woooo boy," he yelled as he held on tightly to the reins.

But the horse was too afraid to slow down. It leaped carelessly over shrubs and fallen trees, forgetting about its rider. Emmanuelle was nearly knocked off its back when it leaped over a log, almost getting him hit by a branch. He didn't know what to do, he had never ridden a horse that was out of control.

All the excitement made his heart race and want to run from out of his chest. Mud splashed over him as the horse sprinted through puddles of mud and water.

Everything about this night made him regret leaving Gabrial behind.

"Herod, woooo," Emmanuelle ordered, pulling onto the reins.

It was as if the horse had a mind of its own and it was heading straight for a rushing river with jagged stones. The prince's eyes widened, there was no way anyone would survive the rage of that river. He clenched tightly onto the horse's neck, hoping the horse would stop before they reached it. Another rumble of thunder sounded causing his horse to rear up, throwing him off and into the muddy water. At one point he attempted to get up, but his eyelids grew heavy and his body felt as if someone had stacked a million bricks on him. His head fell when he could no longer see the horse and he fell asleep.

****

There was a flash of lightning that woke Gabrial up. She looked around her empty room. All night she had been struggling to sleep. Nightmares vexed her, some about losing Emmanuelle because of her failure, then others with a gargoyle hanging above her. But there was no gargoyle in the room so she didn't understand why it was in her dreams. She looked over at the candle as it flickered.

Now that he was gone, she was starting to feel that something was off with this place. It was as if there was something dark hanging around in the atmosphere and it was inescapable. Gabrial picked up the stick of the candle holder and decided to walk around in hopes of maybe tiring herself to sleep. Her door slowly cracked open without a squeak or sound and she stepped into the hallway, lit by torches. At night the place looked more like a dungeon than a monastery.

For a moment she thought she heard screaming or something, but then she thought that it could've been just the rumbling of thunder outside. Her bare feet felt like ice on the cold, stone floor. Then she was startled when she heard the screaming again, this time it sounded to be coming from somewhere down the dark hallway that wasn't lit by many torches. She realized that it wasn't screaming, but sounded more like someone was pleading. Without any second thoughts, Gabrial started for the dark hall.

"Where are you going, Gabrial?" asked a chilling voice, from behind her.

She turned, slowly to see Father Benedict standing behind her. His long dark robe lapped over his feet and he wore his dark hood, being careful to keep his hands together so that both of his sleeves were joined. The hall was empty when she had come out of her room and it didn't seem like he could have moved so fast to catch up with her from the other rooms. Besides that, she hadn't heard anything.

"I thought I heard something and thought to try and figure out what it was," she answered, struggling to control her hand from shaking. For some strange reason, she had seemed to have even lost control of her body to stop it from showing any signs that he had frightened her. "I think I will be leaving tomorrow to find Emmanuelle."

The monk's smile faded away when she said those words and for once a frown showed on his face. "I assure you that your friend is getting along quite finely," he told her as he moved closer to her. "I have much to teach you and if you want me to do so you are going to have to believe what I tell you."

"I'm not sure if I can do so, at least not yet," Gabrial replied, looking at the floor. "Emmanuelle has been with me, when…"

"You must stop this. Can't you see, he is imprisoning your soul so you can't move forward and fulfill your purpose. Learn the truth about who you are," explained Father Benedict, grabbing hold of both her shoulders so she couldn't try and escape him. "Look at me, Gabrial, when I speak to you!" he ordered aggressively as he moved his finger at the bottom of her chin and turned her his way. For a moment she heard someone else, then he softened his expression and said more calmly. "Please."

Her arms felt like it was turning to stone when he touched her. His fiery golden eyes burned into her soft blue eyes as if trying to drain the life from out of her. Gabrial dropped the candle holder with the candle feeling her limbs weaken. When she felt just a little bit of her strength return to her, she tried to get him to release her. But instead, she felt as if something iron were burning through her skin from his hands.

"What's the matter with you?" he snarled when he felt like something had hit him in his forehead making him let go of her. He held his forehead, falling onto the floor, growling with pain.

She didn't wait for him to get back to normal and she ran into the dark hall. There was something seriously wrong with him and now she was certain of that. She had to find a way to get out of this place and find Emmanuelle. If he could do something to her to make her feel weak, then there was no telling what he could've done to him. She had to find Sister Laura and get help from her escape back to Ascedia.

＊＊＊＊＊＊＊＊＊＊

Candles were lit throughout the library, books were scattered all across the floor. More were thrown from the shelves to join the others as the knights and Damien searched through behind every book and shelf in the library. Sir Gilliot kicked down one of the shelves from the upper part of the library, when it hit the floor it broke into pieces.

"Any luck?" inquired Damien.

"No sir," replied Sir Kelvin, throwing books off a shelf.

"Darn, where could it be?" he murmured, looking at another shelf that had been untouched.

The prince approached the shelf, his eyes gleaming on it as if he was trying to see through it. Sir Kelvin had stopped throwing books off shelves when he saw that Damien had stopped. He looked at the shelf where the prince was going. Suddenly books were thrown from that shelf also, Damien looked like a rat tearing through trash as he ripped books off the shelf, then shoving a bunch of them off.

"What are you incompetent fools staring at? Help me!" he ordered.

The knights hopped over the floor covered in books. They helped him throw books from off the shelf, revealing a bunch of writing on an old wall behind it. This was it, the place he had been searching for. He pointed at each side of the shelf as if telling them to get on each side. Two of them went on each side of the wide shelf. When the way was clear of both the prince and the other knights, they began to push on the shelf with all their might. They strained, but the shelf only made a screeching sound, remaining in the same position it had been placed in.

"Sir Gilliot, help these little weaklings," snapped Damien, frowning at them.

The knight came over to help the younger men. He was as strong as a bull when he came and pushed the shelf. It fell onto the floor, breaking into parts and sending a massive dust cloud that left them coughing, afterward, except for the prince. He rolled his eyes at them, then darted over to the wall that had been behind the shelf. Damien tore thick cobwebs and old paper that was hanging from off the wall.

"I've found it," he chuckled as he dug into the wall, where he saw some kind of compass painting on it. "I knew it was here."

"My gosh," gasped Sir Kelvin, wiping his lower lip.

"What the heck," snarled Sir Pelacio.

"It's a map, you fools," laughed Damien, tearing more of the paper off of the wall so he could see the full painting.

"Looks more like a compass," teased Sir Gilliot.

The prince pretended he hadn't heard a word the old knight had said. He tore the last piece of paper off the wall. In the center of the map was a bright star and all around its edges were what looked like constellations like Cancer, Centaurus, Perseus, and so on. There were large letters at the top and sides of the massive star in the middle. His eyes looked across the map as he read parts of the paragraphs that were on the map.

"It's a map of the stars," grumbled Damien.

"Is that all, so we can't search for…"

"It means that none of us here are going to understand or know where it leads," replied the prince, rudely as he glared at Sir Pelacio. "It's going to take someone who reads the stars and who knows how long if ever to find a person who can understand the stars."

"What if it's not a map at all," offered Sir Gilliot as he leaned against a wall.

Everyone turned to look at the knight. Surely he could've seen that it was a map. It was right in plain sight.

"What?" spatted Damien, fuming with anger.

"So you're all familiar with what a mirror does when someone or anything is in front of it," started the knight.

"Don't be silly, of course, we do," chuckled Sir Kelvin, playing with his mustache.

"It reflects, of…" started the prince, suddenly realizing what the knight had meant. "I want these books cleared out of the way! Now!"

They fell to their knees and started to push books aside. As the floor cleared up from all the books a moral appeared on the floor and it looked exactly like the painting on the wall, although it was painted with more colors than the one on the wall.

"Damien!" he heard someone call, from outside of the library. "Damien!"

His eyes narrowed. He was on the brink of finding something great and he wasn't about to stop. The knights looked at the door, knowing that if the person who was calling him got in would be surprised by how they had torn down the library.

"Sir, don't you think you should…"

"Shut up, Sir Pelacio," he yelled. "I'm too close to this and nothing is about to get in my way. I can feel it."

"Listen to me, Damien, there is a place on the wall, where you must put your hand to unlock the secrets below," he heard that same voice that had guided him this far whisper in his ear. When he turned, there was no one there.

"Damien, your brother has returned and he is ill," the woman from outside the room cried. "I think you should visit him."

"Urgh, bolt the door!" he ordered Sir Kelvin. "Crazy woman, I don't care if he was on his way out of this world, let me finish this."

The woman banged on the door outside, but he could care-less as long as she wasn't inside with them. If she did get in, she would have an unpleasant surprise waiting for her. He had given the maids strict orders not to disturb him when he was busy or when his door was closed. They'd have even worse luck than the groom

seeing his bride's dress before a wedding. He chuckled as

he listened to call him from the other side.

✶✶✶✶✶✶✶✶✶✶

The hall was pitch black, it was so dark it was as if

there was some heavenly body roaming the room creating

the darkness. Gabrial stumbled when she stepped onto a

piece of wood. This whole place gave her chills and she

didn't know why. There were a few paintings in the hall

that she could make out since they were painted in such

vivid, bright red.

A few of the paintings had been torn. One of the

paintings looked like the gargoyle in her nightmare. It

looked to have been created from red ash in the portrait

and its eyes were such a lively gold you would have

thought the creature wasn't in a painting. She wondered

420

why might someone in a monastery keep a creature that was so dark.

"Gabrial," she heard voices whisper from throughout the room. "Come with us, Gabrial. Join us."

Portraits and things were broken throughout the room as a minotaur had stormed through the place, but there wasn't a sign of any person in the room, just voices, whispering things. She felt something damp and that felt kind of like a bony grab hold of her ankle. When she looked down, there was nothing there, but when she tried to keep walking it seemed like something was holding her back. Then she felt a few other damp and bony hands grab hold of her.

She pulled and fought, although she couldn't see that there was anything there. Gabrial yelled for help when she couldn't get free. Then she felt something cover over her mouth to make her stop. A light cut on ahead of her as if someone had just snapped their fingers and there everything was brought into existence.

Someone hung over a dark coffin, upon a platform. It looked to have been just like the one she had been at when she had been with the nuns. But then it was darker and there was an eerie light that shined down on the coffin. Instead of lambs, there was some kind of bony dogs with fangs that were miles long and the flowers were shriveled up and dead. Her eyes looked petrified when she heard Father Benedict's voice.

"Ah Gabrial," he chuckled as he turned around to look at her frightened expression. "How I adore everything about you and your personality."

He snapped his fingers, then appeared behind her. She was unable to turn around, but she could feel his finger moving around her neck, then he pulled out a dove. He let it fly from off his finger and into the darkness. His finger felt cold, damp, and bony just like the hands that were holding her still. His eyes were that lively gold like the gargoyle in the painting and his teeth had grown like pricks as he stared at her, menacingly.

"Of course," he clapped his hands, making a ballroom of people dancing appear. "A gentleman's dancing outfit and a gown for you and of course a mask for the lady."

Father Benedict wore a black kind of tuxedo with black short boots. His hair was brushed back, nicely as if he were George Washington. A deep red gown that was sparkly appeared on Gabrial, along with a mask with rubies that decorated it. She stared at all the other people dancing in the ballroom. Every one of their moves seemed to have been so perfectly placed and even their gowns and masks seemed to have been controlled. The men wore white masks that covered their whole faces instead of just their eyes and there were dots on the white mask, each in a certain order. The women wore masks that were feathery and made with precious stones that only covered the upper part of their faces.

"*Help us,*" she heard a few voices call, but when she looked none of their mouths had moved.

"Welcome to my world. Shall we?" he inquired, stepping in front of her and bowing himself.

Gabrial felt like a suctioning mask had been taken off of her face and she gasped for air. "I'd rather not. Why have you brought me here?"

A grin crept on his face and he couldn't help but chuckle to himself just thinking of how she hadn't caught on to things yet. He didn't wait for her to permit him, after all, he had complete control of her now. He took her by the hand and led her with one hand behind his back into the center of the room to join the others. He started with a slow spin like the others, then he took off for a quick dart the other way with her. Making her go up and down with him as if she were his puppet.

"Stop this," she cried as they spun around and danced like they were in some kind of merry go around. "What have you done with the monastery and the nuns?"

He stopped as she told him to, but there was a look in his eyes that said he wasn't done. Suddenly he began to laugh, making her step back and away from him.

His face seemed to have been turning or like it was about to blow.

"Isn't it obvious, Gabrial," he asked before his head popped and turned into Sister Laura's face. "Oh dear, you're lucky I found you," he teased, mimicking the woman's voice. Then his head popped again as he moved closer to her, this time he had Father Benedict's old look. "Don't let him hinder you Gabrial from being so much more. A pleasure for you to join me, Emmanuelle," he said in a woman's voice as his face changed again to the woman who had been in the prince's nightmares. "You're very welcome ma'am and thank you," his face changed again, looking like the child who had taken her to Emmanuelle and his face continued to change along with his voice as he snaked his head out at her as if angry.

She stared at him, frightenedly wondering who or what he could possibly be. All this time all those people had been just him. That was impossible. Gabrial closed her eyes, refusing to look at any more of the faces he was making. At one point it would go up and then the next it sagged like melting ice cream. Then his face would flatten out, it was all too much and him yelling at her made it no better.

"LOOK! LOOK AT ME GABRIAL WHEN I'M TALKING TO YOU!" he growled, getting so close to her face she could feel the spit flopping from off of his tongue. He hit himself in the head, growing frustrated. "TALK!

SAY SOMETHING TO ME! YOU ALWAYS DID, WHEN YOU SLEPT AND WANTED TO DIE! I was there! I had to listen to your sobs every night!" he yelled, his tone growing sinister. "You know exactly who I am!"

"I don't," she cried, keeping her head turned away from him.

"Lies!" he shrieked, leaping up. "All lies!"

He fell silent and seemed to have calmed down and he looked over at a few sages, dressed in black robes. They were carrying a coffin that they set down on the platform. Once they had set it down securely, they vanished into the shadows behind the coffin. He raised his finger a little so the lid of the coffin lifted. She opened her eyes when she heard the lid of the coffin break when it hit the floor.

"Have a look," he ordered her as he pointed to the coffin.

Gabrial looked at him for a moment as if nervous, then slowly approached the coffin. The dancers had stopped dancing and the music had stopped playing. Her gown trailed behind her as she walked up the marble steps. Before she looked in the coffin, she took one last look back at the being. When she looked into the coffin she saw something she wished she hadn't.

"Emmanuelle," she cried, covering her mouth.

Chapter 19

Without the Light of Hope

The other iron angels had left, when Armistice

had ordered them to. She had stayed behind with Arsonist

since she had been immobilized for some reason. A

glowing bright light appeared in the midst of the dust and

it was as if the sun had fallen onto the Earth. Armistice

stared at the glowing thing of light, when she saw the two

sharp edge axes she knew who it was.

"Othniel," she cried as the being came down onto the ground.

His feet that were shod with iron touched the ground so lightly it was like he was a feather. His wingspan was like reaching from the east to the west and he was as big as a bear. It was impossible to see his face since it was covered by an iron helmet that resembled an ancient Egyptian dog. He nodded his head at her but didn't speak. When he saw Arsonist covered with her wings, he looked at Armistice as if talking with his gestures.

"I sent the others away to find the prisoners, but I stayed behind because she doesn't seem to be able to continue for some reason," replied Armistice, shaking her head.

Othniel took one look at Sharon, then at Armistice. They both knew that without her guiding the others they'd stand no chance against those soldiers. He grunted a little

as he lifted his massive wings, picking up some of the dust.

"I will take care of her," he finally said, his voice

sounding as if he were angry, although he wasn't. "You

must lead the others, they will be lost without you."

She stared at him for a moment wondering how he

had read her mind, then she watched as he picked Arsonist

up. He turned his back getting ready to fly away, but before

he was able to fly away he heard Armistice say something

to him.

"You will come back, won't you?" she asked,

worriedly. "Our army needs you."

He nodded his head in agreement, then in one flap

he was gone as if in a flash. There was nothing left here for

her so she decided that she should do as he told her.

Armistice ran for a little while before catching the wind

that made her iron wings emerge from her back and

carried her into the sky.

The prince's face looked as if he had frozen and pale as snow, even the golden brown in his eyes. His frozen face had a bunch of black veins flowing around like little paths of ash on his face.

"Emmanuelle, say something," she cried, shaking him, but there was no response or movement from him. "What have you done to him?"

"I only gave him a taste of his death, your little friend is still alive," he explained, clapping his hands so he disappeared. She turned to look back, but he was already gone. The being circled her like a snake waiting to attack its prey.

"What do you want? Who are you?" she inquired, then he poked her in the sore areas on her back.

"Who else do you think I'd be?" he spatted, aggressively as his anger rose. Steam began to show from his nostrils as if he were a dragon. His eyes became a glowing, possessed red. "Think, Gabrial! He ordered, tapping his finger against her temple. "Think you fool."

Her eyes stared at the ballroom with the dancing people. For some reason the whole atmosphere, the way they danced. It was as if they were trying to send her a code, discreetly, but she wasn't receiving it. Her eyes narrowed and she shook her head, coming out of her thoughts.

"I don't know," Gabrial told him.

That wasn't what he wanted to hear and he banged himself in the head trying to keep it together, but it wasn't working. "Maybe you will remember after this," he shrieked.

Suddenly the place began to shake, making her stagger as she struggled to keep her balance. The being had covered his head as if trying to contain what was trying to come out. He hollered so loud the glass in the room shook, it sounded more like a roar than a holler. She covered her ears to protect them from the loud sounds in the room. Wings tore from out of his back and it sounded like a tree tearing its way through impossible soil.

"URAAAAAHHHHH!!!!" he yelled as he let them free, sending a massive current of air throughout the room.

When she looked at him, she couldn't even recognize him. He looked to have been part bat, dragon, and who knew what else. He was covered in ash and his red eyes stood out from all the darkness. Now she could remember seeing something similar to looking like him in the dark hallway she had taken that had brought her here on a painting, all except he was ash and his eyes were not the burning color of red.

"My name is Erebus, the creature that hung over you at night," he chuckled, looking at her expression. "Now do you remember?"

"Gabrial," she thought she heard Emmanuelle's voice say.

It felt like her heart was going to break into pieces when she heard his voice.

"You can save him," offered Erebus.

"Why are you doing this?" Gabrial cried, frustratedly when she didn't see the prince anywhere.

"WHY? Because I want a life to live, Gabrial!" he yelled at her. "I want to have what belongs rightfully to me. If you had never asked for so many favors in the first place, you wouldn't be here." Erebus began to laugh, sinisterly at her, holding his stomach. "You thought you could escape just that easily. That your sobs came without a price. Well now is your time to pay, by taking my place," he pointed at a coffin that was over in a corner.

Gabrial looked into the coffin to see a place of hands that looked like withered flowers reaching out and calling for help. They were trapped in some kind of lake that looked to have been ablaze in red fire and they were trying hard to fight to get out. She turned away when she couldn't bear to look at any more of it.

"Yes, I've kept many prisoners here to keep this part of me alive, but none have been able to fully bring me back to life," he snarled as his voice deepened. "Then I found you when you were a little girl. Crying out because you were in a world you didn't want to live in any longer."

"I don't understand," she replied.

"I need to trade something more precious than just these wretched humans to get my life back," Erebus growled. "I followed you everywhere you went until you came here with the little prince of yours. Oh, you don't know how perfectly things seemed to be set up so I created the monastery and everyone in it. I even created

Emmanuelle's nightmares and visions about you."

Now it all made sense and she understood why he

had been so strange and different towards her while they

were there at the monastery. He was being mentally played

with like a puppet and being made to see and hear things

that weren't so.

"You're killing him," she yelled.

"Something had to be done to get you here," he

sighed as a grin appeared on his face. "And now that

you're here you can take his place or either leave him to

suffer the rest of his life with me killing him in some awful

ways then making it so he will long to be dead, it'll be just

that bad and of course as long as I keep him alive

somewhat I will live, unlike if I let him die completely I

too shall perish. You see as long as he lives I feed on his

life until I take yours, only then will I be free."

"No," Gabrial said aloud, looking at the floor.

"Oh yes, an angel in my place is most precious and no price can be put on one," he laughed, snapping his fingers. "It's either him or you and if I were you I'd choose it to be me, not because it's a good thing as an angel to do, but because I will be sure you see him suffer every time you sleep."

"Gabrial, come to me, please," begged the prince, standing in the midst of people dancing more slowly in the ballroom.

She couldn't ignore him and just looking at him in such a painful condition made her want to give everything for him to be back to normal. He had suffered enough in his life and he didn't need to pay for her burdens. Gabrial ran over to embrace him, she thought he had perished from her life for good.

The being that had been Emmanuelle, crumpled into a bunch of dust when she had tried to hug him. She gasped, then moved her hands to try and stop him from blowing away in ashes.

"Gabrial, come to me, please," she heard him call again.

When she looked around there had to be about a million of him, all looking to have been trapped or lost. It was too much to watch him look so lost and in agony. Gabrial crumpled down onto the floor and covered her eyes as she wept. She didn't know what to do and she felt so useless at this point. Her gown was across the floor looking like an endless galaxy with black that faded into blue and blue that became lighter until it became green and light green.

✳✳✳✳✳✳✳✳✳✳✳✳

All the books had been finally clear of the center of the floor where the moral was painted, but it didn't have the star in the center. It looked to have been more like the shape of a triangle or rhombus. The knights whispered among one another, wondering what the place could have been for or what was its significance. Damien paid them no mind and stood up, walking over to the wall where the voice had told him to put his hand. For some reason, he could now see the area where it was supposed to be placed. It was like someone had put a light where there had once been none.

"You are so close now, my child just a little further," the voice told him.

The area where he was supposed to place his hand was glowing with a shimmering white light as if guiding him to the right space. Damien reached his hand out until it rested flat on the hand place. His body felt a sudden surge of energy that flowed through his veins and his arms were thrust outward. The knights thought to try and save him from whatever was happening until they saw him turn around.

His eyes were no longer a stone-cold blue, they were white and glowing and so was his body. Damien was still in the same room when he regained consciousness, but the knights were gone and the place looked less like a library. The ceiling was open to the sky above, he could even hear the sound of an eagle. Somehow it all gave him chills.

Then suddenly the doors to the place swung open and he saw three soldiers and a boy, behind them trailed a man with a nicely cut white beard, less savage looking than his father's. He wore rings on his fingers and his face looked as stern as if he was stone himself. The boy cried out to him and called him the man with the rings 'father'.

It wasn't long before he realized who the man and his son were.

It was King Asgard. The first king and founder of Ascedia and his son, who was supposedly said to have never made it. But if that had been so, why was he here and looked to have been the age of seventeen. The king

tilted his head at the soldiers as if telling them to do

something. Damien watched as they struggled to lay the

boy down flat on a place in the middle of the same moral

he and the knights had found. All except the rhombus was

gone and there was a coffin-like area shaped like a body in

the center. In the ceiling was a large hole that the moon

was shining through and onto the boy. For some reason,

when he and the knights were in the library there was no

sign of the hole.

"*My beloved son I give you this very day thy cup of

blood in which thou must drink,*" said the king as he

watched the soldiers tie the boy down to the floor.

Before Damien could see what happened next the

place began to blur and it seemed to have stopped as if he

had been only looking through a mirror at a scene that took

place in history.

"To open the passage, royal blood must be spilled upon the coffin and it shall reveal itself," whispered the dark voice.

The prince came back to his normal self and he slumped down to the floor. Immediately the knights came over to help him. Damien looked at the floor, chuckling lightly, now he understood part of this tangling puzzle.

"Sir are you alright?" inquired Sir Pelacio, worriedly.

"I'm better than alright," he laughed as he stood up from off the floor. He dusted his hands off in case any dirt had gotten on them from the floor. "I have a certain quest for a few of you and I say only a few of you because some of you may not be able to handle such strong meat."

****

The prince breathed heavily as he lay in bed, flat on his back. His head felt as if it were like jello and his whole body felt as if the castle had caved in on him.

Emmanuelle tried to open his eyes, but slowly. The sun's light was so bright it almost made his eyes tear up when he opened them. He realized that he was back in his room, but he wondered how. The last thing he remembered was being thrown from his horse and watching it run off leaving him behind in the dark forest.

He began to cough and it felt like he had a scratch in his throat or something sharp was trying to force its way down. The door to his room opened slowly with a squeaky sound. Damien stepped in, glaring at him. To him, this was a waste of time and if he didn't have to come and get him, he wouldn't have come at all. Seeing him injured and in such a helpless state made him think of something else.

"Happy to see you made it," he laughed. "What was kind of funny was when you got stitches."

"Stitches? What do you mean?" asked Emmanuelle.

"A figure of speech, you...poor thing," snapped Damien, changing his words from what he wanted to say.

If this was his way of saying he was relieved to see he was alright, then he was doing an awful job. He wanted to see Gabrial and he also wondered if she had checked up on him while he was unconscious, he hadn't seen any sign that she may have been there. Seeing his brother as the first face to come and check up on him was a little scary.

"Where's Gabrial?" he asked. "Could you send someone to get her for me?"

"She's gone," he chuckled.

Emmanuelle frowned, remembering how he had left her behind at the monastery. "I have to go back and find her," he said aloud.

"Find her?" Damien looked at him, if he knew where she was then why hadn't he brought her back with him. "Where is she?"

"The monastery. I left her," he muttered, wondering what could've been wrong with him. His whole reason for leaving in the first place was to find and bring her back. "What was I thinking?"

"Where is this monastery?" intruded Damien.

Emmanuelle looked up at him as his brother's question set in. "A town on the other side of the Dark Forest, I don't know…"

He was interrupted by Damien's rude, sinister laughter. "I think you're a little bit more ill than the nurse thought," he chuckled trying to control his laughter. " The town of Cantlemac is what you're referring to. That town has been vacant for centuries, after the death of their queen and that monastery or what was a castle caved in long ago."

"No, I was there and there were people," argued Emmanuelle, growing frustrated. "I and Gabrial lodged there for a while and that is where I left her."

"Are you sure of that?"

"Yes, of course," he assured him. "I was there and so was--you don't believe me, do you?"

The look in Damien's eye was so doubtful and it frustrated him that his brother was starting to think he lost his mind. Emmanuelle threw his blankets aside. If he didn't believe him, then he would just have to prove to him that he wasn't making things up or going out of his mind from being sick.

"And where are you going?" asked Damien as he watched his brother throw some of his clothes from his wardrobe onto his bed.

"I'm going back," he replied.

"Are you really? Because I think you have a much higher calling," chuckled Damien, wiping off a knife the nurse had left in the room.

Almost immediately he realized what he was planning to do. But by the time he tried to run for the door, he was tackled by Damien and back over and into his bed. He struggled to keep the knife away from getting him. The prince rolled out of his bed making his brother get the pillow he had been using as a shield.

Emmanuelle leaped up from off the floor and bolted for the door, then stopped when the knife was thrown nearly cutting him. It stuck out of the door. Had Damien lost his mind? Killing him would only make him look like a crazy person, not a king. Pain surged through his body like electricity and he was forced to fall on the floor. He held his side as he watched his brother near him with a knife.

If he had lived this long, he had to try to still do so for her. His hand grabbed hold of the doorknob and he fell through. He climbed to his feet, then ran down the hallway, nearly running into Sir Hamilton. The knight stared at him when he saw him fall on the floor looking to be fighting someone.

"Prince Emmanuelle, what are you doing out of your bed," he asked.

"Trying to stay alive," answered the prince. "My brother he's trying to kill me, I think he's going after Gabrial and father next."

"Uh-huh," he nodded his head. "I think you need to rest, Prince Damien doesn't know you're here, and um, Gabrial she's…"

"What? Is she alright or…No. No. No. This can't be happening," he cried in frustration, leaning over against a wall and banging his fist as he closed his eyes. "Where is she, where is my mother or Damien?"

"Slow down and take a deep breath," ordered the knight. "We haven't seen your mother and Damien hasn't done anything to her. It's just… well, I kind of lost her." he finally acknowledged, afraid of the prince's reaction.

"Is she here? Has she finally returned?"
Emmanuelle inquired, briskly.

"No, at least I don't believe so. I thought she was
with you," acknowledged the knight, looking at him
suspiciously.

Emmanuelle pushed his way past the knight, he had
to find her before something happened to her or before
Damien got to her. He knew for certain now that since he
hadn't succeeded with killing him that he would go
looking for her next then his father. If only he hadn't told
his brother where she was or of her whereabouts. Sir
Hamilton grabbed him by the arm.

"I'm sorry but I can't let you go, your highness," he
said. "You're not in your mind right now and letting you
leave is too dangerous."

"I don't care, everyone, I care about lives are on
the line and I have to do something," Emmanuelle
replied, pulling his arm free from the knight. Then he

realized something, that the reason he didn't want him to leave was really that he had something up his sleeve also, "You're working with them too, aren't you?"

The knight's eyes looked confused. "I'm sorry sir, but I don't follow you."

"You're working with my brother to kill us all," chuckled Emmanuelle, sickly. "You set this up. You brought me back so I could tell you where she was and so you could kill me also in hopes of helping Damien gain the crown."

"I think you're confused," stated Sir Hamilton, watching as the prince approached him looking dangerous. "Now look, I don't know what's wrong with you but you need to…"

The prince grabbed him by the neck, then squeezed the knight's neck holding him up against a wall and he wheezed for air. He felt a surge of adrenaline rush through his veins making him feel stronger than ever. A maid came sweeping down the hallway and the knight yelled at her to get help.

"If anything happens to her or anyone, it'll be you next," snapped Emmanuelle.

"You're ill sir and you need help, now let me get it for you," Sir Hamilton as his voice grew wheezy and raspy. He looked as if he were growing more chins behind his first one or like he was melting.

"Emmanuelle!" yelled Sir Gilliot, sternly. "Let him go!"

"That's Prince Emmanuelle to you," he snarled, dropping the knight. The prince broke into chuckles as the dark rolls began to show under his eyes as if something else was trying to kick over.

"Get help," wheezed Sir Hamilton, pointing down the hall.

Emmanuelle kicked Sir Hamilton in the stomach, who was on the floor groaning as he rubbed his hand around his neck. "You're all in this together. Working together, I understand now," he chuckled. "Well guess what, if you want to kill the others or Gabrial you're going to have to go through me first. I won't let you lay a single finger on..."

Sir Gilliot knocked him in his neck with the back of his sword and he fell out cold. The two of them stared at each other, wondering what to say if anyone asked what had happened to him.

"What...what are we going to do?" asked Sir Hamilton, worriedly.

The older knight lifted Emmanuelle, straining, then he tossed the prince over his shoulder. "I'll deal with it," he answered. "And if anyone asks where he is just tell them that he's with Prince Damien."

"Okay," Sir Hamilton said, still running his hand around his neck trying to get the pain to leave.

The older knight smiled as he walked down the hallway carrying the prince over his shoulder. This had been easier than he had anticipated.

Chapter 20

Lost After Dark

Words couldn't have even described how dark

the place was in which he was kept. Not so much of the

light but the atmosphere but the depressing spirits of every

person that came into the room. He had given up trying to

get the ropes around his ankles off. If anything it only

made it worse his wrist were burned and caused them to drip blood on the floor whenever he tried to move them.

Never in Emmanuel's life had he experienced pain, not even grief and now he was getting a taste of what the humans must have felt every day. In a way it made him feel some kind of remorse for their state despite what they had done to him. It wasn't the pain from his scars and punctures, the most painful thing was that he was in this desolate place and far from his home, where he was put to service. At this point, he was only good for laughs and kicks. His wings were covered in dirt so that they no longer showed glory, not only that they were messed up since he had lost so many feathers from them plucking them off like leaves.

He heard a long squeaky noise and he looked over at the door where he saw some light seep in. Although he knew what was coming was not light only shadows. For the *past few weeks, he had heard that sound, and every time he*

heard that sound something dark came along. The light

was only a decoy to get his hopes up that something

pleasant was coming.

Some 1,000 Years Later

*E*mmanuelle awakened with a terrible coughing

spell making the dust on the floor blow across the floor. He

could hear Damien's voice along with a few others. The

knights and his brother were seated in chairs at the table in

the library. Suddenly a sword was thrown at him and he

covered his head. The sword hit the floor and slid across

alongside him.

"Pick it up, dummy," snapped Damien, standing up

from his chair.

His brother slowly stood up on his feet feeling as if

he were drowsy. The sword felt as if it would slip from his

hand and when he looked around everything looked

blurred and as if it were shaking, including his Damien. He touched one side of his head as if trying to regain control of it.

"What's the matter with you? Afraid that you will lose in a sword fight to me even after all these years," chuckled Damien, walking closer to him.

"Swordfight, for…"

Damien didn't allow him to finish and swung his sword down at him; his brother stopped it with his sword but struggled to maintain his balance. The knights watched as the two brothers fought with their swords. Emmanuelle backed down as if to be attacked by a dragon and Damien continually attacked him. A few times they heard Emmanuelle groan a little whenever he was slightly touched by the end of his brother's sword.

"I find it funny how you still haven't learned how to master that sword of yours," teased Damien, pushing harder on him.

The sword was almost too powerful for Emmanuelle to hold off and he was using both of his hands to hold his sword so Damien's wouldn't get him. It felt like trying to stop from caving in with only a straw and a few toothpicks. He leaped out of the way, making Damien fall forward and getting his sword caught in the wall. As much as he knew he had the advantage now as Damien struggled to pull his sword free of the wall, something in him wouldn't allow him to attack him.

He pulled his sword free of the wall, swinging it in the air. "Weak," he laughed. "As you always will be."

"Are you sure of that?" inquired Emmanuelle, breathing heavily.

There was a sudden rage that built up in Damien, he didn't like how his brother questioned him. It was obvious that his brother would never be strong enough to withhold anything. Not the kingdom, not the crown, or anything else. He charged at him, swinging his sword dangerously. Emmanuelle held his sword up and in front of him so that it was lined up with him. He stepped back as his brother drew near to him until he stepped too far and for some reason tripped although there was nothing there.

It all had happened so fast he couldn't break his fall and he landed on the back of his head on the moral that was on the floor. A sudden burst of energy blasted from out of the morale and throughout the room. The knights and Damien turned away, closing their eyes.

The floor beneath Gabrial's feet shook as if there was an earthquake happening somewhere. She couldn't help but look around as she heard screaming and voices all rushing to her at once. The images of Emmanuelle being trapped looked to have been scratching up like some kind of hologram and so did their voices. When she looked up at the platform where the coffin was she saw Erebus, but he looked to have been frantic as he looked at his hands.

"Time is running out, now you must hurry," he growled, sounding angry.

She took one look at the holograms that were scratching up, then at the desperate creature.

"For who?" she inquired, frowning.

He rolled his eyes at her as he reached his ash-looking hand out to her. His nails looked like claws; they were so long and dark. "Come on we know for who," Erebus replied, smartly.

"No," Gabrial said aloud, suddenly.

"Excuse me, but what was that!" he asked, almost chuckling.

"No, I don't believe you."

"Gabrial…"

She turned and looked at the ballroom, there were people, children still waltzing in the ballroom just ghostly.

But unlike the ones that had been once dancing all around them, these looked depressed, enslaved. One of them noticed that she could see them and she realized who it was. Sister Laura or whoever she was.

"Help us," she cried, dancing back and forth.

"Shut up!" Erebus growled, showing his fangs as he began to snarl.

"He's not dead and neither are these people are they?" Gabrial asked, noticing the worried expression.

"I can kill you and take you for myself," he acknowledged, unfurling his dark wings.

"You can't answer with a straight answer," she said. "You used him to try and get me to compromise, he's not…"

She felt as if she were being choked when he pinched his fingers together and she held her neck. "I think you've said enough for tonight, my darling," he snarled, flapping his wings.

He lowered one of his hands so that she would kneel in front of him. Gabrial felt as if her mind was free to wander in so many directions and give orders, but her body was unable to carry any of those orders out because some cord had been broken. She felt his massive and scaly hand grasp hold of her neck. When he lifted her from off the floor by her neck, she felt like she was going to choke as she tried to speak.

"Stop trying Gabrial, you are mine now," he chuckled, watching her suffer.

"I…" she felt his grip on her throat tighten and she thought he had broken something on the inside of it "…will not…allow you to…keep doing this."

He chuckled, deviously. "I don't think you have a choice at this point."

Erebus opened his massive mouth and squeezed her neck even more tightly. It started to feel like a thick, sharp rope had been placed around her neck and was being pulled. His eyes began to glow as he transferred energy from her to himself. Gabrial struggled to try to stop him from doing so but began to feel weaker and weaker as he devoured more from her. Glowing gold strands of light ran into his mouth.

Suddenly his body began to shake as if he were going into a seizure. The more he devoured the more he seemed to turn into a glowing creature of light. His entire body glowed from the inside and out making him look like a light bug.

"Urgh, what are you doing to me?" he groaned, dropping her.

Gabrial landed on the floor, but was unable to move as she watched him grab at himself, hollering and screaming as if he were being burned. He covered his eyes as they began to burn, a bunch of black veins began to scurry across his body and then suddenly froze.

Emmanuelle looked up at his brother as he held the sword near his stomach. At this point, he didn't know what to do.

"Damien, please don't…"

His brother's sword pierced through his stomach without mercy and he felt as if it were too painful to even yell no matter how much he wanted to. The last thing he remembered seeing was his brother above him, shoving the sword further through him. Then everything went blank. Damien looked at the floor as it began to open, Emmanuelle was still in the center of the floor so he wouldn't fall through.

The knights stood up when the room began to quake and a few pieces of stone fell from the ceiling. When they looked over at the place where the compass had once been, they noticed a dark staircase.

Lights flashed from out of the coffin as Erebus stepped back losing control of everything. His eyes widened when he saw his prisoners flying free from the coffin in streaks of brilliant light. Slowly his face began to peel away into what looked like pieces of ash and he couldn't keep himself together no matter how hard he tried to.

"No!" he yelled, watching the lights from the coffin shoot out. Gabrial turned away, afraid to look upon him as he wailed with pain like that under the possession of an evil force. His face cracked into what looked like magma. The creature bent over the coffin. "NOOOOOOO!" Erebus wailed as his body began to evaporate and be swallowed by his creation.

The lake dragged him in no matter how hard he tried to hang on to the outer part of the coffin. There were scratch marks from his nails engraving his prints from his nails. Slowly but surely the people that had been kept captive appeared. They looked upon themselves in astonishment to be themselves once more. The coffin closed and sent out a vivid burst of power throughout the place. Gabrial couldn't help but lie down on the floor. It was over, all over.

****

A little while later she awakened in a bed and she suddenly remembered Emmanuelle. Gabrial got up and out of the bed so quickly she almost fell.

"Where are you going?" inquired a woman, who looked familiar. She was wiping her hands on her apron. "You must rest."

"I have to go back," Gabrial answered, sounding as if she were in a daze.

"To where?"

"To…"

"Mommy! Mommy!" cried a voice.

Suddenly, a little boy came running to the woman. He tugged on her apron, desperately. His soft brown eyes staring up at her.

467

"Yes, Jackson," she answered, calmly, "can't you see that I'm talking to our guest. I've told you over and over that it is rude to interrupt mommy when she's in a conversation."

"But there is a man outside and he's from the Ascedia Kingdom looking for her," he explained, pointing at Gabrial.

The woman's eyes met hers and before either of them said anything Gabrial rushed out of the room. She went outside where she saw a man she somewhat recognized upon a white horse. He had a black mustache and bushy shoulder-length hair. The woman and her son ran outside to catch her but stopped when they noticed other people in the village watching them.

"Prince Emmanuelle sent me on a quest to find a girl by the name of Gabrial," he told her. "Are you the maiden he sent me to find?"

She nodded her head. "Yes, I am Gabrial."

"God smiles upon this day for I have found the one who the prince seeketh," he declared, happily as he rested one of his hands on his heart, "you must come with me." The knight stepped down from the horse and helped her onto the back of it. The villagers stared intensely at her, wondering why he had come for her. Some even tried to lean forward to hear better. Gabrial held onto the horn of the saddle. The knight gave a deep sigh after he climbed on behind her.

"Thank you, Gabrial for saving us," she heard the little boy say.

She turned around to meet his soft brown eyes and his giant smile that glowed as if showing the glow from the inside. She waved to him, happily, although she couldn't quite remember why he was thanking her. Then she saw his mom grab and pull him back, scolding him for blurting things out. The knight whacked the reins and the horse ran faster than lightning, leaving behind a screen of dust as the villagers watched her depart.

✳✳✳✳✳✳✳✳✳✳

The castle was so quiet when she had returned, it was as if it had been abandoned. She looked into the kitchen, where she thought she may have found Maid A'Key and the others.

"Hello, is anyone here?" Gabrial said as she slowly walked inside. "Maid A'Key?"

There was not a single person. The dishes hadn't been washed and there was nothing cooking. She wondered what could've happened to make the place so empty. For a moment she thought she heard talking from on the other side of a door that was on the other end of the kitchen. When she opened the door, she found that the hallway was also empty.

Even the knights, guards, and soldiers were gone. Gabrial wandered up a staircase, following the sound of talking. It led her to the parlor area, where she saw Queen Eliza, along with a girl she had never seen before. The girl had sky blue eyes, hair the color of snow and she wore clothes that looked like rebel clothes. Both of them stared at her as if wanting her to leave them alone.

"And where have you been?" snapped the queen, glaring at her.

She wished she had never run into the queen, all of a sudden. "Gone," she replied, finally, unsure of what else to say.

"That's your highness to you and gone where?" inquired Eliza, playing with her teacup. "It isn't allowed in this palace for servant girls to just go and wander off on trips whenever they please."

Gabrial nodded her head in agreement but thought not to say anything else. It would only give the queen a reason to bother her.

"I should be going, your highness," she told her. "I have much to do."

The queen watched as she left the room. Gabrial closed a door behind herself, not realizing that she had stumbled into the king's bedroom. He was snoring terribly and coughed, appearing to have been suffering terribly in his sleep. She knew she wasn't supposed to be in his room and should have left out as quickly as she could, but she couldn't help but feel somehow like she should help him.

She slowly approached him. He rested on his back, beneath a bunch of blankets. There was a cup of water on a little stand. Gabrial stared at the sleeping king to make sure he wasn't awake. Slowly she put her hand out in front of herself and rested it on his forehead. It felt a little bit more difficult to help him, than the people she had helped to sleep.

Glowing strands of gold began to flow around her hand and into him. She closed her eyes and breathed more slowly trying her hardest best to reach him. The king

began to breathe more comfortably as she continued to do

so. Life began to show again in his face and she pulled her

hand away when his eyelid began to move. She headed for

the door, thinking to leave before he awakened afraid of

his response.

"Is that you, Gabrial," he inquired, sitting up in his

bed.

She knew he was probably going to be angry with

her being in his room. But when she turned to look back at

him she saw a grin on his face. He beckoned for her to

come near to him. Gabrial let go of the doorknob and

walked over to him.

"I was wrong about you," Charles declared, staring

at her.

"I'm sorry I intruded into your room, sir," she

apologized, nervously.

"You saved my life, if anything I should be thanking you," he said. "You're not like the others or the one my father told me about. Evil, uncaring, selfish, or any of those things."

She looked at him, wondering if he knew.

"At first I thought you were just a peasant girl who was just seeking a great, easy place to live," he declared looking at the floor, "but now I see different, you truly are good at heart and not just trying to keep up an image."

His words almost made her blush. "You are very kind, your highness," she said.

"I am much obliged to you and thank you," King Charles said, nodding his head. He sighed a little before standing up. "I guess there's no better time than the present to start something. I will see you soon."

She smiled, then headed for the door leaving the king alone.

"Oh and please, if you see Emmanuelle tell him…"

"Your highness you are conscious," cried the nurse as he charged into the room.

Gabrial took one last look back at the king as he smiled at her. It was as if the two of them were exchanging a message, then he nodded his head at her as if telling her that her secret was safe with him. She smiled, then left out the door.

"Gabrial, you're back," cried Maid A'Key, grabbing hold of her so quickly to embrace her that she was surprised. "Oh darling, I missed you so much. Look at you, dressed as if you had been at some kind of ball.

She blushed a little, the dress was pretty, but the place it had come from was a place she had rather left in the past. "I'm so happy to see that you are doing well," she replied.

"You speak as if I were ill," teased the maid, waving her finger. "Now old Maid A'Key may have some years, but she is not quite ready to be ill."

The two of them broke into laughter. It was just like the first day she had met the maid, not a thing had changed about her. Not her smile. Not her personality. Not even her hair. It was just like the Maid A'Key she remembered. Now that she was here, she saw things differently. It was so much more joyful somehow and she realized how much she had missed this place.

"Oh Gabrial you don't know how it's been here these past few weeks without you," declared the maid as the two of them started to walk along the hallway. "I mean take the princes for instance."

It suddenly all came back to her that she hadn't seen Emmanuelle and she was worried about how he may have been. "Do you know where I may be able to find Emmanuelle?" she inquired, hastily.

The maid looked almost as if she had been slammed with a bookshelf when she said his name. "I'm sorry, but I'm afraid that he is dead," she admitted nervously.

Everything about her dreams collapsed in on her and immediately the smile was wiped away from her face. This couldn't be happening. How could he have been dead? Erebus had been locked away for good, it should have never affected him. Gabrial turned away from the maid feeling as if her heart had completely been taken from her. He couldn't die, not with those thoughts of believing that she didn't love him and not knowing the truth.

"Do you know where I can find him?" she asked, sounding as if her voice were muffled by something.

"His room for they are preparing the...Gabrial wait, you can't go in there," cried the maid, chasing after her.

Before she could catch up with her she vanished around a corner and Maid A'Key decided that there was no use in trying to stop her. No matter what she tried to do she knew that Gabrial would not allow it to keep her from seeing him, even if the image of him being in the condition he was in was awful.

✳✳✳✳✳✳✳✳✳✳

The prince's door was shut, then it slowly opened when Gabrial pushed on it. She saw him lying in his bed, his face was so lifeless and pale. There were a few bruises and scratches on it as if he had been in a fight. When she was close enough to his bed, she knelt beside it and rested her head on his bed, wishing she could just feel his hand stroke her hair so she would know that he was still alive, but to her disappointment, he didn't.

She sat up, then looked at her hands. Her powers may have been strong enough to heal people of sickness and pain or anything like that, but she wasn't sure if it would be strong enough to save him. But looking at him like this was terrible and she had to do something. Gabrial placed her hand on his forehead and tried to transfer her

478

energy to him, but when she tried the golden strands of glowing gold flowed around her wrist and to him, but then stopped and she felt as if something were jammed between the two of them.

It made her feel completely hopeless and she let her head fall onto him and she began to cry.

"I'm sorry, Emmanuelle," she cried, then she thought to try one last thing to save him.

Gabrial climbed onto his bed with him, keeping her eyes focused on his face. Something had to work to save him. If she couldn't save him, then she wondered why she even still had powers. She slowly laid her body against his feeling the coldness of his becoming warm as she became closer to him. Her head rested against his heart and she placed her hands on either of his sides.

The golden glow began to transfer from her hands and body into him. Slowly curls of the glowing gold strands appeared on his face. She could feel as the power was exchanged from her to him and he began to heal, but she started to feel the pain he had no doubt felt when it all occurred to him. It was something that had never happened to her when she had done so. Her eyelids became heavy and they closed and she lost control of what she was doing.

Emmanuelle sat up in his bed as if he had only been asleep, he rubbed the sleep out of his eyes. "Gabrial!" he called, looking around his room, convinced that he had heard her.

He pulled his blanket off himself and got out of the bed, believing that she may have been somewhere near the pavilion like he had told her the other day. When he stood up he immediately noticed her on the side of his bed on the floor.

"Gabrial," Emmanuelle said, walking around his bed to see what was wrong with her. He lifted her a little. "Gabrial?"

A smile appeared on her face and she reached her hand out to touch him again. His face felt so smooth like she had remembered. He looked a little confused as if wondering why she was being so strange.

"Is everything alright?" he inquired.

"It is now," Gabrial cried, happily. "You're alright."

She embraced him warmly. Now he felt very confused, but he ignored it thinking that maybe she hadn't slept very well in a few days and was not thinking straight. Gabrial felt like everything was going to turn out just perfect now. He was fine and after all this, she would never leave him again.

As If There were Stars

Chapter 21

You Changed My Mind

Arsonist awakened on the battlefield feeling

as if she had a weight inside of her head. When she looked

up she saw Othniel, hovering over her. Immediately she

wondered where Armistice and the others had gone. She

stood up feeling a little shaky on her feet and he put his

massive hand on her shoulder to give her support.

"The others have headed for the prison, they believe they'll find the prisoners," he explained.

"I must help them," she cried, attempting to flap her wings, then suddenly felt a surge of pain run through her body and to her head.

"Are you sure you're up for that?" he asked, concernedly.

"I think so," she replied, rubbing the side of her head.

The massive iron angel nodded his head in agreement, then flapped his wings, sending a storm of dirt back at her. Arsonist was finally able to move her wings again and she didn't fall to the ground like she had done the first time. She followed behind him for a while until she noticed her necklace was glowing. Not once had she seen it glow, but there was something strangely familiar about it. The necklace flowed around her neck as if pointing the opposite way of where Othniel was heading.

She thought to ignore it and continue, but when she tried to follow him she felt the sudden weakness again and she thought she may fall again. In a way she kind of understood what it must have meant so when he wasn't looking she turned and flew the opposite way of him, hoping that her necklace wasn't leading her into more danger than she could handle.

Some 1,000 Years Later

Praise that both the king and Prince Emmanuelle being healed went throughout the kingdom. Though there were some that had been skeptical believing that the king may not have been sick at all and they hardly believed his son had been dead, after all, he was living now. Miracles like that just didn't seem to occur and they were convinced that it could've been a part of some scheme that was happening within the royal family. Either way, the prince and his father didn't pay much attention to their opinions, they were just grateful to be alive.

The roses always bloomed a vivid crimson red in the early spring, giving the garden behind the castle a radiant kind of look. There were many fountains and statues placed throughout it and there was even a stream that flowed through the garden.

"For you, my lady," said Emmanuelle, giving Gabrial a rose he had just picked.

"Thank you," she replied, looking at the rose.

"You know I had one of the strangest dreams, the night before last night," he announced, looking at her as she touched the soft petals of the rose. "You had gone off somewhere and I had gone after you and there were so many strange things that happened after that, some parts I kind of enjoyed like there was this time I… there were just some enjoyable moments."

It was a little strange, although it was obvious that he had thought that everything that had occurred to them was just a dream and she thought that maybe that was a good thing. At least he wouldn't have to deal with feeling like he had messed everything up. Gabrial sat down on a marble bench to settle for a moment. The prince looked back at her just thinking of all the strange feelings he was feeling for her. He was nervous, excited, happy, unsure and so many other things all at once. He didn't want her to refuse him if he asked, but then if he never asked he would continually be vexed by all these feelings. Emmanuelle didn't know which was worse.

She looked so happy and at peace and he didn't want to seem like he was bothering her. But he couldn't shake off how he felt either. Everytime he looked at her soft, pale blue eyes and even touched her, he felt as if he was going to lose his breath. He had to try, if she refused him he was just going to have to find a way to accept it. The prince slowly approached her.

"Gabrial, I have something to ask you," he told her, nervously.

When she looked up at him and smiled at him, it only made things worse to see her eyes sparkling in the sun's light and he was sure she could see straight through him. If he asked her, she was going to tear him in two with the word 'no'.

"I...um...oh no," Emmanuelle muttered.

He knew he had messed up, he hadn't even started properly. Right now he wished someone would just kick him and make him go through with what he had to say. The words felt like coming out of his mouth, it was just every time he tried to put them together it was like they got caught in his throat or like his tongue had been tied in a knot. Things were so much easier when he was a lion, for some reason he never had a problem telling her anything when he was like that.

"Is everything okay, Emmanuelle?" she inquired, noticing that he seemed to have been fidgeting.

"Yes. Everything is okay or it will be once I figure out how to say this," he declared, watching as she stood up in front of him.

"Say what?"

"I would be more than honored if you would be…" Emmanuelle bit his lower lip, he couldn't bring himself to ask her for some reason "… my friend."

She smiled at him trying not to laugh. "I thought we were," she replied.

"Oh yes. We are, I mean. Take it a little further," his words became more jumbled the harder he tried to speak and it made him feel so silly.

"And what do you mean by that?" inquired Gabrial, looking up at him.

Now he didn't know what to say to her, it was like everything he wanted to say was fleeing from his tongue like a runaway horse and wagon. Emmanuelle tried to grin to hide how awkward he was feeling. He just knew he messed up or beyond messed up and he suddenly wished he hadn't even attempted to say anything.

"That we should… Ummmmmmmm… evolve a little more with it," he explained, hastily. "Like…"It was one of those times he wished someone would just come and interrupt and say he was needed somewhere "…do you like flowers?"

"Emmanuelle, what is on your mind?" Gabrial asked him, noticing how bad he was stammering. "It's better to get burdens off your shoulders by discussing it with someone and you know I will help you."

He sighed deeply, wishing it was just as easy as she made it out to be. Despite everything they'd been through he somehow still struggled to tell her certain things no matter how much he tried to change. The prince turned around when he heard someone coming. When he turned around he saw Sir Hamilton.

"I'm sorry, sir, I hope I am not disturbing you," he told him.

"No, not at all," Emmanuelle said, feeling relief take over. "Gabrial, I'm sorry but I have to go and Sir Hamilton has something to do before the ball and it almost slipped my mind."

"We do, your highness?"

"Yes, actually we do," chuckled the prince, wrapping his arm around the knight as if to make sure he got the message.

"Oh yeah," laughed Sir Hamilton, playing along. "That is exactly why I came to get you, sir."

"Can we talk more later, Gabrial?" he inquired, smiling at her as he hoped she didn't know how he was trying to escape the mess he had started.

She nodded her head, knowing that he was trying to escape her. She didn't understand why he was so afraid to ask her anything. By now he had to know that she would never cut into him, no matter what he said. Gabrial watched as he and the knight left the garden.

"Later, remember," he assured her, cocking an eyebrow at her.

There was a slight bit of breeze that blew past her face after they left. Gabrial started to walk through the garden. Crossing over a little wooden bridge that ran over a little stream. She stopped and looked down at the clearness of it, then noticed some little fishes swimming around, almost looking transparent. He would get around to telling her about whatever was bothering him, in his

own time or so she hoped. She wanted him to trust her,
knowing that she would never criticize him for anything he
said.

Emmanuelle closed the door to the sitting room.
The fireplace crackled looking like a group of screaming
flowers made of fire. He watched as Sir Hamilton sat down
in a chair at a table in the room. He gave a deep sigh as if
he were relaxing. The prince picked up a book that he saw
hanging off the edge of a bookshelf. He browsed through a
few pages.

"So is there any specific reason you brought me in
here, your highness?" inquired Sir Hamilton, slouching in
his chair? "Or did you just want a little company?"

"No," answered Emmanuelle, closing the book
with one of his hands. "I mean, I need some help. I mean
serious help right now," declared the prince leaning over
the table.

"How serious is this problem, because you know if it's too serious I may have to get the other knights and soldiers to…"

"No, not like that," he answered, standing upright again. "It's Gabrial and…"

The knight waited a few moments for the prince to finish what he was going to say. "And what, your highness?" he inquired, noticing the blank expression on his face.

"I think she's going to say no," finished the prince, nervously.

Sir Hamilton broke into laughter. "Say no, is that serious your highness? I mean, say no to what?"

Emmanuelle didn't answer him, he just gave the knight a long peaceful silence. His eyes staring at him as if he already knew what she was going to say 'no' to.

"Oh, you want to take her to the ball, is that what this is all about?" Sir Hamilton answered, catching on.

"Yes and I don't know what to say to her. I don't even know how to ask her," he acknowledged, shaking his head. "I do know, but then it's like I don't know how to keep the words in my head to say for my mouth to speak. I don't know!"

"She's just some old peasant girl, she couldn't say no to the prince even if she…"

"She's not just some old peasant girl. She's… So much more, beyond even a magnificent person," argued the prince. "And she can say 'no' to anything she wants to," Emmanuelle realized what he said. "I mean I don't want her to say no to me but…" he growled in frustration.

"You do have a thing for this girl, don't you, sir?" chuckled Sir Hamilton, looking at the prince, who had his hands on his head as he looked at the floor.

"I owe it to her is more of the reason I'm trying to ask her," Emmanuelle stated.

"Well I'm sorry your highness but all I can tell you is this. Tell her the truth. Tell her what you'd like her to say before she says anything and most importantly tell her how you feel," chuckled Sir Hamilton, taking out his flute. "Play music for her, write her a poem or sonnet. A song, do something that might impress her that no one has ever done. In other words, change her mind before she even says the word is my advice."

The knight pulled his legs up into the chair and crossed them and started to play a soft tune with his flute. The prince watched him for a moment thinking of something to do that might change her mind or something that might impress her. Then it came to him what he was going to do for her.

"I think I have an idea," he declared, happily. "Thank you, Sir Hamilton." He rushed for the door leaving in a hurry.

"For what?" asked the knight, being answered by the door.

He shrugged, then began to play his flute again. If it were important he was sure he would find out about it sooner or later.

****

Damien's torch began to dwindle as he and the knights walked down the snaking, long staircase that was so dark you could almost feel its presence. The torch was almost not even worth having when the place was so dark. Suddenly the staircase came to an end after hours of walking.

He opened the book that one of the knights had been holding. He flipped through the pages, looking for the right place to find what he was looking for. When he struggled to go through the pages with one hand, he decided to hand the torch to Sir Kelvin, who was right beside him. Immediately the knight grew frightened when the fire seemed to leak from off the torch and he yelled, throwing the torch.

"Noooo!" cried Damien trying to stop the torch before it touched the book.

Unfortunately, his efforts were unable to prevent the torch from falling onto the book that Sir Gilliot held, only noticing at the last minute the torch. He dropped the book to the floor, diving out of the way. The fire devoured the book page by page without mercy. Damien grunting, annoyedly as he stepped on the book trying to put out the fire knowing that it was hopeless now.

"What were you doing, you incompetent fool!" snarled Damien, approaching Sir Kelvin dangerously.

"I'm sorry sir. It was an accident, sir," the knight stammered. "Honest."

The prince was so angry he could've killed the knight with his sword and he may have if he wasn't surprised by a massive current of wind that blew through the place carrying the sound that someone was breathing. The knights gasped, worriedly as they looked around only to see darkness. Suddenly there were torches that all lit up in the place all at once making it so they were able to discern what was in the place.

They all gasped as wonder-filled their minds. The floor looked to have been made of pure glass. It was so clear or even water that had somehow been stuck in the solid form. There were columns built of stones that had vines winding around them and there looked to have been other corridors, but they were pitch black and they weren't sure if it was a good idea to venture off into them at least not yet.

"My goodness," they heard Damien say.

He was standing in front of what looked like some kind of wall that had been shaped like the sun from a child's picture. It had rays on the outside of it and between those rays were skeletal-looking creatures with wings. One of them looked to have been trying to creep over the boundary of the center of the sun shape. In the circular part of the sun was a woman carved into it seeming to be tied on a cross and above her head was a being that had a hood over their head so they couldn't make out who or what it was. On her right side was a bunch of skeletal beings that had wings, looking to have been attacking her.

On her right side were what looked to have been angels, a few of them blew trumpets as if to make the other creatures leave. Beneath her feet was a much larger angel and skeletal creature. The two of them looked to have been trying to kill each other, but it looked like the skeletal creature was winning and was pushing the knife closer to the angel to kill him and he looked to be struggling to keep it from reaching him.

"Damien, look down, there is a little nitch," gasped the faint voice.

The prince knelt and moved his hand around the surface of the stone, only getting a bunch of dust on his fingers that made them look like ink. Then his hand felt something, it was a nitch just like the voice had told him. He reached inside but was surprised when he got a handful of millipedes in his hand. They were miles long and thick as a semi-truck. Damien's eyes widened and he whacked his hand away quickly. The insects went scurrying across the floor in all kinds of directions, then vanished into the darkness.

Sir Gilliot and the others looked over at him to see if he were okay and they saw him pull out what looked like another book. He blew across the surface of it so all the dust would fly off of it. Some of the dust got into the air and caused Sir Pelacio to sneeze.

"Ga zone tight," said Sir Kelvin, pulling out a handkerchief and handing it to him.

"Look at this," Damien told them as he flashed through the book, excitedly. "The other book didn't have pieces torn out of it, there was another half of it."

"So, the person just decided to split the book in half, sir, big deal," snapped Sir Gilliot, unamused as he rolled his eyes.

"But why?" inquired Damien, waving his finger. "Nothing is just ever done out of just the impulse of actions, everything has a reason and I'm going to get to the bottom of it all."

They gave each other a bunch of weary-eyed looks as if knowing what those words meant for them. Another long quest to who knew where. They just hoped they wouldn't be digging up the cemetery next.

✳✳✳✳✳✳✳✳✳✳✳✳

Gabrial sat on her balcony, looking off into the sunset. She hadn't realized how much she had missed this place while she was gone. The fresh air and the freeness it brought to her were somehow all very consoling. Her cat climbed onto the banister of the balcony, then carefully walked across.

"Oh, come here," she laughed, picking up the cat. "You shouldn't be up there, you could hurt yourself."

"Meow," went the cat, staring up at her as if confused.

She laughed again at how much she had missed him also. She walked into her room, moving past the silky curtains that flowed in the wind. Her bedroom was lit up by a bunch of candles she had placed in a certain pattern. In the center of her room, she had decorated a small table with the roses the prince had given her. There was one thing she had forgotten to put away and that was her dresses. They were lying across her bed and she only noticed them when she had laid down on them.

"Do you think he'll like it?" Gabrial asked her cat.

The cat responded to her question by rubbing his head against her shoulder.

"You're right, I think he will too," she said, happily as she stepped from off of her bed.

The dresses were placed inside her wardrobe in a certain order. Tonight she was going to finally do something right or so she hoped. Emmanuelle wasn't very picky about things, but still, she wanted to do her best for him. Doing anything for him just because he wasn't picky wouldn't show how much she appreciated having him in her life. There was a knock on her door and her heart felt like it had stopped for a moment, then she took a deep breath and looked at her cat.

"Gabrial," she heard the prince call. "I would like to finish speaking with you now if you're not too occupied or tired."

"Just a moment," she answered, smiling at her cat as she placed the last dress in order with the other ones.

"Take your time," he said, happily.

Emmanuelle couldn't wait for her to come out, he had a wonderful surprise for her and he was going to finally be able to ask her to go with him to the ball since he had all the words he was going to say written out on a sheet of paper. Now he didn't have much of a fear that he would mess up by jumbling his words or something.

He fixed his sleeves so that they were perfect, then stood upright. He noticed a little window outside her room and looked into it to make sure his hair was still in order. When he saw that a piece of his hair was out of place he moved it back into place, then fixed the collar of his jacket. The prince couldn't help but smile at himself when he saw how nice he looked. This was going to be a night he would want to remember forever because it was going to be the night he finally took a step forward and not backward.

"Tonight's the night," he said to himself as he looked into the glass.

Chapter 22

A Night Away

There were now storms of fiery arrows, stones

that rained from the sky like hail, along with the shouting

of men as they attacked the remnant of iron angels. Unlike

the warriors they had faced before, these were far more

advanced, some looked to have been like their own.

Wearing iron helmets in the shapes of serpents and

animals. They even had sharp claws made of steel and the

ends of their iron gloves. Armistice and the others didn't

know how the human world could've advanced in their armor and weapons.

Laonacia laid siege to one of the creatures that dared to stop her from entering the prison area. His eyes were pitch black as if he had none at all. He roared, swinging his massive hand of steel in the air to knock her down. She took out her spear, stretching it out in front of her, then pierced straight through his armor. The creature gave a growl of pain, then slowly fell back to the ground.

The other angels had already begun to do the same with the others. Armistice looked to the skies when she thought she heard something familiar. Suddenly her eyes caught sight of a great winged being, who was shielded by his iron armor and he wore the steel mask that was shaped like a hound. He came down onto the ground with such impact that it almost knocked everyone off balance.

"I lost her," Othniel told her, worriedly. "I lost

her."

"Arsonist?" she inquired.

His dark eyes met hers and she knew that just by

the look he was giving her that he was telling her 'yes.'

Some 1,000 Years Later

Slowly the door to her room opened. The first

thing she noticed was Emmanuelle looking to have been

rehearsing something. He looked nervous or awkward

when he saw that she had opened the door. The prince

quickly hid his sheet of paper in his pocket as if to act that

he wasn't doing anything.

"You look very formal tonight," Gabrial said,

smiling at him.

"Oh yeah, I had something formal to go to, but it's over now and I decided to just leave it on," Emmanuelle explained, quickly.

"I think it makes you look very pleasant," she complimented.

"You do? I mean, thank you," he replied, feeling as if his mind was going to blow.

She walked back inside her room and he thought to follow her, but he didn't want to seem like he was intruding. It was her room and space.

"You can come inside," she laughed, noticing his expression.

The prince walked inside immediately, noticing the table that was so neatly decorated and made. He saw the roses he had given her in a little glass full of water. It made him wonder if she had been expecting someone.

"Gabrial, were you expecting someone or had other plans?" he inquired, looking around the room from her. "I can leave and we can talk sometime tomorrow."

"Expecting someone," he heard her voice from another corner. "No, only you."

She emerged from around the corner and when he turned around he saw her in a long dress that looked like the galaxy. The dark black faded into blue and the blue faded into a greenish-blue. It sparkled a little whenever the light flashed on it. The only thing it was missing was a necklace that was made of diamonds. Her hair was pinned up in a halo braid that crossed over her bang.

"I don't quite remember that dress," he admitted as he approached her. "But it's just as beautiful as the one wearing it."

The prince took her by surprise when he wrapped his arms around her and leaned her back. There was a glow in his eyes when she looked at him. He wasn't just here to talk about what he had been saying earlier, she could tell by the way he was acting. A grin appeared on his face as happiness flooded over him. His heart just wanted to fall from him and let everything he was thinking in his mind become words that were so poetic and carried such a rhythm that even he wouldn't realize what he was saying. He knew the words, but then it was like he didn't know them. Even his paper couldn't come close to what he was feeling for her and the things he wanted to say.

"A lovely night to go exploring," Emmanuelle declared, trying to snap out of his daydream.

"Yes, it is," answered Gabrial. "But where?"

"That's a surprise. The real question is will you join me, I mean…" he began to chuckle, bashfully "…as a friend so we can finish what we were talking about earlier. It's important.

The way he was speaking in such a jumbled but kind of normal way made her smile. He was just himself, nervous, despite being a prince, but very thoughtful at the same time.

"Of course," she told him.

His face almost lit up like a candle, when he heard that she would go with him. Emmanuelle took her by the hand, slowly, then led her toward the door.

"Oh," she said, remembering that she was forgetting something.

"What is it?" he asked, nervously.

Gabrial picked up a dark cape that was red on the inside. The prince looked at it, remembering the one he had lost. This one was far better than that one though. He looked at it in astonishment, he couldn't remember a time when someone had given him something except for when he was a boy and that was only from his dad. She gave it to him slowly, noticing the expression on his face.

"Is there something wrong with it?" she asked, finally.

He looked up from the cape, then a grin appeared on his face. "No, I love it. It's just… I don't know what to say. Thank you," Emmanuelle told her as he brought her closer so he could hug her. "Now it's my turn for surprises."

****

The prince and Gabrial went down a staircase that led to the hallway, where the library was located. It was now lit by a bunch of candles and was very bright even though it was night. For the most part, the halls were empty, there were only a few guards they walked past ever so often.

"I still can't believe how quickly my father recovered, it still amazes me," he declared, moving closer to her. "He was so ill and with a disease that even the nurse couldn't identify and it just cleared up as if it were never there."

She smiled a little, if only he had known how he had been. He was way worse off than his father and he had still survived. "Miracles do happen," Gabrial said, happily. "Some smaller than others and some greater."

"Years ago I probably wouldn't believe in such a thing, but after everything that has happened over the past few months, I don't doubt anything is possible," he replied. "Not even that there is a God that watches over this world and maybe angels."

There was kind of a doubtfulness in his voice when he mentioned 'angels' as if he wasn't sure that they existed. Suddenly the library door swung open and she was grabbed by Emmanuelle, who had stepped in front of the door to stop it from hitting her.

"Are you okay?" he inquired, holding the door.

"Yes, thank you," she said, startled.

He nodded his head at her, the grin still on his face. Then he turned and looked at the door when he heard laughter that sounded sickly, but somehow familiar. Damien emerged from the other side of the doorway, he immediately stopped and glared at his brother as if disappointed or confused.

"I killed you," he muttered, silently.

"What?" asked Emmanuelle, catching only a few of his words.

"You're not alive, you're dead," chuckled Damien, stepping closer to him. "You were stabbed to death. I was sure of it."

"I'm not dead, if I were I wouldn't be standing here tonight," he chuckled, softly meeting his brother's cold blue eyes. "Look I know we've had our differences, but proclaiming me to be dead won't solve anything."

"Dear mother," cried Sir Pelacio, when he walked into the hallway, also noticing the prince. "He's dead, he couldn't have risen from the dead, it's not possible."

"What are you men talking about?" laughed Emmanuelle, confusedly. "I'm here and alive."

Damien noticed Gabrial behind his brother and realized that it may not have been possible unless he was healed by an angel. Now he knew for certain that she had powers, but there was no telling what kind. She could grant him immortality, wings of his own, and the list could've gone on.

"You healed him, didn't you?" the prince asked, attempting to walk closer to her. "You know he was dead, but you couldn't just let him die, could you? If you can save him with your powers, then give me what I want."

Her eyes looked over at him when she realized he was talking to her. Emmanuelle gave his brother a warning look to stop talking and he acted as if he hadn't seen it at all.

"Damien, you need to stop this," he warned him as he moved away from the door. "So I'm not dead aren't you at least…"

"Should've died, you must be crazy to think I'd ever been satisfied with you being alive," snapped Damien. "I could've had everything I wanted if you were dead."

For a moment everything fell silent as Emmanuelle stared at his brother feeling like a rock had been thrown at his head for the seventh time. He knew he had messed up in the past, but now that he was back he was kind of hoping to establish things between the two of them. But now that seemed like that would just remain as a dream and only that. He still wanted the crown and he wanted him dead just as bad as a rat wanting to be free of a trap.

"Gabrial, I think we should leave," he told her without turning around.

"You? Yes, you may leave, but her. No," announced Damien, glaring at her.

"I don't have to put up with this," chuckled Emmanuelle, frustratedly.

"Then don't," laughed his brother. "Leave like you said you were."

"You don't run everyone around here," he argued, stepping closer to his brother, who was standing on his toes so that he was leveled up with his brother.

"You haven't been around, dead man, so I don't know who else could," chuckled Damien, giving him a devious grin. "I certainly hope you don't think you run things at your young age. Why you are younger than me."

"Wrong," laughed Emmanuelle, annoyedly as he glared at him. "Do you even know what you are saying these days because to me you are starting to sound…"

"Oh dear brother, I'm a lot of things but not crazy and we have plenty of witnesses that knew you were dead," he explained, glaring over at Gabrial. "No one has ever lived again after death, only Christ and you are certainly nothing like him. That girl has powers and both you and I know that."

"She's no witch," snapped the prince, fuming with anger.

"Then explain how you lived."

"I never died," answered Emmanuelle, feeling like his head had a cramp inside of it. For some reason, he still couldn't convince himself that he hadn't, but he kept feeling like he remembered some kind of darkness that had imprisoned him. It had felt like he was bound in chains of shadows that vexed him every moment when he had been at that place. "Damien I advise you to stop running that creature of yours. I don't feel like I can deal with it tonight."

His brother shook his head, smiling at him. "Look at you after all these years you still haven't learned who's in control of things."

"Emmanuelle, please don't argue with your brother," she begged him as she grabbed hold of his hand. He turned and looked at her as he began to feel the rising anger or pain slowly go away. "I don't want to cause conflict between you."

"Let the little peasant girl speak the message," he teased, trying to annoy him.

"Will you ever be quiet," growled Emmanuelle, pulling his hand away from her.

"Emmanuelle, please don't," she cried.

Damien glared at her, then made a daring few steps toward her, but was stopped by his brother. He gave him a deceitful smile as he looked at his soft brown eyes that looked to show so much weakness just like when he was a boy. "And you think you're little stepping in front of her is going to stop me?" he laughed, pushing up even more on his toes so that he was in Emmanuelle's face.

"I intend to keep things…"

Before he finished he was punched in his face so hard by his brother that it almost knocked him backward. He groaned a little and Gabrial quickly moved closer to him to make sure he was alright. His lip was busted and so was his nose, crimson red blood ran down from his nose and onto his lip like a stream.

"Here," offered Gabrial as she handed him a handkerchief.

"You can't stop me from anything, so why would you even try," Damien acknowledged, looking down at him. "Stop trying to fight, you're weak and you can't even protect yourself so what makes you think you can protect anyone else?"

He narrowed his eyes at him just when he felt like grabbing his brother. It almost hurt not to get him as much as he wanted to, but something was keeping him from doing so. He didn't know what it was, but he had sometimes felt it even as a lion before he had met her. There was always something keeping him from hurting anyone no matter how much they hurt him and how much his heart would ache to hurt them back. For some reason, he couldn't bring himself to do it and he took her hand in his as if to make sure she was still with him.

Damien chuckled, sinisterly as he watched Emmanuelle walk down the hall leaving him behind with Sir Pelacio. "This isn't over yet for either of you and I mean that," he bellowed as he watched them turn down another hallway. "Especially not for you my dear brother."

****

Dust trailed behind massive wagons that were pulled by what looked like an ostrich mixed with a dog since it had a tail and paws instead of the toes it normally had. What made it look like a wolf was its hairy face that

523

had a golden beak sticking from underneath all the fur. Esmeralda closed her book when something on the wagon caught her eyes. Immediately she stood up when she saw the name of the kingdom she had first landed in and first ran across her sister.

She tore the paper from off the moving wagon and looked at it, letting her eyes scan across the paper like a pair of lasers taking in all the information. When she saw that there was going to be a ball being held in the kingdom, the first thing she thought of was her sister being there. After all, her sister had left with the prince in the arena.

A grin appeared on her face when she thought she may have another chance at getting her sister so that the two of them could go home. Things would go back to normal in both the human world and there's. Then they would both be happy, their father could work something out so that neither of them would have to die.

It was a brilliant idea. She looked back when she heard her hawk making screeching noises. Perhaps she wouldn't have to go alone, the palace would be heavily guarded since it was a ball and they wouldn't just allow anyone into the building. In that situation, she would most definitely need help and she was sure Achmed wouldn't mind helping her, not if there was something in it for him, anyway. Esmeralda let the hawk land on her arm when it decided to fly down from the building above.

The hawk had feathers that were as silver as the speckles that had been on Gabrial's wings that had sparkled every night and sometimes even during the day, sometimes leaving a storm of star-like flurry's in the air whenever she flapped or was nervous. Now the wings she had once bared had been taken by their father and kept as his souvenir or trophy behind a glass in the place they had been fighting. She petted the hawk, gently as if stroking her sister's hair when the two of them were girls. The feathers were soft and fluffy making her miss her own with her wings she had felt so free and powerful without them her back felt so bare and lifeless and she didn't feel that power she had felt with them.

It wouldn't be long now before the two of them would be doing those things again. Everything about her success in her plan just made her heart feel like it was fluttering like the wings of a butterfly.

****

The prince and Gabrial had finally reached the place he had been trying to take her. It had been the garden, except it was far more dreamy at night. The trees had some kind of substance on them that made them sparkle as if it were winter, all except the leaves were on the trees and plants and it was during the spring. In the midst of the garden over the little bridge she had crossed earlier, she noticed a bunch of doves looking to have been waiting patiently for something. There was also a table with a candle and rose petals scattered all across it.

Gabrial looked up at him, knowing that he must have had something to do with it. Even though the soreness of his face he was able to return her a smile. He reached for her hand, slowly without looking down, being careful to keep his eyes focused on her face. The prince began to kneel in front of her and she thought to do the same until he stopped her and made her stand in front of him. She grew confused, he was the prince he wasn't supposed to bow before anyone especially not his maids or servants.

"I don't know how to say this," he started, nervously. "For quite some time now I have been waiting for this moment to ask you…" he took a slow deep breath, then looked up to meet her soft pale blue eyes. They looked as if they were aflame or like there had been a light shining into even the darkest parts of the eye so that the true color of them could show. She looked almost like she was blushing as a smile tried to make its way onto her face "... I know it must be old by now but you look so beautiful I would have thought I was dreaming."

Her head turned as she lowered her head and pushed a piece of loose hair behind her ear trying to hide how badly she was blushing. "Thank you," she replied.

"I'm sure you must be told a lot how charming and calm you are."

"Actually, no," Emmanuelle chuckled. "But besides your beauty, you have brought me great pleasure since you entered my life and I must admit for the past few weeks I have been with you I have felt something I have never felt before."

Immediately she looked at him, wondering if he could have been feeling what she had been feeling for the weeks they had been together. He could've easily not have said anything about it, afraid that she hadn't felt the same way. In his eyes now she could read the whole message and it was like she had been wearing a blindfold for so long she had forgotten she had been wearing one in the beginning, but now she thought she may have seen what was truly there.

"It's been a little confusing, I know with the princesses, but the truth is none of that is real," the prince told her, standing upright in front of her. "There was nothing there when I came in contact with them, unlike you. There's something there whenever I'm in contact with you, it makes me feel--I don't know--alive somehow or enlightened in places that were dark."

"I felt the same way," admitted Gabrial, finally looking straight up at him. "I don't understand it, but I don't believe it's wrong."

His heart felt like it had almost stopped when he heard her say those words. It felt like a heavy weight had been lifted off his chest. He almost chuckled trying to contain all the feelings he was feeling right then. His stomach felt like butterflies were fluttering inside of it or like he had lost his heart.

"Honestly?" the prince was finally able to say.

"Yes," answered Gabrial, happily.

"Then I'm not wrong or I wasn't, those feelings whenever we were together weren't just my own," he acknowledged, realizing what must have been happening. "They were both of ours. That's why it was stronger whenever we came in contact."

She nodded her head in agreement as she watched his face glow like a candle with happiness. "Emmanuelle?"

"You're the one I would love to have come with me to the ball," he said, as he lifted her. "I'd dance with no one else but you. That's if you want to accompany me, I mean," he finished, setting her down and rubbing the back of his head.

"Of course, I'd love to accompany you there," Gabrial answered happily as she cupped his face in her hands, then she suddenly wondered what she was even thinking. He was still a prince, even if he wanted her with him at the ball she wasn't sure how he would feel once he was there and with her once they were around all the others.

"And don't worry, you will not embarrass me," he laughed as if reading her mind. "If they can't accept you, then pretend like they're not even there. I mean it shouldn't be a problem for them at least it's not them with you."

"You're right," she said as he moved closer to her face.

Slowly his face grew nearer to hers and he kissed her. His heart felt such an explosion of excitement on the inside of him that it felt like it may leap from out of his chest. She smiled as she looked down at the ground.

"There is one last thing I have planned before this night is over," he told her as he took her hands in his.

"Oh and what might that be?" she inquired.

"Follow me and you will soon know," Emmanuelle told her.

The prince led her across the bridge of the little rushing stream that ran over stones that were the size of maple leaves. Tomorrow was the night of the ball and she couldn't wait, although she did feel a little nervous. On the other side of the stream was the table he had set up. The vivid white of both the chairs and table cloth almost looked like it had been sprinkled with stardust whenever a few of the pieces of the sparkling plants fell and glinted in the moon's light. The place looked like something from a

snow castle in the summer. Emmanuelle pulled out a chair

for her.

"Thank you," Gabrial said, taking a seat.

He nodded his head. "Of course, it is quite an honor

to serve you Madam Gabrial," he replied, taking a little

bow in front of her. "Can I get you anything special?"

"Emmanuelle," she laughed, listening to how his

voice had changed to a much more debonair voice. He

looked up from the ground with one of his hands behind

his back and the other in front of him still. She noticed him

cock an eyebrow at her and she wondered if he had been

serious. "Well since you ask, could you tell me where to

find an optimistic prince that has both a nervous and

generous kind of attitude and who has also experienced

being a lion, please?"

"Why now, Gabrial, that is quite too much to ask for," chuckled Emmanuelle, standing up. "There's no one like that, except for me."

"Of course not," she laughed as she leaned over to hug him. "Because you are the only Emmanuelle that is mine."

The prince smiled as he hugged her. The ball was going to be the most memorable night of his life, he was going to be with the one he knew was right for him.

Chapter 23

The Ball of Celebration I

Light suddenly poured into the dark room from

the ceiling that looked to be cracking above, making

Emmanuel's eyes tear up since he hadn't seen light in so

long, he had begun to forget what it looked or felt like. He

listened when he heard a bunch of groaning and yelling. As

soon as he tried to move and see what was happening his

chains clanged together reminding him quickly that he was still restrained.

The feathers that had fallen from his wings that had now created a bed beneath his knees flew everywhere when he had moved. Suddenly the entire ceiling melted away and it didn't even fall in, it was like it had just vanished.

He heard the flapping of wings from above and the first thing that came to his mind was a dragon, but when he looked up he saw light as bright as a star and knew that light as luminous as that one would never come from a dragon unless it was setting something on fire. Behind the being of light were dark clouds and rain poured into the building.

A girl with long snowy white hair appeared from within the light. She had eyes the color of sapphires and wore armor that was silver that glinted the light from her. A massive halo of silver hung above her head and in her *right hand, she held a circular kind of silver thing that*

swung by a chain.

There wasn't a single weapon in her hand and he

wondered how she could've ever got by all the soldiers and

guards that had been around the place. Then he saw her

take a spear out from behind herself and realized that she

had a weapon with her. Her glowing sapphire necklace was

the first thing he noticed and the first thing he had

remembered.

"Sharon," he muttered, confusedly.

Some 1,000 Years Later

The day he had been waiting for had finally come

and he couldn't wait for everything to start. He couldn't

wait to be dancing with Gabrial in the ballroom, he

couldn't wait to have anything but the enjoyment that

night. Emmanuelle sighed deeply as he looked up at the

tapestries of the royal families before him. Every one of

the families looked so serious and not only that none of

them had more than one child, which had always turned

out to be a son. The only royal family tapestry that had two

sons was the one with him and Damien.

He ran his hand across the tapestry, then was

startled when he heard his brother's voice. He noticed

Damien walking down the staircase to join him.

"What are you looking at brother?" he asked,

calmly.

At first, he didn't want to answer him, after how he

had treated him the other night he didn't want to be

bothered with him. But the look in his brother's cold eyes

looked as if he had forgotten about what had occurred and

he thought for a moment that maybe he hadn't meant to

say all those things. He thought that he could've been

under a lot of pressure and didn't know how to deal with it

so instead, he took it out on him since he was the only one

there.

"The tapestries and our families," answered Emmanuelle, finally.

Damien nodded his head as he approached his brother. "Interesting."

"Yeah," he answered. "Have any plans for the ball tonight?"

"Plans?" he broke into laughter, touching the tapestry.

There was an awkward silence between the two of them for a while as if neither of them knew what else to say. They had been so distant since boys and the only time they had communicated the older they had become was either when they argued or wanted something from one another, but communicating or even talking to each other was nothing they had ever liked to do.

Now that they were trying to talk without fighting it was strange but at the same time kind of nice or at least to Emmanuelle. After his homecoming, he had wanted nothing but a moment like this where they could talk together like brothers or family was supposed to.

"I wanted to apologize for last night, I don't know what came over me," admitted Damien, uncomfortably.

"Apology accepted," said Emmanuelle, happily.

He wrapped his arms around his younger brother and hugged him. It was almost too good to be true, it was the first time he had ever let him do such a thing without fighting him or the first time he ever felt like hugging him.

Damien winced a little as if in pain, he wished he wasn't so huggable or so hands-on with everything. It made him want to go to a window, he felt so sick on the inside, but he allowed him to do so anyway.

"You do know that this ball will not change anything as far as the throne, right?" inquired Damien, stepping back.

"Of course I do, but Damien let's try and put that behind us, I'm your brother even if I do become king," he explained. "That doesn't change who I am."

"No, I mean as far as me becoming the king," he chuckled, glaring at him. "It's my dear brother and I want you to hand it over just like that, no problems at all. Not for you or Gabrial."

Emmanuelle cocked an eyebrow when he heard him mention her. "What about Gabrial?"

"I know your secret and I've known since the second day you were here. I know of your little schemes and thoughts," acknowledged the prince. "I hate to break it to you though, but it won't happen, especially not once I become involved and she finds out the truth about you. She'll hate you."

"No, she won't" argued Emmanuelle feeling like a storm cloud was hovering over his head. "She's different from everyone else. I don't know how, but she is."

"I don't know if she'll be that much different after she finds out. You might just feel more of a hole in your heart than the first time," snarled Damien. "Of course you can always change all of it if you just hand over the crown now and I can make everything else clear up."

He stared at Damien complacently, wondering how he could've just turned from apologizing to this. It made it seem like he hadn't apologized at all or like it was just a cover-up to get what he wanted.

"I'm sorry, but I cannot do as you want," Emmanuelle replied, frustratedly. He turned his back and started walking down the hall, then he turned around. "I thought that after all these years of me being gone would change you, but you haven't I guess. It's still the same thing in your mind, every time you look at me all you see is the crown you so badly want from my head."

"It's rightfully mine, Emmanuelle!" he yelled, angrily. "You disappeared and was dead."

"You wanted me to be, but I wasn't," he told him.

Damien clenched his teeth tightly together, looking down at the floor. "I'm not done with changing your mind, yet," he muttered, watching his brother leave. "I will have that crown and I will have your body hanging upon a cross I have created just for you and that angel as my slave. Mark my words."

Laughter and talking could be heard from outside of Gabrial's room door and Emmanuelle wondered where all the laughter and talking was coming from. It completely slipped his mind to knock on her door, before he entered.

The maids screamed when they saw him enter and one of them poked her with a needle. Gabrial looked up from the floor and noticed him as he pushed the door.

"I'm sorry," he said with embarrassment, then quickly left back out.

The door slammed behind him and he felt like such a clown for walking in like that. It wasn't long before the door opened and she saw him leaning against a wall. He glanced over at her slightly, then sighed as if relieved.

"Is there something wrong?" she asked, looking at his expression.

"No. No. Of course not," he chuckled trying to smile, then he saw that even his efforts to try and act like nothing was wrong were even failed. "Yes, there is. I messed up. I'm sorry."

She couldn't help but laugh, the look in his eyes made it seem like it was something far more serious. "I accept your apology."

"So you still want to go with me to the ball?" Emmanuelle asked.

"Why wouldn't I," Gabrial inquired, walking beside him as he started to walk. "Of course I do."

He sighed again with relief. "I promise I'll make this night the best of your life," he told her. "Along with being memorable and nothing will change between us after this night, at least not the way I feel about you."

"You make every day of my life the best and memorable," she assured him, happily.

"Same here," the prince declared.

"Gabrial!" yelled Damien from behind them.

The two of them turned around and saw him standing by her door. Emmanuelle looked at her as if trying to tell her something with his eyes. For a moment he thought that maybe Damien hadn't been bluffing with the threats he had made and if he was telling the truth he didn't want her anywhere near him. He approached her quickly and Emmanuelle walked forward to meet him.

"You don't have to go all out slandering my name to her like this, it's just a crown," whispered Emmanuelle, worriedly.

"Oh, but I must," laughed Damien, staring up at him. "You may be able to take that from me, but as for her. I found her and she's not yours. So don't even try and play like I'm always the bad guy. At least I didn't steal what was mine anyway."

"You're nuts aren't you. Gabrial is…"

"A servant girl and my servant at that," he snarled, pushing him out of his way.

At first, Emmanuelle thought to fight him and would've, annoyed by how his brother thought of her. He struggled to control his anger as he watched Damien walk away with her. For a moment he was about to stop him.

"Emmanuelle, remember tonight," she told him, trying to smile.

He nodded his head, he couldn't let Damien ruin what was going to happen that night. Even if he did try to slander his name he trusted that she wouldn't hate him after and he had to try and keep believing that. The door to her room slammed behind them and he suddenly wished he had found her first when he was a human before his brother. Things would've turned out so much easier and differently.

Gabrial sat on her bed watching as Damien locked her door with a silver key he had been concealing in his pocket. He looked both angry and as if he were losing his mind. Once the door was locked he walked over to her.

"I see you have feelings for my brother, don't you?" he inquired, crouching in front of her. "And don't just leave my question for the air to answer."

She looked at him but didn't say a word. The prince couldn't force her to speak against her will. He grew annoyed, he had enough of her silent treatment and now he was going to get some answers out of her.

She felt his hand grab her mouth and squeeze it so tightly she felt as if he were trying to put finger impressions into it. Every time she tried to take his hand from off her mouth he would increase his grip.

"Answer me, when I'm talking to you just like you do with my brother," he ordered her, his tone growing aggressive. "I already know the truth. I just wanted to see if you were going to say a word."

He released her mouth, shoving her away from himself. "But the truth is you're engaged to me! Engaged to me! Or have you forgotten?" he bellowed. "Have you told him that?"

"I'm not!" she cried, frustratedly. "You're not like him and you can't force me, I'll never vow to anything for you!"

"Shut up!" Damien ordered, standing up and grabbing her by the wrist when she tried to get away from him. "I don't ask for your love. I don't need any of that, but you're still my wife," he told her, taking out a ring from his pocket.

"Stop!" she yelled, struggling to get him to release her. "I will not marry you."

"We'll see about that," he chuckled, bitterly as he shoved the ring on her finger and it felt like it was cutting through her skin. It was so tight against her skin as he pushed it on.

The prince threw her aside once the ring was on her finger. She tried to pull it off but it was too tight around her finger. He laughed at her as he headed for the door, knowing that she was unable to get the ring off.

"You'll never get it off," he told her, watching her struggle.

The door closed behind him and she was left alone in her room, fighting to get the ring off her finger. A few tears of frustration burned down the sides of her face. She didn't know what she was going to do or how she was going to explain to Emmanuelle. There was no time to think like that, she had to get the ring off.

****

Today was the day, after all these weeks of trying to get her sister back she finally was going to be able to do so. Through the fogginess of the mirror Esmeralda could see her reflection. She touched her lower lip, thinking of how Gabrial had been hit in the mouth by their father.

After that, she had never spoken much again and she never knew why. She pulled her dark cloak up and over her shoulders, letting the golden lions rest on her shoulders.

She smiled at herself in the mirror, admiring how clever she was as she played with a white feather that had silver speckles. It was one of the feathers from her sister's wing and the only one she had been able to take after their father took them.

Beneath all these clothes no one would be able to tell the deadly weapons in which she concealed. Her door suddenly opened and she set the feather down on the desk, knowing that it was finally time.

"Esmeralda are you ready?" asked a man.

She threw her hood over her head, then said. "Let's get this party started."

The two of them started for the door, but before she closed it she took one last look back at the feather that lay flat on her desk, reflecting the sun's light making it look somehow alive.

Esmeralda turned her head and closed the door feeling a surge of excitement creep its way up her spine. It wasn't just the thrill of getting her sister back that made her excited to be going to the ball, she knew she was going to do something she hadn't been able to do in a long time or rather be what she was.

✷✷✷✷✷✷✷✷✷✷✷

Maid A'Key looked at Gabrial's door when she thought she heard her weeping from the other side of the door. She couldn't help but open the door and see what was wrong with her. When she entered she noticed

Gabrial laying flat on her bed with her face buried in her pillow. The maid approached her slowly, then stroked a few strands of her hair softly.

"Gabrial?" she said, calmly. "Is everything okay?"

Slowly she sat up from her pillows, all around her eyes were red and puffy. "No," she answered, looking away trying to stop the tears from coming from her eyes. "Emmanuelle wants me to join him at the ball."

"Is that all?" asked Maid A'Key. "You should be proud, he's a prince."

"It's not that at all," she cried, wiping her left eye. "His brother is convinced that I'm entitled to marrying him and he put this ring on my finger and I can't get it off," Gabrial explained, attempting to pull it off once more. "Emmanuelle, will be disappointed and probably will never trust me again once he finds out. But I don't want to marry Prince Damien, he despises me and his brother doesn't. I don't want to be despised if I'm married, but I can't find any way out."

"My goodness," gasped the maid, thinking of how unhappy she would be with him.

"Oh, Maid A'Key you have to help me. I couldn't bear to have Emmanuelle despising me," explained Gabrial.

"He won't Gabrial," she assured her.

"I wish I could be sure, I've messed things up."

"You can be," Maid A'Key told her, petting her on the shoulder, soothingly. "You and I both know how he feels about you, he won't just walk away like that. If he asks, all you have to do is tell him the truth."

"But it'll anger him," she said, worriedly.

"Not as much as if you don't tell him and he finds out on his own," Maid A'Key stated.

Gabrial looked over at her and smiled. "You're right," she admitted, deciding to forget about the ring on her finger.

"Now do you want to also add being late to the ball to your list or are we going to start to get you prepared?" asked the maid.

She nodded her head in agreement, the maid was right. They didn't have much time now before the ball started. It was already sunset, the people would start to pour in. The maid helped Gabrial to her feet, the maid always knew how to make the best of everything and she hoped the maid knew that she would be there for her also, whenever she needed her.

The prince had already started to get ready for the ball. He swung his sword around playfully until he heard his door swing open. Immediately he turned around with his sword, startling Sir Hamilton, who put his hands up.

"Okay, you got me, your highness," he cried, frightenedly.

"Sorry," chuckled the prince as he put his sword back into his halter. "I guess the excitement must be getting to me."

"Yes of course, but maybe you could kind of calm it down a little, sir so no one ends up with that thing through them," explained Sir Hamilton, pushing the end of it away from himself. "Also your green mask doesn't suit you."

Emmanuelle rolled his eyes, frustratedly, all this time he had spent mainly looking for a mask and not a single one seemed to fit him. "Thanks," he said.

"I think if you wore a black mask, it would suit both you and the outfit, your highness," he advised, looking at his clothes. "And could you possibly do something about those white boots, they make you look out of league, sir."

"Well maybe you wouldn't mind giving me a little hand," chuckled Emmanuelle, fixing his collar.

"Of course I wouldn't, that's why I'm here, your highness," declared the knight, moving over to help him.

The knight and Emmanuelle went through his things searching for the right thing for him to wear that night.

✳✳✳✳✳✳✳✳✳✳✳

Gabrial sat in a chair, patiently as the maid wandered around the room looking for the things she needed to help her get ready for the ball. Somehow she felt different about Emmanuelle since he had become himself. She couldn't tell whether it was good, but she felt like hiding from him. There was something about his whole personality, it was familiar and still, she couldn't figure out how. She felt as if they had met sometime before she had even encountered him as a lion, perhaps as a little girl.

"It's been so long since we've had a young maiden so beautiful enter with our prince, well I mean it has been a long time since he's been here," she said, dancing with an elegant light blue gown. "We thought he had given up with ever loving anyone again when he stormed out the night he learned the girl he had admired was with someone else. She broke his heart, yes indeed she did."

"Please tell me Maid A'Key what happened that night, I really want to know. Why did everyone believe he was dead?" she begged her. "I feel as if part of him is incomplete if I don't know."

Maid A'Key sighed as she put jewels in Gabrial's hair. "I guess the time comes when you can no longer hide the past," she chuckled softly. "It is a long story, but to shorten it up some, Prince Emmanuelle loved a girl named Veronica, but what happened was that she pretended to love him, but the day came where he decided to propose to her on his eighteenth birthday at a ball.

If only you could have seen the glow in his eyes, you could see that he loved her, but when he proposed to her, she refused him in one of the rudest ways possible, breaking everything on the inside of him." she took in a deep breath, then started again. "He was so hurt that night, he couldn't bear to stay any longer so he ran out that night, and as far as we knew he had been slain by a gigantic lion or that is what his brother had told us."

"But that's not true, he was cursed somehow to become the lion," explained Gabrial, becoming more tangled in confusion.

"Gabrial darling, you are truly an angel sent from heaven, we would have never known." she cried, happily as she started to brush her hair. "Anyway, would you prefer a blue or black mask?"

"Blue, please," answered Gabrial, feeling a chill climb up her shoulder, remembering Erebus.

Gabrial stood up slowly from the chair taking the dress and walking to a changing area when she walked out, the maid stared at her, curiously. She was wearing a white cloak that almost took away from the design of the dress.

"It is a lovely dress, it's just could you leave the cloak, darling?" asked the maid.

She looked at the dress, then at the cloak, she felt her heart sink. What would they think if they saw her bloody streaks on her back, they would think she was from some kind of troubled family.

"Come on!"

The cloak slipped from her fingers slowly falling to the floor.

"Ow my, you are so beautiful in blue just one more thing," she said, wrapping a diamond necklace around her neck. "There you are darling, he won't be able to take his eyes off of you, when he sees you, anyone for that fact."

Gabrial nearly blushed. "Thank you!"

The maid hadn't seemed to have noticed the bloody streaks on her back. Then, of course, it may not have been showing right now and she hoped it stayed that way for the rest of the night.

"I suppose you're all ready for the ball, are you excited?"

She looked at the maid, happily, then answered. "Yes and nervous."

The maid broke into laughter. "Ow darling you'll be with the prince, don't be nervous."

The two of them walked out the door and down a long hallway that led to two large doors that had lions engraved in them. The maid pushed open the doors, music poured in from the ballroom and into the quiet hallway. People danced, while others played music and ate some of the grand food. A young man pointed over to her and signaled her to come over, but she couldn't tell who he was behind the mask he was wearing. It wasn't long before she realized it was Emmanuelle but she could hardly tell it was behind his dark mask.

"Go on, it's the prince he wants to probably dance with you." explained the maid, giving her a little push out and into the ballroom.

Gabrial was suddenly nervous and felt as if she might faint when the maid closed the doors and left her all alone. Everyone stared at her and she didn't know what they were thinking. She rubbed one of her arms a little as she made her way over to the place where Emmanuelle and his brother were standing.

"Isn't she just beautiful?" asked Emmanuelle, happily with his hands crossed.

His brother nodded, somewhat annoyed. "I suppose, but there are better women here, along with being more mature."

"No, none like her," argued Emmanuelle, staring at her as she walked closer. He reached his hand out to take hers when she was finally close enough, she felt less nervous. Then he whispered something in her ear. "Don't be nervous, you'll be their princess soon they can't laugh at you and besides you look wonderful."

She looked at him, had he said, princess? Was he planning on marrying her soon? A bashful smile appeared on her face and she tried not to stare directly at him."Thank you!"

"Princess? I think you've lost more than your gentility dear brother." laughed Damien. "She'd never be fit for you, not after what she did with me."

"What are you talking about?" questioned Emmanuelle, glaring at Damien. "She was never involved with you."

"In more ways than one, dear brother."

Gabrial frowned, feeling a little uncomfortable as he laughed. He was working on making Emmanuelle question her about things that were not what they had appeared or had never even happened.

"She's engaged to me," chuckled Damien, deviously.

"Stop it, now. This isn't…"

"Funny? It's not, because it's the truth," he snapped, grabbing her hand so quickly she couldn't stop him. "Is this proof enough? I sure hope that wasn't the scent of a proposal, because you and I both know what will happen."

Emmanuelle frowned, feeling betrayed as he wondered why she hadn't said anything about her engagement to his brother, but that wasn't what really had hurt him. What hurt him most was that he remembered why he may not have been able to marry her. He threw her hand down when he knew he had seen the ring on her finger.

"She's to be my wife, well actually weeks ago until you came along."

"Emmanuelle, please I can…"

"Shut up!" laughed Damien, watching as his brother turned his back. "Hurts, doesn't it?"

Gabrial moved away from him when he tried to grab her again and went after Emmanuelle. "Emmanuelle, please listen to me," she cried, only to be ignored by him as he vanished into the people.

As she tried to catch up to him, he vanished into the people until she could no longer tell who was from the others. She felt lost in a sea of masks and dancers. At this point, she didn't know if she would be able to heal what she had caused. She felt like shedding tears because her heart was overwhelmed with grief and hurt. Nothing was going to be the same if she lost him in this way.

Chapter 24

The Ball of Celebration II

And they entered the prison field, raining

down from the sky with their bows pulled back and their

arrows ready. Armistice with all the power from the inside

of her holding her hands above her head with a ball of

blue fire. Othniel and a few other male iron angels close

behind them having their backs.

"Stand back," she ordered them, deciding to finally give the soldiers below them a taste of their own medicine.

A luminous light spread across the land like a force making every one of them fall. They landed on the ground since it was safe and walked around the men that had been scattered abroad like a bunch of ants in a lab case.

"Are they…"

"No, but it won't be long before they awaken and hopefully by that time we will have retrieved all the others," Armistice answered Ambassador.

The iron angel looked down at the men, then when she saw that they were still breathing it made her feel less nervous. Ambassador didn't like to harm anyone unless there was no other alternative and she didn't like to harm mass bunches of anything, even if it were evil. The prison door was placed in the ground and they could hear the wails and cries of so many. It was chained with many thick chains and locks.

"Stand back," ordered Othniel, lifting his two-sided ax up and above himself.

He slammed the ax into the chains, breaking every one of them. Armistice and Laonacia helped themselves to pull the door open, although they didn't know what to expect to come out first.

Some 1,000 Years Later

*H*er black gown flopped over her feet as she stepped from out of the carriage. The castle was far more beautiful than she had anticipated, but she still loved the palace in the world beneath the Seven Sands far more. It carried a kind of freshness along with coolness to it since it was completely made of water and glass and there was only sunlight at the end of the week, but the other days the moon just showed.

"Do you have an in…"

Before the guard could finish Esmeralda held up an envelope but said not a word. A grin appeared on her face when she could sense he was growing nervous when he saw six men get out of the carriage. A few of them were short and others were tall as Goliath. The guard took the envelope from her and stepped out of her and the men's way.

"This indeed shall be a night to remember," she chuckled as they started up the steps and towards the palace doors, where light poured out.

The prince sat alone outside the ballroom with his hands together, frustratedly. He had worked so hard to even get this far and now everything seemed to want to come storming in and just uproot it all like it had never been there. His heart felt so heavy, it felt like it was crying on the inside of him or bleeding. Not because of her being engaged to his brother, but because of all the consequences that came along if that were him marrying her.

"I thought it was supposed to be a night to remember," said Gabrial, walking into the hall.

Immediately he sat up looking at her in her glowing pale blue, slender gown. She tried to smile since it was what he had done for her whenever she hadn't felt so great. The prince turned the opposite way of her trying to make the feelings for her go away. Gabrial sat down beside him and touched him lightly on the shoulder.

"Please listen to me," she begged him. "We're still friends, aren't we?"

Emmanuelle turned and looked at her, his eyes showing a little glow when he looked at her. "Not anymore," he replied, staring at her face.

For a moment she thought she might have lost her breath, it felt like part of her heart had been pierced through by a dagger. She knew he was angry with her, but she never wanted it to tarnish their relationship. She didn't care what Damien said, she wouldn't marry him and

Emmanuelle had to know that she wouldn't do that to him, not after everything they had been through.

"Emmanuelle, I…"

"It's more than that now and I think both you and I know that," he explained, regretfully. "I knew I should've never let it happen, but I lost control, and now…I regret ever letting myself feel like that."

The prince turned away from her, getting ready to stand up.

"No," cried Gabrial, taking his hand. "You shouldn't regret it. I don't."

He looked up from the floor at her trying to make himself feel a little hopeful even though he didn't. She stood up in front of him, touching the side of his face as she stared into his soft golden-brown eyes that looked as if they were so lost as he stared at her.

"Don't let this get between us," she told him. "We're meant to be.

As much as he knew he should've stopped himself from listening to her, he couldn't. Everything she said was true, but even so, it just didn't seem like it was meant to be. Outside of her engagement to his brother, he still had secrets of his own that he knew could put her at risk if he let himself go through with sharing those feelings with her. Gabrial began to move her face closer to his face, slowly as if hesitating, then they kissed deeply.

"I love you, Emmanuelle," she admitted.

Emmanuelle's stern face that acted as a gateway into his thoughts slowly began to return to his hopeful smile. "You love…"

"I beg your pardon sir, but the dancing has begun and Prince Damien wishes you to be in the room," interrupted a butler.

At first, he wanted to just ignore Damien's wishes and finish talking with her. Right now he felt like there were so many things that had been left unsaid and needed to be said right now and at that moment.

"I'll be there," he replied, finally with his eyes focused on her. "Come with me?"

"Of course," she replied.

When they went back into the ballroom his brother was still standing in the same place as when they left. He was talking to a few other men that Emmanuelle had noticed were dancing with a few of the princesses before. Damien smiled when he noticed the two of them enter the room.

"Excuse me," he told them as he walked away from them and over to his brother. " Sorry dear brother, but if I may say, it appears that I am the older brother now and I should be king next."

Emmanuelle stared at him, almost frowning. "I prefer not to discuss that besides today's is a special day. Can't I at least have a day or two without you pestering me about the throne and who goes next?" Damien bit his lip and glared at Emmanuelle when he wasn't looking. "Now if you would be so kind enough to excuse us. Would you like to dance Gabrial?"

"I'd love to," her face glowed with happiness. "I must warn you, I've never danced."

"Don't worry, a long time without..."

"Emmanuelle now is not the time to fool around, we must decide this now on who becomes our father's successor."

He was ignored by his brother as he and Gabrial walked out to join the other dancing people. It amazed Damien how after all these years he was still not worried about becoming king or fighting him for it. There had to be a way to still become the next king, even if he didn't have the birthright. He walked after his brother to catch up with him.

Everyone had been so occupied that they hadn't seen that Esmeralda had slipped into the room, along with the men. They attempted to blend in with the others, keeping their eyes on her sister, who was walking into the center of the ballroom with the prince. At this point, she wanted the young man dead more than ever. He was getting too close to messing up that relationship between her and Gabrial that she sought to restore.

"Now?" asked Gordan, from behind her.

"No, not yet," she answered, pushing her hand against him to stop him from moving.

Her green eyes eyed the prince with every move he made. At the right moment she would attack him without any mercy and this time Gabrial wouldn't be there to save him. She still remembered how her sister had taken his side and acted as if he had been the one hurt when he had attempted to kill her as a lion.

Damien tapped Emmanuelle on the shoulder before he had started dancing. "Fine if you want to dance, let it be for the best at dancing to the fastest music, be our father's successor," Damien said, knowing that Emmanuelle was hardly paying attention.

"Whatever, let's just dance," he said, signaling his hand to the musicians to play some other music.

The two of them stood side by side with their partners, Damien laughed deviously, then said. "Let the best dancer be king."

"Yes and let the best dancer be king," muttered Emmanuelle, rolling his eyes.

The music started slowly, Emmanuelle spun her around. "For someone who has never danced, you sure are graceful," he whispered in her ear.

She chuckled softly as she let her hand lay on his shoulder. In a few moments, they were twirling and spinning around like ballets in the ballroom as the music grew more intense. At times it sounded like someone could break their violin. His brother teased and yelled things at him as he and Gabrial danced.

He leaned her back a little, then quickly pulled her back up, holding her up against himself, her arms wrapped around him. When she let go, she leaned back again. It wasn't long before Damien and his partner were hardly able to keep up with the fast and difficult moves Emmanuelle and Gabrial had been performing.

The music suddenly stopped and so did the dancers. Gabrial's forehead was pressed against his as he held her up. Her left leg secured one of his sides. At first, they were silent, but when everyone began to clap, they broke into laughter, then he slowly moved his face closer to hers and kissed her, deeply. His brother and his partner, however, were in a wreck staring over at them. His stomach felt as if it would give way as he looked at them.

Gabrial's sister's eyes widened when she noticed what she was doing. He had stolen her heart away, him and whatever magic he possessed. Her mouth dropped and she wanted to start the riot now before things got any worse. "No. How could you, Gabrial?" she cried, a spark of lightning flying from her eyes.

"Repulsive!" growled Damien, his face pinching together as it became contorted.

Emmanuelle slowly let her go and set her back down. "Well Damien, looks like I'm the king still so you don't have to worry about that," he laughed, then took her hand in his.

Anger showered over Damien behind his pasted smile. He looked at his brother leaving the ballroom with Gabrial, noticing the bloody streaks on her back and it came to him about her identity. Ruining his love for her in one moment would be easy if he knew what she was. If he couldn't have the throne, then his brother didn't deserve to be happy. He tapped a woman on the shoulder pointing at Gabrial's back and whispering her a message.

"What?" the woman asked, looking around, then passed the message.

It continued until the whole room was in an uproar of voices. Gabrial looked back, when she heard something about blood, remembering the marks on her back. The prince looked at her, seeming confused, but he didn't say anything to her. Damien ran over to him, bowing before him as if humble.

"My king," he panted as he bowed before his brother.

"Stop it, Damien." snapped Emmanuelle noticing how the people had begun to stare at them, a few of them chuckling.

"I have a confession to make before the night is over." He stood up, wrapping his arm around his brother and pulling him alongside him. "My beloved brother is planning on proposing to that girl. An angel. Why take a look for yourselves you can tell she's different if you don't..."

He was immediately pushed away by his brother, who was boiling with fury. "Don't you ever say that about her, you could get her killed," he yelled, lunging at his brother and shoving him away.

He was stopped by Gabrial grabbing hold of his arm to stop him. "No."

His eyes stared at her, he was hurting from the inside and that had just added the last brick to his collapsing wall. "Don't stop me."

Damien laughed at him. "Taking orders from her, what a sissy thing to do," he teased, hopping around.

Emmanuelle chased after his brother, furiously as he pushed and ran through people. She thought to go after the two princes, but suddenly the people screamed when a knife flew through the air, almost hitting Gabrial. She turned and looked around, noticing a girl with long black hair and a dark dress standing in the midst of the dancers along with five men.

Each of them wore wrappings around their faces and clothes that were the color of sand and shoes that had pointy tips. The girl's green eyes were what helped her figure out who she was. The girl from the arena, who had attempted to kill Emmanuelle and she looked to have help.

A short man swung on the chandelier like a monkey on a vine, gathering up all the food he could fit into his bag. Guards charged into the room for everyone's protection but were knocked out by some kind of dust that was thrown in front of them.

Esmeralda threw the hood of her cloak off. "Let the party begin," she chuckled.

The place became an uproar of the guests running and screaming in no time as they all headed for the exit to escape the place. But almost all the main doors were bolted by wood so they were unable to escape, letting

Esmeralda's friends rob them of all their precious

possessions. Gabrial noticed the door that Emmanuelle and

her had come through the second time they had come into

the ballroom and left for it, hoping to find help.

Unfortunately, she wasn't able to leave unnoticed.

"You two after her," ordered Esmeralda. "And you three

get all you can get, I'll find the prince."

Gabrial ran as quickly as she could through the

dark, empty halls. There had to be someone in the palace

who could help. When she heard a bunch of growling she

soon realized she had been followed by two gigantic men,

who carried grave weapons and they weren't too far away

from her. As soon as they saw that they had been noticed,

they sprinted down the hallway after her.

They were too close and she knew she wouldn't

escape them if she were to run. She opened a door to

another room and shut it quickly, bolting it with a chair so they couldn't get in. The door shook as they rammed their bodies into it. Fear aroused her as she tried to think of what to do if the chair gave way and they got in.

The doors were shoved in and sent swinging backward. Emmanuelle noticed Damien laughing as he stood in a dim corner of the room.

"You see how scared she looked, that is completely the reason she looked like that, my brother has no doubt been beating on her," he laughed.

Emmanuelle laid hands on his brother and shoved him into a wall. "How dare you spread those ugly lies about her." he scolded, holding Damien up by his collar. "You can hurt me all you want but I'll make sure you don't forget to lay a hand or spread a lie about her again."

"You know what brother it would have been better if you had never returned because what is going to happen to you and that creature is going to be terrible and I'm going to make sure…"

"Of nothing," finished Emmanuelle. "Tell me Damien, is it me you hate, or is it just the thought of me becoming king?"

"Both. You're not fit for the position, you're weak and timid," he insulted, bitterly.

Emmanuelle glanced down at the floor, angrily, then he looked up into his brother's evil and jealous eyes, which were so full of hate. For some odd reason, Damien began to laugh gently, then said in a raspy voice. "Just like your bride, I want to tell you something before the night is over. If something happens to you I will be certain that I plague her every day of her life, because every time I look at her I see you and I would beat that out of her every day! I'd be afraid to leave her out there right now, she could be dead, those people aren't very fond of angels if you haven't seemed to notice."

The prince could no longer hold back and he suddenly punched Damien in the nose, releasing him to the floor as the blood from his nose ran down his face, it was like the colors of rubies. He would've said something to him if he didn't hear the screaming from the ballroom and the first thing that came to his mind was that Gabrial may have been in trouble, especially after what his brother had announced in front of all of them.

Damien touched his nose letting the blood paint his fingers, then he licked them as he watched his brother walk away from him, knowing what might happen if he stayed any longer with his crazy brother or what might become of Gabrial if he didn't find her soon.

"That's right, run like the coward you are!"

When Emmanuelle entered the ballroom he noticed the guests were in disarray, but they had stopped screaming. Food was everywhere and the women were missing their jewelry.

A few of the women that were standing alone were pointing at him and whispering things. He walked out of the ballroom and into a dark hallway. A sparkling bracelet

caught his eye and he quickly picked it up, it was hers. She

couldn't be far, but where?

"Gabrial!" he yelled through the dark hallways.

Although she hadn't heard him, someone else did.

Emmanuelle heard the sound of the men pushing on the

door. When he looked a little harder down the hall he

realized that two men were shoving on a door. Their

clothes were what made him able to notice them since they

were the color of sand. One of them looked over when they

heard him approach them.

"Who are you?" inquired the prince.

One of the men snarled, then reached into his

pocket drawing a knife that was curved at the end.

"I order you to lay down your weapons," said

Emmanuelle.

"And who are you? We have our orders to capture that girl and kill the prince if necessary," declared a taller man in a raspy voice.

As much as he didn't feel like fighting anymore, it appeared that they were not going to listen and were leaving him no choice.

"Come at me prince," chuckled a familiar voice from behind him.

It didn't take Emmanuelle long to realize that she was the girl from the arena. She grinned at him, pulling out a sword from a holder she had concealed beneath her dark skirt. The girl charged at him with the sword trying to stab him. He stepped out of the way and her sword collided with the door.

"I don't know what you want, but I'm sure it isn't anything we can't discuss," he told her, resting his hand on his sword.

"Huh. You tell me if there's anything left to discuss," snarled Esmeralda.

They attacked Emmanuelle all at once, driving him up the large stairway. Three other men came out of the shadows of the hall, joining her and the others. He became surrounded, fending off any one of them that attacked him. Esmeralda swung her sword making him leap onto one of the banisters. A dagger was thrown at him but missed tearing a piece of his jacket.

"Give up," she laughed as she leaped onto the banister with him. "You can't defeat us all at once."

Emmanuelle looked up at the chandelier that was giving off no light since the candles hadn't been lit. He may not have been able to defeat them with just his sword, but he knew how he may have been able to stop them. Just when he was about to cut the rope so the chandelier would fall he heard something that sounded like a horse stampede.

In no time guards swarmed into the place like bees. Esmeralda looked at Emmanuelle thinking to attack him, but as soon as she tried to he cut the rope and the chandelier fell. He jumped down from off the banister, slamming into the floor below.

The girl screamed when the chandelier fell on her and her men. He breathed heavily as he looked back at the stairway. The guards ran over to see if they could find the intruders. Gabrial knelt down in front of him. A smile of relief glowing on her face when she saw that he was alright.

"Are you alright?" she asked as the prince slowly sat up.

"Yes," he chuckled, standing up as he brushed himself off. "I guess this night will be most memorable."

"Your highness," said one of the guards. "I'm afraid there is no sign of the intruders."

Emmanuelle narrowed his eyes, confusedly. There couldn't have been any way for them to escape that quickly. "Are you sure of that?"

"Yes, sir. There were only broken pieces of the chandelier," explained the guard. "We will search the outer premises, they couldn't have gone far."

"Of course," he answered.

The guards left the place in a hurry. He sighed deeply with relief, then embraced her, happily.

****

The ball went on even after all the chaos, but as for Emmanuelle and Gabrial, they decided to retire. He didn't want to have another run-in with his brother and besides the guest would be eyeballing them the whole time after what Damien had said. So the two of them went outside beneath a pavilion. Water flowed from out of the mouth of a valiant statue horse and into a basin below. Showering over the water lilies that floated above the water.

So much had happened all in this one night. So much had been said, maybe telling the truth was the only way to avoid learning the truth from someone else. He looked at Gabrial as she sat down on a marble bench, her fingers touching the water in the fountain.

"Gabrial I have something to tell you before time runs out and I'm unable to." his tone was low and his head was down, as his eyes gleamed into the crystal clear water.

She nodded her head, smiling at him. "As long as you feel like you're ready."

"I know I will never be ready, to tell the truth about your painful past, but sometimes that's all a part of being married," Emmanuelle tried to smile. "You have to be able to confide in the person you're married to, otherwise conflict in the future could arise."

The hint was clear that he was planning on marrying her, but was that the only thing he had plans on telling her?

"To every firstborn son born after the third generation of his blood is said to be cursed, ever since my great grandfather slew millions of angels, he's a great hero in books and myths but is thrown down by those who believe in angels such as the Southern Kingdom, the kingdom who cursed us," he announced. "In a way as a boy I envied my brother, he wasn't cursed so he had a happy living and I used the crown as a way to pay him back whenever he teased me. In return I cursed myself twice more since I became a lion and missed so many years with my parents," he explained. "I'm cursed Gabrial, I could kill you if you have any children with me, even if we're married. But I love you and I guess it'll have to stay just that. Love, never marriage."

None of it made sense to her, but what about the girl he loved a long time ago? She would have died if he had married her or would she?

"Emmanuelle, I don't want to seem as if I'm prying, but Maid A'Key said that you were engaged to someone some time ago," she said, calmly, "she would've died if you had married her, wouldn't she?"

"I never loved anyone, I found that the only reason I wanted to marry a woman a time ago was to pay their kingdom back for what they had done to me. It was evil and now I see my sin and that's why I never wanted to remember my past because what I was then. A monster, but looked upon as an angel; was the person I never wanted to remember or want you to see me as," Emmanuelle explained, looking at her.

She stood up and touched the side of his face

feeling the smoothness of it beneath her hand, all of him

wasn't bad. He had been hurt and because of his hurt, he

had felt the need to hurt others, and that part that was

concealed by that hurt she saw every night in her dreams

calling to her to release him from his sin someday.

Everything made sense now.

"I love you too and I don't believe that any curse is

more powerful than the two of us together," she said,

tousling his hair. "You've changed and you've always had

a glorious side of yourself even when you were convinced

you were evil."

He reached into one of his pockets taking out a

white box with a red ribbon tied around it. A necklace with

a blue gem sparkled as he put it around her neck. "You are

the most beautiful person I've ever met." His hand moved

slightly around both sides of her waist, then he lifted her

from off the ground. "It may be wrong of me to ask and if

you refuse me I'll understand, but if you'll marry me

Gabrial?"

"Look at me," Gabrial said as their eyes met. "I

could never refuse you, no matter the cost."

She cupped his face in her hands, closing her eyes

and kissing him as if saying "yes" to his question. A

glowing mist of gold wrapped its way around them

bringing them closer together and suddenly the water from

the fountain shot up into the air, raining down on them like

magic. Doves flew into the pavilion and started to circle

around them, some of their snowy feathers falling.

"Stay with me beyond forever. Hold me in your

arms," she told him in nearly a whisper.

"I will. I promise," he answered her, breathing

heavily.

He pressed his lips against hers again, kissing her

deeply with their eyes closed. Her hands held his face as

he held her against himself. There were so many heartfelt

emotions they couldn't explain, but it felt like they knew

what this was like they had felt this sometime before or

that this was something they had wanted long ago. The

moment could never end, it was all too sensational, almost

like a real fantasy.

Epilogue

 Dried, dead flowers floated in a bowl of black

water that had begun to boil from the fire below. The

flowers were retrieved from the water by hands that were

covered with black gloves. They were carried over to a

coffin that was covered with many other types of flowers

that were also dead. The coffin was brown with golden

trimming. Above it was a skeleton head that looked as if it

were smiling down upon the coffin.

The hands set the flowers down, then picked up a little piece of wood. The piece of wood was scratched up against the side of the coffin so that there was a little flame on the very tip of it. The flame was carried and placed just above the skeleton's head, where it slipped off and into the inside. The eyes of the skeleton lit up and so did its mouth as if it had awakened from a long slumber.

"The time is near," whispered a gentle voice from the person that had lit the skeleton, "Summon the one of many faces, whose cloak is as dark as raven's feathers and who rides upon the night itself."

"Your wishes are my commands, master," answered the skeleton head in a cold, raspy voice.

"And say this unto him and he shall know who hath sent you," she told it. "Little Mrs. Milled sat in a field, watching her colts and wrote. Along came a spider that benighted little Mrs. Milled away."

www.ingramcontent.com/pod-product-compliance
Lightning Source LLC
Chambersburg PA
CBHW051113300726
48981CB00001B/118